FIGHTING ENVY

deadly sins series

BY JENNIFER MILLER

ISBN: 978-098407427
Copyright © 2015

Cover design: Wicked by Design
Cover Photo: Dollar Photo Club
Editing: CDK & Associates
Formatting: Allusion Graphics, LLC

Other books by Jennifer Miller
Pretty Little Lies
Pretty Little Dreams
Pretty Little Vows – A novella
Perfect Little Plan
Whispering Wishes

DEDICATION

To my husband, for giving me such a great idea, and for showing me what it means to have love that's worth fighting for.

PROLOGUE

"You'll never be anything special. Do you hear me, Rowan? No one will ever love you. No man will ever stay. You're worthless, good for nothing."

Words I've heard over and over again so many times, I've lost count. How could I have thought today would be any different? It may be my sixteenth birthday, but the shameful truth is, my mother doesn't care. It's not special, not to her at least. Just another day.

When I arrive home from school she's actually sober for once. I'm momentarily excited and relieved thinking it will be a good night and just maybe it will be what I hope. The fact that she actually remembers that today is my birthday is a good sign. When she suggests that we go ahead and leave for dinner even though my twin brother Tyson isn't home yet, I quickly agree. I'll agree to anything if it means she will keep her good mood. I've learned any hesitance, disagreement or question can make her mood change in the blink of an eye, and I really, really don't want that to happen today of all days.

Feeling excited that she lets me pick my favorite diner, Al's, to go to for dinner, I'm positive we are off to a great start. Maybe this birthday will be different. Maybe she'll even take Tyson and I to get our drivers licenses this weekend so we don't have to take the bus. I momentarily feel bad again that Tyson isn't here because it's his birthday too, but I just go with the flow and do what she wants me to do.

Ordering my favorite BLT sandwich with fries, I happily begin digging into my food as soon as it arrives making small talk about my day. "I saw Tyson at lunch and he seemed like he was having a good day too. His friends even sang happy birthday to him. He acted like he didn't like it – even started punching a couple of them, but I know the truth," I laugh.

My first warning came as she orders a beer. She drinks it quickly and promptly orders another, as the little hairs on the back of my neck rise in trepidation. Forcing myself to ignore the feeling and her drinking, I keep talking.

"Then Mia, you remember her, right? She gave me a gift and it was wrapped in really pretty blue paper that said happy birthday all over it. I tried to open it slowly because I didn't want to rip it, but she laughed and told me to go faster. It was a book I've really been wanting to read. It's the one about the girl that likes a boy only she finds out that his family isn't what they appear; they are all vampires. Mia told me that he even sparkles in the sun, mom. Isn't that cool? Remember, how I told you about that book?"

I'm babbling trying desperately to hold her interest. She looks at me a couple of times and nods absently, but I lose her completely when a family sitting in the booth across from us distracts her. Out of the corner of my eye I see a mother, father and two children enjoying a meal together. Upon closer inspection it appears that the boy at the table is about my age, and he has a younger sister. He parents are sitting on one side of the table, the children on the other. My mom is facing the parents and I can tell she's taking in the couple, the envy mixed with curiosity. Want and anger settle clearly on her face.

"My gift from Erica was this bracelet," I hold up my wrist and watch how the thin silver bracelet with the small half heart sparkles even in the poor lighting of the diner. "Isn't it pretty? She has one that attaches to the heart; see how it's only half? She laughed that it may be kind of immature for our age, but I don't think so. I really love it."

She doesn't answer. She's too busy flagging down the waitress to order another beer. A bad feeling churning in my stomach grows and my heart starts to beat faster. I feel tears press against the back of my eyes. I blink and look up at the ceiling to keep them in their place.

She hasn't looked away from the family so I turn to look at them as well, too curious at what she's finding so interesting. I stare openly, even though it's rude, desperate to understand what it is that's holding her attention. The man is sitting close to his wife, her hand in his on top of the table. They are listening to something their son is saying and when they laugh, they look at each other clearly passing a sharing of amusement. When the man catches me in mid-stare, my cheeks flush with embarrassment, but he gives me a soft smile. As I start to return it, I'm quickly pulled back to my reality as my mom hisses my name, "Rowan!"

Turning to her wide eyed and embarrassed at being caught, my stomach drops, painfully familiar with the tone of her voice. Her mood has officially turned and the night will be far from pleasant. She's clearly feeling the buzz of the alcohol she's consumed so far, and I know she's far from finished. Ripping money out of her wallet, she throws it on the table, not caring that I haven't finished my food, or that we haven't received a bill. "Let's go. Right now."

Knowing better than to argue, I slip out of my side of the booth and wordlessly make my way out the door with my mom. I can't help but allow myself one last look at the family over my shoulder, longing filling my heart and soul.

Gripping my arm tight enough to create a reminder in the morning, she drags me to the car. Knowing better than to cry out at the pain she's causing, I bite my lip and walk as fast as I can. When I trip, her nails slice my arm, drawing blood. "Dammit, Rowan. You're such a fucking klutz. Move it."

Finally getting to the car, the minute our doors slam, she starts in. "Did you get a really good look at that family? The family that you wish you had instead of the one God gave you?"

"Mom, I was just-"

"Shut up, stupid girl. I saw the way you were looking at them. Do you think I'm stupid? You were looking at them wishing you could be with them, instead of me. Don't you dare judge me, you stupid bitch! It's not my fault your father left us. He didn't want you two brats. It's the family curse. I knew it would happen, I knew it. But I hoped… I hoped, but I was wrong. My mom warned me, but I didn't listen."

I remain silent. I've heard this so many times I've lost count. I find myself once again wishing for Tyson. For some reason she isn't as harsh to me when he's around. Not that he hasn't heard the same thing I have over, and over, but he always does his best to protect me – a soft of buffer when it comes to our mother.

"She told me that just like her, and her mother before her, that men always leave. We aren't worthy of love. We aren't worthy of commitment. Our family is cursed. Men come and go, but never stay. Believe me, I've tried. I stupidly thought your father was the one. And he would have been, but then I fucked up and got pregnant. As soon as he found out, he was gone. I should have gotten rid of you but I didn't have the chance. He was gone the same day I told him and what the hell did it even matter at that point? At least I would have two children that have to love me. That have to stay."

The only time I learn tidbits about my father is during her painful rants. She reveals a little bit more each time. I don't even know his name. I know that they went to high school together, that he played basketball, and that she says he was very smart. My mom got pregnant with us right out of high school, and while he went on to college, she did not. We lived with my grandmother for a while and then jumped from house to house. Usually we'd move in with whatever man she was dating at the time – until they'd leave or she would leave because of "the curse" and then we would go off somewhere else. Always staying at my grandmother's in between men. When my grandmother died from lung cancer, my mom moved into her house permanently. Now, even though men still come and go, at least we don't have to go from place to place any longer.

"Did you see the way that man looked at you? He may have been with his family and looking like he cares about them, but he looked at you with lust in his eyes. I can tell you right now if his family wasn't with him, he would have tried to have his way with you." Her words disgust me and I know they aren't true, but once again I know better than to argue with her. My thoughts on the subject aren't relevant to her. "Just remember that, Rowan. Men are assholes and aren't worthy of your love and attention, because they won't stick around long anyway. You're a Martin. You aren't worthy of love any more than the Martin women before you."

We pull into a gas station and I wait in the car as she gets out, knowing she's going to stock up on beer. Hopefully it's only alcohol and not drugs this time, but really, I should know better than to hope. She's worse when she mixes the two. With alcohol she remains somewhat coherent, but when she adds the drugs, her words are harsher and she can get physically violent until she eventually seems unaware of herself and anything and anyone around her. She'll say all kinds of things, throw things and invite men over and eagerly do inappropriate things right in front of me. Even boast about it. One time a man tried to leave her and hurt me. He had me pinned against the wall when suddenly Tyson was there with a knife in hand. The man laughed but backed off and Tyson and I left the house for several hours until they both had passed out.

Both of us spend a lot of time behind locked and closed doors when we are home. A lot of times when Tyson and I leave the house we go to the library. It's my favorite thing to do. I love to lose myself in someone else's world. Sometimes, I dream that I'm one of the characters that I'm reading about and that I'm far away from here.

Tyson promises me we will get out of here as soon as we turn eighteen. I hope he's right. The thought of going somewhere new, somewhere we can start over, is one of my favorite. Starting over with just my brother and no alcohol, no drugs, and no mom. Maybe it's wrong because she's my mother, but I want to get away from her. I don't want to hurt like this anymore.

Immediately feeling guilty for my thoughts, I try to give my mom a smile when she returns to the car.

"What are you smiling about? Still dreaming about what you'll never have? When we get home, I want you to get your ass to your room. And your brother too, if that little troublemaker has decided to grace us with his presence by then. Where the hell is he anyway?"

"I'm not sure," I lie. "He said he had to get something from his friend Jeffrey after basketball practice today." Truth is, he's working his after school job at the car wash. He's saving every penny he makes so when we leave, we have money to get an apartment and live for a month or so before we have to get jobs. Or at least, that's the plan. If my mom knew, she would take all his money and spend it on drugs and alcohol, so I make excuses whenever she's aware enough to notice he's not around. Sometimes I work in the library after school. They pay me too and I save every penny, dreaming of the day we can start over.

"Yeah right. He just doesn't want to be around you anymore than I do. Even on your birthday. He probably hates the fact that he's your twin and has to share a birthday with you." She laughs at herself and that's all it takes for a tear to slip from my eye. I was holding it in as tightly as I could, she doesn't deserve my tears, but the dam has sprung a small leak at the constant pressure. I feel angry with myself. I know better than to let her see any emotion.

"Oh that's right you big baby. Cry. Cry all you want. It's not going to matter. News flash. No one cares." She's wrong. Tyson would care.

When we finally pull into the driveway, I practically throw myself out of the car and run into the house not stopping until I get to the safety of my room. Locking the door behind me, I shut out my mother's cruel laughter and the words she yells. Walking to my bed, I stoop down and reach under it and pull out the gift that Tyson gave me this morning. It's a travel book. Inside are thousands of places in the United States. The book talks about each. Closing my eyes, I flip through the pages until I randomly land on one and begin to read. Columbus, Ohio. I wouldn't mind moving there. Fact is, I would move anywhere if it meant not being here.

Reaching back under my bed, I take out my old CD player. I hide all the things I don't want my mom to find under here, she's too lazy to check under my bed. Putting my headphones into my ears, I turn the music up loudly, and then begin to read. Flipping pages and dreaming about a new place, I use music and the captivating pictures in front of me to drown out the words that keep replaying in my mind, "*No one will ever love you. You're not worthy. You'll never amount to anything. When God gave out looks and brains you were obviously in another line.*" Closing my eyes, another tear falls down my face, and I know full well that like it or not, the words I run from have embedded themselves in my heart and soul.

CHAPTER ONE

Rowan

"Come on baby, I really want it."

"I said I'm not in the mood, Jason."

"I promise I'll make it good for you, baby. I just really need this."

Sighing, I rub my swollen belly. One week past my due date and I've never been more uncomfortable. Instead of massaging my back or rubbing my feet to bring me a bit of comfort, he's more concerned with his own needs. Then again, I have heard that an orgasm can help kick start childbirth. When I tell Jason as much, he smiles his manipulating smile, knowing he's about to get his way.

Several minutes later Jason is bucking and moaning while on his knees inside of me. He could give a shit about getting me off and is lost in doing whatever he needs to get himself there. I stare at the ceiling and just wait for it to be over. "Oh yeah baby. I'm coming. Yeahhhhh."

Jason falls to his side next to me trying to catch his breath, oblivious to the fact that I just let him use me, and I turn away from him, curl up with my body pillow and close my eyes praying for sleep to take me. I sigh, pretty sure that to start labor, I would have actually needed to orgasm. I can count on one hand how many times I've had an orgasm with this man, and when it happened it was because I helped myself. Sighing, I do my best to let go of my thoughts and relax.

Something wakes me.

Feeling a strong kick from the baby as he or she shifts, I feel the urge to go to the bathroom. Shuffling my way there, I make my way to the toilet and squat. Before I can be seated, water pours out between my legs. Furrowing my eyebrows, I stand back up. Nothing. Then as I sit back down again, water comes from between my legs again. I am not urinating. Holy hell, my water broke!

Pulling my pants back up, I make my way back to the bedroom as more water falls between my legs. Quickly going to the closet, I change my clothes and then grab my over night bag. Making my way back to the bed, I shake the snoring oblivious man lying in it.

"Jason? Jason!" He groans and turns over, so I shake harder. "Please wake up! My water broke. It's time."

He turns to me, stretches, then opens an eye and squints, "What?"

"It's time. My water broke."

Both eyes open now and he looks me up and down. "What? Are you sure?"

Any other time, I might have laughed at such a stupid question. Key words? *Might have.* "Yes, I'm sure," I spit out between gritted teeth.

He looks at me disbelievingly and I have an almost irresistible urge to smack him up side his head, "How are you sure?"

"Seriously, Jason? I have water pouring down my legs and it sure as hell isn't pee. Now please get up so we can go to the hospital."

"Don't pregnant chicks have bladder control problems?" When I just glare at him, he sighs, "Alright, just a second."

He takes longer than a second. He leisurely rubs his eyes, sits up and rolls his head around his neck like we have all the time in the world. Yes, it's my first pregnancy and this will likely take hours, blah, blah, but I don't care. I want to get a move on and I'm trying desperately to keep my mouth shut and not yell at him, because I know that won't get me anywhere. So instead, I count silently in my head trying to be patient. I do that sometimes when I feel anxious. The counting sooths me in some way I don't quite understand.

I've known from the beginning Jason's less than thrilled about my pregnancy. It was crystal clear when upon hearing about the baby growing in my body, his first response was one of laughter, thinking I was joking. Next came disbelief, then when he was shown irrefutable proof, his words to me were, "Take care of it."

I adamantly refused and expected him to leave me. Yes, I was scared, because no, it certainly wasn't planned. In truth, I never pictured Jason as the father of my children. It wasn't like this was the ideal situation for me either. But, never the less, it happened, and 'taking care of it' wasn't an option for me.

Staring at him blatantly as he saunters into the bathroom, I begin tapping my foot in impatience. When I hear water running in the shower, I let out a sound of disbelief. Peering into the bathroom, I see him feeling the temperature of the bath water. "What the hell are you doing?"

He looks back at me like the answer should be obvious. "I'm going to jump in the shower really quick."

"Are you fucking kidding me, Jason?"

"It's just to wake me up a bit. It's the middle of the night, and I have to drive a car. Just give me five goddamn minutes, alright?"

Tears spring to my eyes and I do my best to push them back. I'm scared, I'm tired, I have more water trickling between my legs and I just want to get to the hospital where I know people will take care of me. I know I'll feel relief as soon as I'm around the doctors and nurses that do this for a living. Sure, I read a ton of books and attended all the newborn, breast-feeding and child care classes I could, but anticipating what's ahead, and being in the moment, are two very different things. I can't contain the fear and nervousness in my heart right now, no matter how hard I try.

Sitting on the edge of my bed, I feel the baby in my belly move and place my hand there to connect with this wonder inside of me, feeling grateful that somehow this simple act calms me down a bit. I don't know yet if it's a boy or a girl. I want to be surprised and Jason never seemed to be curious about the sex. He never asked or suggested that he would like to know. This is one of the few genuine surprises we get in life, and I want that. Many surprises in my life have been hell and this will not be, so I feel a unique eagerness and excitement.

Meeting the little person that has already stolen my heart is something I've been imagining for months. Will he or she look like me? Have my dark hair and hazel eyes? Or will he or she have Jason's blonde hair and blue eyes? Whenever I imagine the baby I'll hold in my arms, the appearance is slightly blurry; the features not defined. I'm anxious for the mystery to be revealed – no matter what it is. I will be happy for ten fingers and ten toes. None of the rest matters.

I've put up with all of Jason's shit because I know that once he meets our son or daughter, it will change everything. How could it not? How will he stare into the tiny face of a person he helped create, and not feel something? So many times during my pregnancy I've felt alone. I've gone alone to doctor's appointments, and experienced the baby's first movements by myself. Every class and shopping trip spent buying tiny outfits and diapers, or hunting second hand shops and garage sales for gently used items for the baby's room, has been done in solitude. There have been many times I wished so hard for him to hold me, rub my belly, kiss it and tell me how much he loves me, and our child. I kept hoping he would attend just one appointment and ask the doctor a question with excitement in his eyes, and anxiousness in his voice. But, to no avail. The loneliness has been suffocating at times, and I can ache so badly for his attention that it physically hurts. But, I keep holding on. I know he will come around.

I hear Jason step out of the shower and dry off. When he's finished he walks into the bedroom naked in order to get clothes from the closet. Seeing him nude used to immediately make my thighs clench. I'd feel desire deep in my belly and shiver all the way to my toes. Somewhere along the way, that's disappeared. I've read that some women's hormones and lust during pregnancy are off the charts. Not mine, at least, not with Jason. However, there was this one guy I saw at the grocery store one time, and lord, I had to hide myself behind the stack of bananas to keep myself from jumping him. Although, bananas weren't exactly a great diversion when sex was on the mind. I felt ridiculously guilty when a feeling of heat washed over me out of nowhere making my nipples tighten and need clench in my belly. I stood and shook for a long time watching his every move, feeling a mixture of relief and regret when he walked away.

Shaking my head trying to push the thought away, I admit to myself that somewhere along the way, things changed with Jason and I hope like hell this baby brings us back together in every way.

Finally, Jason emerges dressed and begins putting his shoes on. He looks at me, raising a brow, "You ready?"

"Are you kidding?" He just sighs and I roll my eyes and nod my head, then follow him out of his apartment into his car.

I'm glad I stayed the night at his place. I haven't been doing that much lately. Stupidly, I thought he would ask me to move in before the baby comes, or at least give me a key or something, but he never asked and I never suggested it. Part of me didn't want to let go of my place anyway – maybe it has something to do with trying to hang on to the little bit of independence I still have before my life completely changes. Maybe it's because I'm not ready to move out from the place I share with Tyson, even though he's not there. I'm not really sure. I just know I've never pushed it, but now on the way to the hospital to have this baby, I can't help but be nervous about what will happen when I walk out of the hospital. Will I go to Jason's place or mine? Will he stay with me? We haven't really talked about that. Will I really know how to take care of this baby? Will I be a good mother? Will Jason and I become the parents and family to this child that I never had?

How does a woman that's never truly had a mother or family of her own be that for someone else? I'm scared - so scared. I don't want to fail at this. It's too important to me. There have been times during my pregnancy that I actually wished for my mother. I almost laugh out loud at the thought. Maybe a child never truly stops wanting and needing her mother, I don't know. Tyson and I left her five years ago, and never looked back. She's rarely been a thought in my mind since - until I became pregnant. Then, thoughts of her – and her words - would come at the most random moments.

When we pull into the hospital, Jason pulls right up to the curb down the sidewalk from the emergency room and sits there not looking at me. Looking at him in confusion I point to the road turning right just ahead, "The maternity center is on the other side, down that way."

He clears his throat, "I know, but the parking garage is here," he points to the covered parking tower ahead. "Just go on inside. I'll go park the car."

Sighing, I murmur, "Okay." Arguing isn't going to make a lick of difference.

Unbuckling my seatbelt I glance at him and momentarily think about leaning over to kiss him on the cheek. When I see his clenched jaw, the impatience as he white knuckles the steering wheel, I change my mind. To aid my decision, my stomach tightens with a contraction. As soon as I stand up I feel a sizable trickle slide down my leg and grimace. I look over my shoulder at Jason, "See you in there." He still doesn't look at me – he just nods and drives away as soon as I shut the door.

Shuffling my way to the entrance, I can tell I'm full on waddling. The water that continues to fall between my legs does not make this comfortable. I'm glad I had the foresight to put on dark sweats. Hopefully I won't have to wait long to get into a hospital room.

Stepping through the doors, I realize it's busy. Several people are occupying the seats available in the waiting area and there are more than a few nurses behind the registration desk. Low murmurs and a buzz of activity fill the space. Deciding to take a seat while I wait for Jason, I try to make myself comfortable and relaxed on the stiff chair. You would think that they would make these seats more comfortable considering people who wait here are generally hurt or sick. I close my eyes, think of my happy place, and take breaths like I practiced in class.

Calmer, opening my eyes and looking around the room, I take in everyone sitting around me. No visible blood or bones to be seen, thank goodness. While I'm trying to be patient, I feel my stomach tighten into a hard ball as a contraction begins. It's short and doesn't last very long, but they are definitely coming a little faster. It's okay, I tell myself. Jason will be here any second and we can go to the maternity ward.

"Tommy! I told you to keep the cloth on your cut. Now you're getting blood all over yourself and the chair. Can't you listen?"

Swallowing thickly at the mother's words, I wonder how I'd deal with something like that when it comes to my own child. Would I speak like that? I've never been one to handle blood well, not even my own. One time when I fell down and busted my knee open, I couldn't even look at it without feeling bile rise up in my throat. Tyson took me home and cleaned it up and bandaged it for me. A small smile curves my lips at the thought. Tyson was always taking care of me. He is someone who will make a great daddy someday. I know he'll be the best uncle. Me, on the other hand? I wonder if God is upstairs laughing over this one. Maybe he needs some entertainment or something. Perhaps the angels are getting boring, all that singing and playing of the harps becoming repetitive.

"Mr. Hansen?" a nurse calls looking around the room for the owner of the surname. A gentleman that looks to be in his mid thirties walk towards the nurse. He's holding his arm close to his body and winces in pain as he walks.

Another contraction comes and this time it takes my breath away just a little. When it's over I feel angry at myself for not looking at the clock when it began. I'm supposed to be timing how frequently they come and how long they last. People continue to get called back one by one. Meaningless conversations continue all around me and I start to worry about Jason. Where is he? What's taking so long?

Taking my phone out of my purse, I check to see if he texted or called to say something happened, but the screen is blank. Calling him, the phone rings over and over. When the voicemail picks up I leave a message, "Jason, where are you? My contractions are picking up. Please hurry."

Hanging up, I feel another contraction and this time, I glance at the clock, checking the time it began. Trying to think about things that bring me peace, I think about the songs the birds sing outside my bedroom window in the morning. How sunshine feels on my face and how I love the smell of rain. I think about how in a matter of hours this child will finally be in my arms. Looking at the clock when it's over, I see that it lasted almost a minute.

Picking up my phone I try again to call Jason. And again. And again. Each call goes straight to voicemail. Getting up I shuffle out of the hospital doors and look towards the covered parking garage. Nope. It's still standing. No accident. Nothing appears to be a problem.

The man I saw with a hurt arm a while ago, now leaves the ER with his arm in a sling. He nods at me as he passes and I make my way back inside, once again sitting in the chair. My contractions continue to come five minutes apart. Distracting myself by looking around the room, I realize that everyone is different. No one from when I arrived is still here.

The big hand on the clock keeps moving and I'm still sitting here… alone. I try his phone, again. "Hi, this is Jason. You know what to do." Lowering my arm slowly, I place my phone back in my bag.

It doesn't take this long to park the car.

He's not coming back.

No man will ever stay.

He doesn't want me, or this baby.

No one will ever love you.

He left both of us.

You're not worthy.

My mom's words haunt me once again.

CHAPTER TWO

Jax

"Motherfucker!" I put my hand over the top of my eye and immediately pull it back seeing blood covering my fingers. It continues to fall like rain down my face and I glower up at the asshole that's to blame.

"Dude. I'm so sorry!" Zane flinches from the look on my face and runs to the bench to grab a towel. When he returns he presses it against my eye.

"Ow, fuck. Don't touch me!"

"We need to stop the bleeding." He keeps pressing the towel against the cut he gave me.

"What the hell, man? We're just supposed to be sparring and you nearly took my head off with that hit."

"I know! It was an accident." Zane looks at me with guilt in his eyes. "Levi!" Zane yells. "Get me a wet towel."

"Get it yourself douche!" Levi yells back.

"We have an injury out here," Zane yells back.

I keep myself from rolling my eyes – barely. Fucking adolescents. A few minutes later, Levi comes sauntering into the room with a wet towel in his hand. He takes one look at me and starts laughing. "What the fuck happened to you?"

I want to smack the look of amusement off his punk ass face. "Zane got in a good right. Ow!"

"Sorry, but I need to clean the blood off." He continues to swipe and poke at me with a towel covered finger. "It's deep man and is bleeding like a bitch. I think it's going to need some stitches."

"What? No. Just butterfly bandage it and let's move on."

"A butterfly isn't going to hold it. It's too deep and wide."

"Aw man, Zane. You are going to scar Jax's pretty face. That alone is going to deserve an ass kicking." Ryder obviously can't contain making a sarcastic comment as well as he walks over from the other side of the gym.

"What the hell? Is this a group event? If so, I'm selling tickets for ten bucks each." The guys laugh and all peer at my face making me feel like I'm going to suffocate. "Alright, everyone back the hell up. I'll go look at it myself."

Passing Cole and Dylan on my way to the office, I give them the finger when they smirk at me. Pricks. Some group of friends I have. Looking in the mirror, I take the towel away. Blood immediately starts flowing again and I curse as I see the guys are right. It's going to need stitches. Dammit. Well, at least we are here after closing time, so all I have to do is kick them out and not worry about getting anyone to close up for me.

"What's the verdict?"

Turning to Ryder I take in his concerned expression. "Zane's right. I need stitches."

"Don't worry, Stone. The ladies think scars are sexy." I scowl at him and he smirks. "I was just heading out, but I can take you to the ER then back here to get your truck afterwards."

"No," I shake my head, "it's cool. It isn't far and I can drive."

"How are you going to drive and keep pressure on the wound at the same time?"

"I'll manage." Brushing past Ryder I yell to the guys, "Alright assholes, practice is over. Get your asses out of here so I can get to the hospital."

Zane, Ryder, Dylan, Cole, and Levi all gather their stuff and walk to the door, while pushing and shoving each other like a bunch of idiots, and blaming Zane for breaking up practice time.

"Jax, let me take you to the hospital, man. I feel like shit for getting you."

"Nah, it's late. Who knows how long I'll have to wait there. I'll be fine."

Zane looks at me helplessly, "You sure?"

"Yep."

"Whatever dude," Ryder takes the keys from my hand and after Cole turns out the lights, he locks the door. "Don't let him off that easy. He should be your bitch at the gym for at least a week or so."

"Yeah, I second that idea," Levi chimes in.

"I may be on board with that myself," I confess. I probably won't really make him do that, but I don't think there is anything wrong with making Zane suffer a little longer. When I reach my truck and unlock it, I throw my bag in the back being sure to hold the towel to my head at the same time. Giving a nod goodbye to the boys that makes my head ache a little, I head on out.

When I take in how busy the emergency room is, I mutter a curse under my breath. I'm going to be here forever. Giving my name to the registration clerk, I explain why I'm there and pay my co-pay, then try my best to wait patiently until I'm called in.

Fortunately, I don't need more than a few stitches when it's all said and done. The doctor agreed that a butterfly bandage wouldn't have done the trick, so I guess it's good I came – pain in the ass as it is.

Checking my phone as I walk out, I see a text from Zane asking how I'm doing. I can't help but smirk to myself knowing he's feeling bad. He should. Sparring means holding back with the punches, not going all out like it's a real fight. I text out a reply telling him I needed three times the amount of stitches I really did, and that they're monitoring me for a concussion, because he deserves it. Smiling to myself I shove my phone into my back pocket, and as I round the corner, I look up to see a very pregnant woman standing up from her seat. When she suddenly bends over and cries out, I run to her.

"Whoa, whoa!" I immediately grab her elbow and hand to help support her into a standing position. She continues to breathe rapidly while looking at the ground and squeezing my hand. After a few minutes, she appears to calm herself. Taking a deep breath, she finally looks up at me and I'm surprised by the instant reaction I have to her when she looks into my eyes. It takes my breath away.

She's beautiful. Huge green, or are they brown, eyes. Long dark hair. A smattering of freckles cover her nose, and her long lashes make her eyes look big and dark. Her lips are full and pouty and currently parted as she takes rapid breaths in and out which draws my gaze to her chest. Realizing I'm looking at her full breasts, I look back at her face just in time to see her lick her lips. My eyes automatically follow the movement and it makes my dick twitch in my pants. Realizing I'm lusting after a pregnant lady, I put my focus back on her eyes. *What the hell, Stone? What's wrong with you?*

Tilting my head, I narrow my eyes - she looks familiar. "Are you okay? Do you need some help?" Before she can respond, I look over to the registration desk and see a male nurse standing there staring at us like an idiot. "Dude! There's a woman in labor here. Can we get some help?"

He runs into action and comes around the corner within seconds pushing a wheelchair. "Ma'am, what are you doing here? If you're in labor, we need to get you to the Family Place, where our maternity services are." He's coming across kind of harsh and I feel an immediate possessive and protective feeling run through my body making me scowl at him. He must feel the heat of my stare because he glances up at me and immediately adjusts his tone. "How long have you been in labor?"

She lifts her head and looks at the clock on the wall, "Um, my water broke about three hours ago I guess."

My eyes widen as does the nurses, "Three hours ago? Have you been sitting here the whole time?" She nods. "Why didn't you say something?"

She opens her mouth to respond, but her eyes meet mine and then she looks down instead and shrugs. The nurse and I help her into the wheelchair and then he immediately begins pushing her through some double doors and down the hall. I give her hand a squeeze, feeling almost anxious at the thought of letting go, but know that I need to. About to wish her luck and tell her goodbye, she grabs my hand and squeezes it like hell, "Ow, fuck!"

The nurse looks at me with a raised brow at my outburst, but I'm too focused on the girl breathing through her contraction to care. He begins wheeling her faster and she doesn't let go of my hand, so I do my best to keep up.

When we arrive at the part of the hospital stupidly named the Family Place, the nurse brings her right through the doors and into a room. "I'm going to get someone to come in here and check you out. They'll be here in a moment to take your information." She just nods and takes deep breaths appearing to try to calm herself again. "In the mean time, go ahead and change into this gown, then get up in the bed, please."

When he leaves, I stand there awkwardly and start to tell her good luck once again, but then feel nailed to the floor and struck dumb. She sets her bag down and pulls her shirt over her head. Swallowing hard, I turn my back to give her privacy although that didn't seem to be a concern of hers.

"You can turn around now," she says.

When I do, I'm thankful to see she's all covered up. She may be pregnant and in labor, but I'm not dead. Her tits looked luscious and huge spilling out of the lace enclosing them when she pulled her shirt off. When she begins to get herself up in the bed, I immediately walk towards her and offer stability as she climbs in. They should have helped her, the asses, how can any pregnant woman do that easily? She looks at me in surprise and murmurs, "Thank you." Before I can say another word someone comes in with a clipboard and begins asking all kinds of questions.

"Hi. I'm Nurse Diaz and I need to ask you a few questions. First of all, did you preregister with the paperwork your doctor should have given you?"

"Yes."

"Okay, great. That will make this fast then. What is your name, honey?"

"Rowan Martin."

A sound of surprise instantly leaves me drawing Rowan and the nurse's attention. I cross my arms and stay silent through the rest of the nurse's questions about insurance. When she leaves telling her another nurse would be in to check her progress and confirm if her water did in fact break, I finally tell her the reason for my surprise. I know her. Well… of her anyway. "Your Ty Martin's sister," I say as fact, not a question.

Her eyes widen with surprise, "Yes, I am. He's my twin brother."

I knew it. I met Ty several months back when he started coming into the gym. We became friends and he was shaping up to be a great fighter. He hasn't been in the gym for quite some time and we've all wondered where he's been. We tried calling his cell phone with no luck.

Her face screws up in pain and I know another contraction has hit her. Without thought I walk over to her and take her hand vaguely wondering what the hell I'm doing. I should leave, but somehow I can't seem to help myself. She squeezes my hand immediately, making me glad I took hers, and pants through her pain.

Looking worriedly at a new nurse that walks in I blurt, "This seems to be happening a lot. Doesn't that mean something?"

Before she can respond a doctor breezes into the room behind her. "Hi there, my name is Dr. Sutton. I'm the doctor on call this evening and I'm going to check you to make sure your water did in fact break, and to see how far you're dilated, if at all, okay?" Rowan nods and I start to pull my hand away but she squeezes it tighter.

When they begin to lift up the sheet that covers her legs, I politely look away. I hear him ask her to move down a bit and readjust the sheet. I don't know what the fuck the doctor does under it and I don't think I want to know. Watching her face as her nose wrinkles with discomfort, I can't help but wonder why she's here alone. Where is her family, her brother? Hell, where is the baby daddy? All I need is for him to walk in here ready to kick my ass because I'm seeing his girl in such a vulnerable and personal state.

"Your water definitely broke and you're already at an eight dilation, and about eighty percent effaced. At this rate, it won't be long before you'll begin pushing. This baby doesn't appear to be waiting around. I need to know what your birth plan is?"

She looks at the doctor in confusion, "Birth plan?"

He smiles kindly and I'm glad. I think I'd punch him if he weren't nice to her. "You need to decide now if you want an epidural or not. How much pain are you in? Are you managing it well? Do you need help with the pain?"

"It's bearable. I don't want an epidural, I want to be clear headed for the birth."

"Okay. Just so you know. You're at a point where we won't be able to do it later. So, just want you to be sure." I see her nod her head yes. "We are also going to get you to a labor and delivery room now, put an IV in and attach you to baby monitors. I'll be back as soon as you're dilated to ten centimeters. Did you take any labor and delivery classes?"

"Yes."

"Okay, good. Then you know what I mean when I tell you to breathe the best you can through the pain. As you get closer to ten, your contractions will come faster and harder."

Way to be encouraging there, asshole. I keep my thoughts to myself although I can't contain the glare I give him. A nurse notices and I swear I see her smile at my obvious protectiveness.

"Okay, Rowan. I'll be back soon." He pats her leg and heads out of the room.

Finding myself staring at her, I realize that I don't care for the thought of her being in more pain. When her face twists again and her hand tightens in mine, I grit my teeth wishing I could take it from her.

When it subsides she looks at me, "So, you know my brother, Tyson?"

Smiling, I think of the guy that looks so similar yet different enough to the girl looking at me. "Yes. He came to my gym all the time and started MMA training."

"MMA training? What's that?"

Her breathing is harsh and her words come out like bullets between pants. I'm assuming keeping her in conversation is helpful, so I squeeze her hand and keep talking. "MMA stands for mixed martial arts. I fight professionally, and own a gym for training and fitness. Ty came in a lot and had begun training too. When I met him, he told me he wanted to get into fighting. In fact, I think he said he needed to." When her brows furrow, I shrug. "He's really great and I've been excited to sponsor him. My gym sponsors several fighters and we have someone that helps get fights scheduled. We were planning on doing just that for him."

"Oh. I had no idea. He didn't mention it."

"Where's he been? Is he okay? I haven't seen him lately and we've tried calling him a few times and left messages, but he's never gotten back to me, or one of the other guys. He never said he wanted to quit. He's always been really into it, so I never expected that he just wouldn't return."

Before she can answer, two guys come in to wheel her to the labor and delivery room and somehow, I find myself walking along side her bed without question. This is the craziest shit ever. I came here to get a few stiches and now I'm going to be here for the birth of a baby? Am I? How did this happen? I watch with wide eyes as nurses bustle around her connecting her to wires and poke and prod her. She reaches for me when another contraction hits and I automatically give her my numb and tingling hand. When it passes, she puts her big eyes back on me, "I'm sorry. I keep squeezing the hell out of your hand. I'm just… not myself. I…" she stops and her eyes well up, but she lifts her chin and clears her throat trying hard to get control of her emotions.

"How can I help, Rowan? Can I call Ty? Your mom or dad? Your boyfriend or husband? Are you married? Just give me their numbers and I can let them know what's going on, or maybe they are already on their way and I should go watch for them and tell them where you are?"

"No," she whispers. "There's no one."

"What do you mean? Let me at least call Ty. He talked about you all the time. I know he would want to be here."

Another pain grips her and she seems hesitant to say more with the nurses all around her clearly listening in on our conversation, so I don't push it. When this pain passes she finally says, "Tyson's gone."

"Gone? I don't understand. Did he move away?"

"No. Kind of, I guess. Only temporarily." She sighs and blurts, "He's in jail."

"What?" I stare at her in disbelief. "Jail? What the hell happened?"

"He…" her breath is taken from her and she begins to take short breaths, working through the pain. I think I feel something pop in my hand. Gritting my teeth, I do my best not to call out like a pussy, but hell, it hurts. This little woman has some power in that grip of hers. "Oh god, I feel like I need to push," she yells.

"Let me take a look, honey." According to her name tag, Nurse Johnson lifts the sheet that's covering Rowan's legs and takes a look and once again, I divert my eyes to Rowan's face. She's watching the nurse intently. "You're at a ten. Let me go get the doctor right now."

Rowan nods her head and a tear falls down her cheek. It breaks something inside of me to see her hurting. "Hey, its okay. I'll be honest, I don't know shit about this, but I can tell you are doing great. Don't cry."

Eyes full of tears, wet hair plastered to the side of her face, cheeks and lips flushed, she gives me a soft smile and something inside of me completely flips over. She undoes me with that look. I'm gone. Even in the midst of pain and obvious fear, her beauty and strength shine through whatever darkness her earlier words made her feel. She's the epitome of strength and I feel humbled to be in her presence and I don't even know details. I don't need to know. It's written all over her. "I know you don't know me. But please, can I ask you a favor?"

"You can ask me anything," I answer.

"Don't leave me." Her words are soft as if she's afraid to confess them for fear of my response. "I don't have anyone else and I don't want to be alone."

An overwhelming feeling of possessiveness and the blatant need to protect her once again takes me over, making me grit my teeth and my toes curl in my shoes. The strong feelings make me unable to answer her for a full minute.

I'm not one of those guys that believe in love at first sight and all that girly shit, but hell if this girl doesn't do something to me that I don't understand. She makes me think that maybe it's not so impossible after all. So, instead of questioning it further, I do what I always do, I take a chance. It's no different than when I stand up to my asshole of a father. It's no different than when I took over the gym I now own. It's no different than when I step into the cage, each and every time. All of those times, I fight for what I want. And now, I want her, no matter how crazy or fast it seems.

"I won't leave you. I promise."

I don't take my promises lightly.

CHAPTER THREE

Rowan

Breathing through another contraction I want to find Jason and rip his fucking head off. I feel a mixture of sadness and anger laced with despair. My mind is all over the place. I've become this scared shell of a person and it's pissing me off. I've dealt with much more than this, and alone, so why should this be any different? But it is.

Right now, I'm angry not only for him leaving me like a piece of trash he threw away, but for getting me in this condition. Yeah sure, it takes two to tango and blah, blah, stupid blah. I don't care. This hurts, so damn much. Not that I didn't think it wouldn't. I know what to expect, but I didn't expect to do this on my own.

The squeeze of my hand makes me remember that I'm not alone. Before I can glance at mystery man, I focus hard on getting through this pain. *Breathe… breathe… in…. out….in… out. I can do this. I can do this. I can do this. I'm fucking strong, dammit.*

I want to find out mystery man's name. It's ironic that he knows Tyson, and somehow that comforts me. I feel a twinge of guilt for squeezing his hand so tightly and for practically begging him to stay. He looks terrified, yet determined. He keeps swallowing a lot and gritting his teeth to stay under control. He's running his other hand through his thick dark hair and I can tell he's stressed. It isn't like I really made the choice easy for him. Who the hell can say no to a girl in this condition anyway? Oh wait, I guess I just asked myself a rhetorical question. I know the answer to that, don't I?

The doctor walks in with a big smile on his face and claps his hands in excitement. "Okay! Let's have ourselves a baby. You ready?"

Is he serious? I glare at him and almost smile when I see mystery man doing the same, until I get another contraction that distracts me from him. The asshole doctor is smiling like this is a picnic. I'm getting ready to squeeze a fucking watermelon out of my vagina hole, and he's clapping? I'd like to tell him to shove it. This is what I get for not choosing a specific OB and going to the free health clinic instead. They told me that all the delivery doctors are great, but hell, what else would they say? Oh well, no use in thinking about that now. Instead, I nod and try not to get nervous when they push a button that lifts the bed into more of a sitting position.

Oh god, I will never, ever have more children. This is awful. The pain is debilitating, and what the hell is up with me deciding to do this naturally and wanting to be clear minded? There's no award to be won here, what am I out to prove? Clearly, I've lost my mind. My abdomen tightens and I feel so much pressure, "Oh! Here comes another one. I need to push! Now!" I scream but can't find it within myself to feel embarrassed.

"Alright, Rowan, listen. I'm going to count to five and at the same time, you push as hard as you can, take a breath, then push again for another five. Got it?"

Nodding, I grip the handles on either side of me to have something sturdy to hold onto. One nurse holds my leg back and gestures for mystery man to do the same. Now, I feel a flash of embarrassment and if my cheeks weren't already red from exertion, they'd redden at the horrified look on his face. All that quickly fades when I start pushing. "One... two... three...four...five...." I take in a deep breath gulping as much air as possible and then start pushing again, "One... two....three...four....five."

Falling back, I pant from the exertion while sweat pours down my face, neck and back. I jerk a little when a cool towel brushes over my forehead. Looking to my left, mystery man seems focused on his task of cooling me down. "Thank you," I tell him in between pants.

He nods at me and tries to give me encouragement, but he looks a little green. "You're doing great. You can do this."

Before I can respond, it's time to push again. When I'm finished the doctor does his best to encourage me, "You're doing exceptional, Rowan. I can already see the baby's head. Do you know if it's a boy or a girl?"

"No. I want to be surprised."

"Well he or she has a full head of dark hair just like you!"

My toes curl with the pain from the next push. "One… two… three… four…five." I gulp in air again but feel the need to push again immediately. "One…two…three…four…five. Great job, Rowan. We need one, maybe two more pushes, and then the head will already be out. This is going so well, you're doing amazing for your first time."

Amazing? I feel like I'm being ripped apart from the inside out. "I just want it out!" I scream.

Mystery man rubs my leg and looks at me, "Hang in there. You are so strong, and you can do this." I look at him and surprisingly want to laugh. Truth is there's a mix of amazement and terror on his face that's comical. Poor guy. I'm going to have to bake him something after this. I wonder what he likes? Maybe cookies or brownies or something. "Oh hell! I need to push again."

"One….two…three…four….five," the nurse counts. I take a deep breath through my nose and then push again. While they count I hear the doctor tell mystery man that he should take a look and can't even bring myself to care when they ask, or when he declines. Can't say I blame him.

"The head is out, Rowan. The rest will be easy." Somehow I manage not to scoff or laugh hysterically at that comment. "Hold it until I tell you to push gently, okay?" I nod and do my best to catch my breath and breathe deeply while thinking of all the ways I'd like to murder the doctor for suggesting anything about this is easy.

Men! Fucking men! Sweat pours down my head, my hair is sticking to me and I'm exposed to the world, but all I can think about is that I'm almost done. I'm going to meet my baby. I can do this. I see the finish line and it's glorious.

"Okay, Rowan, this is the final stretch. Give me a gentle push."

I do as he asks and am thrilled when after a moment, I'm rewarded with the sweetest cry I've ever heard.

"It's a girl!"

I begin crying and when they place her on my chest, I wrap my arms around her the best way I can considering she's still attached to me and I'm panting from exertion. "Hi there my sweet, sweet baby girl," I say to her in between pants and tears. Her little eyes open and she looks at me and in that instant, my heart no longer belongs to anyone but her. I never really understood what people were talking about when they said that in an instant my whole world would change and my heart would become full to bursting. Their words would make me nod and smile in agreement, but I didn't really understand – not really. Now, I know exactly what they mean – I understand with my whole heart and soul. My heart feels like it's overflowing with love and awe and protectiveness at this little life so entwined with mine. The empty, broken pieces in my heart are mended together with one look from a sweet precious baby girl. *My baby girl.*

"We just have to take her to clean her up a bit, honey." The doctor has cut the umbilical cord so the nurse takes her off of my stomach and a small whimper escapes me at the loss of her heat on my belly. Then I moan in pain when another nurse starts rubbing hard on my stomach. "I'm sorry dear, I know this is uncomfortable. We just have to make sure the uterus doesn't retain clots and contracts back." That's an understatement I think as I groan in pain. The nurse smiles softly at me, "I'm sure you're tired honey, let's make sure you get some rest once the baby is sleeping. Do you have a name for your sweet girl yet?"

"Yes, it's Lily. Lily Rayn."

"Aw, what a beautiful name." She takes a dry erase marker and writes Lily's name and birth statistics on the board. She finishes cleaning me up, and when Lily's ready she places her back in my arms and says she'll be back to check on me and move me to a recovery room shortly. I nod absently, all my attention on the treasure in my arms.

When I finally manage to look away from my baby's sweet face, I see that I'm alone. I have no idea if mystery man is coming back, or if he left for good. I really hope he comes back, I'd like to thank him for being here for me.

Returning my attention to Lily, I take in her sweet face. I smile when I see she has my full lips and certainly my dark hair. Her eyes are blue, but I know they could change. So many emotions swirl through me as I watch her. Love. There is so, so much love. It's a wonder my heart can contain it all.

"I promise to love you the way you deserve to be loved," I whisper to her. "You *are* worthy, you *will* be loved and you will never, ever be alone my baby girl. I promise you that."

Tears make silent tracks down my face and I marvel at how I can feel so complete yet so lost at the same time. I wish my brother were here. It's been so hard while he's been gone. We spend all our time together whenever possible, and I even miss his over protective ways. The time left before his release seems to be crawling by. The occasional collect phone call isn't enough. He's careful not to call too often knowing it's quite expensive to do so, and of course I can't call him, though more than anything I wish I could. I smile to myself knowing how proud he would be if he were here.

My missing him turns into fear. I thought when Lily was finally here that Jason would be too. How am I going to do this alone? No Tyson. No Jason. Just me. It's a physical pain in my chest that wants something more, for some*one* more. Jason didn't just abandon me. He abandoned our daughter too. What kind of father does that?

My eyes feel heavy and though I want to continue staring at my sweet baby's face, when I'm finally moved into a room of my own later, I place Lily in the bassinet knowing I need to get some rest. Turning on my side, I wince at the pain I feel at the junction of my thighs. Feeling utterly exhausted, emotionally and physically, I close my eyes and tears fall from behind my lids, down my temples, to become lost in my hair.

"You're not worthy of love. You will always be alone."

It doesn't matter how many miles separate us, her words are still the poison that runs through my veins. They've scarred me; they've branded my soul and no matter how hard I try, I can't escape them. Then, I open my eyes and look at the child sleeping next to me and know that she's wrong. Now, I just need to believe it.

CHAPTER FOUR

Jax

Slipping out of the delivery room, I make my way to the waiting room, which signs indicate is down the hall. Taking a seat in the corner of the room away from a man that's pacing back and forth and another person talking on the phone, I try to rub out the kink I feel in my neck. I'm exhausted from being up all night, but I also have adrenaline running through me after what I just witnessed.

I can't stop playing the delivery over and over in my mind. You would have to be one hard son of a bitch to not be affected by something as amazing as a woman giving birth. I'm simply astounded at not only how strong Rowan is, but how amazing her body is to physically go through what it just did.

Seeing her lying there with her new baby in her arms, even I was brought to tears. I'm not ashamed to admit it. It was simply breathtaking. Giving her time alone to bond with her child seems like the right thing to do. It felt intrusive being there to witness something so special and sacred between a mother and child, yet my heart felt full at being privileged enough to see the little bit that I did. I had to physically rip myself from the room in order to give her the privacy she deserves.

"There's no one."

Her words ring in my ears and make my fists curl. I want to rage at the person that has obviously left her. I can see the fear, despair and anger in her eyes. Whomever put it there should be castrated. Something about her has completely flipped my heart, mind and body to full on want and need. How am I going to leave her alone?

She seemed so sad and vulnerable with her confession. And she said Ty is in jail. I wonder what the hell happened? The last time I saw him, he had car trouble and I offered to drop him off at his place. I remember seeing Rowan from a distance when Ty gestured to her walking toward their place. He waved a quick goodbye to me and bounded over to her. I stood there transfixed as I watched her radiant smile as he ran up to her hugging her in greeting, their love for one another clear to anyone that watched. Plus, Tyson talked about Rowan a lot when he came into the gym for practice. It was "Rowan said…", "Rowan went…", "I need to tell Rowan….." He very clearly loves her and considers it his job to take care of his sister. I need to find out what happened there. Especially since she said she has no one else.

And how can that be? I find myself curious about the man who is her baby's father. Where is he? Why isn't he part of the picture? The need for information is making me crazy.

I can't help but think that I ran into her for a reason. I don't believe in luck or coincidence so I know that I happened to see her just when I needed to most. It's obvious why. Someone needs to help take care of her and I intend to be that person.

Looking at my phone I see I have another message from Zane spouting out his apologies and a text from Cole asking how I am. Checking out the clock I see that it won't be long before the gym needs to be opened. Time apparently flies when you are an active participant in a birth that managed to make you feel both awe and terror at the same time. When she screamed in pain, I don't think I've ever felt more helpless and I really don't like that feeling.

Refusing to call my father to ask him to help out at the gym, I dial Cole instead, thankful when he answers, "Lo?" His greeting combined with the gravel sound of his voice tells me I woke him.

"Hey man. Sorry to wake you, but I need your help."

"What's up?"

"It's a long story, but I'm tied up at the hospital and I need someone to open the gym this morning. Can you do that for me?"

"Yeah of course, but I thought you just needed a few stitches?"

"I did. I just ran into someone here that I can't leave right now. Like I said, a long story for later. And I don't want to call my dad."

"I get it. No worries."

"Thanks for helping me out, man. I'm not sure how long I'm going to be."

"Any time - you know that, and I'll just cover you as long as needed. I'm off the next few days from work and planned on being at the gym anyway. I figured that's why you gave me the extra set to begin with, yeah?"

"Yeah. And nothing major is expected today – no deliveries or anything. Thanks again."

"No problem. Talk to you later."

Hanging up, I run my hands through my hair and over my eyes and try to make myself comfortable in the chair so that I can nap for just a bit while I give Rowan some more time alone.

Closing my eyes, my dad's angry face comes to mind. I can already hear the nasty words that will come out of his mouth if he goes to the gym and I'm not there. Fuck him. He doesn't deserve to know anything about my life. He can talk smack all he wants. My guys know the truth. Shaking my head, I'm relieved when Rowan's big hazel eyes and soft smile as she looks at her baby's face are there to greet me instead.

Jolting awake I forget where I am for a moment until I look around and see the waiting room and the armchair my body is contortioned in trying to find comfort. Rowan. Shit. How long have I been asleep? Looking at my phone, I see it's only been a couple hours. After I find a bathroom, I make my way back to the delivery room to see that she's no longer there and I almost walk in on some other woman. Wouldn't she have been shocked! Not to mention the hospital staff will start to think I'm some creepy guy that likes to assist with childbirth or something. That or gets off looking at woman's anatomy. Um, no thanks.

I quickly get her room number from the nurse's station and head that way before deciding to make a quick detour to the gift shop. Standing there I look around feeling unsure of what to buy. I have no idea what kind of flowers she even likes.

"Hello," a kind voice interrupts my thoughts. "Can I help you?"

Turning to my left, an older woman wearing a bright yellow shirt with kind eyes behind her glasses, smiles at my obvious confusion. Smiling in return I confess, "I need to bring something to a woman that just had a baby girl, but I'm not sure what she will like. I don't even know her favorite flower."

"Oh, I think I can help you with that, sweetie."

Ten minutes later I'm walking out with a mixed arrangement of pink and white flowers, a fluffy lamb and an "It's a girl," balloon. Feeling much more prepared to see Rowan again I make my way back to the room she's in. When I peek inside, she's sitting up picking at what must be some breakfast on her tray.

"Hi," I say quietly, not wanting to startle her.

Her eyes widen a little in surprise when she sees me and then her surprise turns into a smile at the items I'm carrying in my arms. "Hi back. I'm surprised to see you."

Cocking my head to the side I look at her curiously, "Why's that?"

"When you weren't here, I figured you left. Not that I would blame you after what I forced you to witness and participate in." She giggles and I find I love its tinkling sound.

"You didn't force me. I'm glad I could be here for you." Walking to the table next to her bed, I sit the flowers down and hand her the lamb. "For you and the little one."

"Lily," she says.

"Lily," I repeat softly while peeking at her in the plastic rectangle thing she's lying in next to her mother's bed. She's wearing a knitted pink hat and is swaddled tightly in a blanket. She's sucking on her bottom lip in her sleep and my heart can't help but flip and tighten at the sight. God, it's like I have girly hormones. "She's so small. So sweet."

Rowan smiles beautifully, "I think so too."

I take in her wide smile and how her eyes are alight with love and my chest tightens further. I can't put my finger on what the feeling is. Clearing my throat a couple times, I hesitantly set the lamb in the corner of the bed where Lily is lying, then sit in the chair next to Rowan's bed.

I'm startled when suddenly Rowan starts to laugh. Looking at her curiously only makes her laugh harder. In response, I let out a chuckle as well in an automatic response to her infectious laugh, but I don't know why she's laughing. "What's so funny? Oh shit! Is it the lamb or the flowers? That lady at the gift shop told me you would like them. I blame her."

This only seems to make her laugh harder. Standing, I start to remove the items I bought. I mean hell, I don't know dick about this kind of stuff. What am I even doing? "No," she gasps making me freeze. "No, don't touch them." She tries to calm herself, placing a hand on her chest as if that helps, and I hand her a tissue to wipe her watering eyes. "I'm sorry." She swipes at her eyes and then gestures wildly with her hands while trying to explain, "I think my laughing got out of hand because I'm tired, but it just struck me as funny."

"What did?"

"You."

"Me?"

"Yes. You know my brother, Tyson. You held my hand all through giving birth. Plus, you were up close and personal with my vagina and likely not in the way you're usually up close with them from the various looks on your face during the whole experience."

Smirking at her very true comments, I still feel lost as to her point, "That's true. So what are you getting at?"

"Well, the reason I'm laughing is because I have absolutely no clue what in the hell your name is."

I immediately chuckle with her. After everything we shared, and everything I've seen, she doesn't even know my name. I guess I never did tell her.

"I just think that given all of that, I should know. Don't you think?"

I nod in agreement and she smiles bigger, dragging my gaze to her mouth. It makes my stomach flip, yet again, and my dick twitch.

"So, handsome mystery man that came to my rescue when I really needed someone..."

"You think I'm hot?" I can't help but tease her. I want to keep that smile on her face a little longer. She should smile all the time - the sight is fucking gorgeous. Stunning. Maybe giving birth really agrees with her because I don't know if I've ever seen anyone more beautiful.

"I said 'handsome'."

"Yeah you did, but you think I'm hot," I state with not just a little confidence. I'm not stupid. I have a mirror. Doesn't mean it's not nice to hear though.

"You know you are," she says with a smile as if she read my mind.

I have mercy on her, "My name is Jackson Stone. My friends call me, Jax."

"Well I would certainly say we are friends after our experience together, wouldn't you, *Jax*?"

The sound of my name on her lips makes me smile wide, knowing in doing so, I'm flashing her my dimples. Women love them. When she said my name, immediately a need to hear her say it in all kinds of ways rushes through my mind making me shiver. Whispering it, saying it with need, saying it in a whine because she needs and wants more of me, saying it in lust. Fuck me I want to hear her scream it. Her eyes widen likely at the look on my face. I wonder if she can see the heat in my eyes? I don't want to scare her, so I lean back in my chair, cross my ankles, and do my best to look comfortable when I feel anything but. "I would definitely say we are friends."

She nods and holds my gaze for what seems an eternity. I'm immediately lost in her eyes. Those green but sometimes brown eyes. Her dark hair is gorgeous and while she has tired lines around her eyes, she's simply glowing. No makeup, freckles across her nose prominent. I want to get to know each one, see if she has more on other parts of her body, kiss across her nose and suck her lips into my mouth.

Shaking my head I try to rid myself of the thoughts. The woman just gave birth. I can't explain the feelings she invokes in me. Distracting myself I ask the question that's been on my mind. "You mentioned earlier that Ty is in jail. What happened? If it's okay to ask, I mean. You don't have to tell me."

"No, it's fine. Besides, it's a matter of public record anyway." She's momentarily distracted when Lily begins making little noises. She peeks at her in concern and I follow her gaze. She's fine and Rowan focuses her big eyes back on me, "He got in a fight at a bar. It wasn't his first and unfortunately this time, he got in a fight with the wrong person. I don't even know what it was about." She shakes her head in obvious irritation at her brother. "I honestly don't even know if I asked him," she laughs sardonically. "He was arrested because the senator's son he was fighting with pressed charges. Since it wasn't the first time he's gotten in a fight and been arrested, this time around he was given six months in jail and six months community service when he's out. He was warned if it happens again after he's released, his jail time will be longer."

"I had no idea, Rowan. I'm sorry. Like I said, we became friends when he began practicing at my MMA gym."

"It's your gym?"

"Yes. My grandfather left it to me," and that's enough about that. "Anyway, like I mentioned before, Ty is a great fighter. I'm surprised he never mentioned it to you."

"Well, he knows I was never thrilled with his fighting, but that's only because he did it as an outlet where he was always getting busted. I would have welcomed his involvement in MMA as opposed to letting his temper get the best of him and getting in random fights with people and getting arrested."

"Well, like I mentioned before, we were hoping to line some professional fights up for him, but one day he just quit showing up."

"Yeah, he's been there for two months already."

"Do you talk to him often?"

"Um, not really. I went and visited him a couple weeks ago. He calls when he can, but collect calls are expensive, so he doesn't do it often."

"So, he doesn't even know yet that you had Lily." I don't know why but this troubles me and an idea starts to take form in my mind.

"No, he doesn't."

"Can I help? I'd be happy to go and see him for you and let him know."

She looks at me as if she's trying to look for sincerity in my words. Then something that looks like apprehension crosses her face and I can almost see the solid wall she puts up between us.

"Why?"

"Why what?"

"What would you do that?"

"Well, it would help you out. Plus, I wouldn't mind seeing him myself now that I know where he is."

"If you'd like to see him I'm sure he would love it, but don't worry about going on my account. I'm sure he will call eventually."

Yeah well we'll see about that. But for now, I change the subject. "How long do you have to stay in the hospital? A week? Two?"

This makes her laugh out loud, "No, not at all. I should be released tomorrow."

"Tomorrow?" I yell out shocked and then wince when I realize my mistake. Peeking at Lily, I lower my voice, "What the hell? Why so soon?"

She shrugs, "It's pretty fast, but typical. Usually forty-eight hours or less for a regular birth."

"Regular?"

"Vaginal versus cesarean."

"Cesarean?"

"That's when they have to cut open your stomach to take the baby out."

"But what you did is considered regular? They are messed up." She laughs again. "Seriously, Rowan, that's ridiculous. After everything you did? I should complain to someone." She starts to laugh again until she sees me rise half way up out of my chair. She holds up a hand as if that would stop me. "No, Jax. It's okay, really. I'm only a little sore, and tired, but otherwise fine. I want to go home. Trust me. And truly, that is a normal release time."

Sitting back down, I can't help but frown. I don't like this at all. I mean, how is she possibly healed in twenty-four hours? That just seems dangerous to me to send her home before she's ready. After what I saw... I just can't see how that's possible. "Well I'm not leaving here until they release you. Do you need a ride home? Or did you drive yourself here in your condition?" I feel almost sick at the thought

Looking down in obvious embarrassment her face reddens, "Um, a ride tomorrow would be great. Are you sure you don't mind? I'm sure you have to get back to your gym."

"Don't worry about me." How the hell did she get here if she needs a ride home? Some things don't add up. Suddenly a frown mars her pretty features, "What is it? Are you hurting? Do you need me to get the nurse?" I hop up out of my seat.

"No, I'm fine. It's just… I thought of something."

"What is it?"

"Can I ask you a favor?" she asks sheepishly.

"Of course you can," I smile encouragingly. She looks like a dog that's been kicked and it makes my gut burn. What the hell has been done to her? My fists clench at my side feeling the need to punch whatever's put that look on her face.

"Well… the hospital won't let me leave if the baby doesn't have a car seat. My ride…" she clears her throat, looks away, takes a couple breaths and then looks back at me. "Well let's just say my car seat is no longer here. If I give you some money, would you run to the store for me and get one? There's this great second hand baby store not too far from here that will have something."

"Absolutely, and I don't need money."

She immediately frowns and argues, "You aren't buying a car seat. I have some cash in my wallet if you will just hand me my bag."

"You can just pay me later, okay?" Like a lot later, or never, I think but don't say.

"Okay," she looks relieved and I'm happy to remove a tiny amount of stress from her. "Thank you so much."

"I told you I'm happy to help you and I meant it."

She looks at me thoughtfully for a minute and I can see the question brewing in her eyes. I wait patiently for it to leave her lips, "Why?"

My brows lower in confusion. This again? "Why what?"

"Why are you so willing to help me?"

She looks uneasy as if she's afraid of my response and it makes me feel irritation. Has no one ever been nice to her? I don't understand. There are so many things I want to know about her, and I'm determined to know them. I have no fucking idea what has happened to me, but all I know is that I want to be someone she can trust. Someone she can count on. I have the feeling she can use someone like that in her life. "You told me earlier there's no one to help you. I don't believe in coincidence and I think I ran into you here for a reason. So, I want to see you and Lily home safe and sound. I wouldn't feel right otherwise. Especially since I know Ty isn't around right now."

Her eyes flash anger, "I don't need your sympathy."

"Good, because that's not what I'm giving you. Ty is my friend, and I'd like to be your friend too. Is that so hard to believe?"

She looks at me for a few beats before saying softly, "No."

"Good, because friends help friends. Okay so I'm going to head to the store for the car seat now. Is there anything else you need?"

The tentative look falls off of her face and she gives me a soft smile, "No. Thank you so much."

"I'll be back," I inform her gruffly trying to shake the want I feel when I look at her. Leaving the room, I adjust myself on the way out. *What is she doing to me?*

CHAPTER FIVE

Rowan

This is an indescribable feeling. I may have arrived here alone in many ways, but I leave with so much more. A mother. I'm a mother. The thought alone brings tears to my eyes. I seem to be doing that very easily – crying. I should be feeling more happiness than sadness, but there's something that's not quite letting me get there and it isn't Jason's abandonment. I'm not sure what it is.

Looking down at the little darling in my arms I chalk it up to this precious little prize evoking feelings in me I couldn't have imagined even when I tried. I love her more today than I did yesterday. How is that even possible? I had no idea my heart was capable of containing this much love. If this happens every day, how will I not burst from it? She's everything. My everything.

Jax sits quietly next to me as we wait for the nurse to get here with a wheelchair so I can be taken to the hospital exit. He was true to his word, staying with me all night. I slept off and on and when I needed to go to the bathroom, or feed Lily, he would make himself scarce, always returning, always making small talk about nothing or just being a constant presence that I found soothing.

But now, I'm so glad we've been discharged – I have this overwhelming need to get home. Running my finger softly over Lily's cheek, I smile when her little mouth puckers in response. I wish Tyson were here to meet her. He didn't like Jason, but he couldn't have been more supportive when I told him I was pregnant. I thought for sure he would be angry with me. Over the years since escaping California and our mother, we've worked long and hard for everything we have. While at times it's been exhausting for both of us, for the first time there's a freedom we never had before. A freedom from nearly daily verbal and emotional abuse. A freedom from feelings of unworthiness. Adding another mouth to feed and more responsibility to our chaos worried me, but Tyson was thrilled and he became the person that asked the questions I wished Jason had and helped take care of me. Until he left.

Looking at Lily in my arms, I flash again to my own mother. I'll never understand, especially now, how my own mother could not love us. How could she think I'm not worthy of love? This baby in my arms is worthy of everything. I want her to have the world. I tear up again when I feel hope rise in my heart... maybe just maybe... Lily will love me too. Perhaps I am worthy of love after all.

"Rowan?"

I look to Jax and see him standing, "Yes?"

"I'm going to go pull my truck around so that when they bring you out, we can just put Lily right into the car seat, and you won't have to walk too far, okay?"

"Okay. Thank you."

He smiles, grabs my overnight bag, then leaves the room. Turning my attention back to Lily I place a soft kiss on her cheek and hold her a little tighter to my chest. "I promise to be a good mom to you, Lily Rayn. I will love you, encourage you, support you and want the best for you. Always. There will be times when you won't like me much because you disagree with things I say or do as I raise you, but know I will always have your best interests at heart." Tears once again fall down my face with my words. I will never be the kind of mother to her my own mother was to me. Never.

I never admitted to Tyson the way Jason had been acting about the baby – not entirely. I think he had his suspicions, but surprisingly he never asked. Missing him is an ache in my chest and as much as I wish he were here, part of me is happy he isn't. He would go absolutely ballistic if he knew what Jason did. His temper would be lost in a moment and he would hunt him down.

My attention is diverted to the nurse when he finally comes in with a wheelchair. "Are you ready, Miss Martin?"

"Yes, absolutely." I get out of the bed, sit in the chair and hold Lily tight as he begins to push me through the halls making our way to the door. I can't wait to sleep in my own bed and not be interrupted every hour with a nurse coming in to take my vitals and Lily's. I can't wait to get her to sleep in her little nursery. Tyson and I moved into a three-bedroom townhouse several months back. He insisted on it when he found out I was expecting. I hedged because I wasn't sure what mine and Jason's plans were. I had still been hoping he'd ask me to stay with him, but Jason insisted. It was more expensive, but together we could afford it. I don't think it hurt that the landlord was clearly lusting after my brother and gave us a "special" rate for our rent.

One of the first things we did together was decorate the nursery. We found sweet little bird décor at my favorite second hand shop and we snatched it up, painted one of the walls a pretty pale green, and Tyson even surprised me one day by buying a stencil of a large tree with birds on the branches. He painted it black and it's so perfect. So sweet. I would sit in there sometimes and dream about the baby I would be bringing home.

As we approach the hospital doors, I catch sight of Jax standing by his large black four-door truck waiting for us. When he sees us approaching he smiles and opens the passenger doors. I'm so grateful that he's here. I'm not sure who I would have called to help me if he wasn't. Maybe Jane or Stacey from the diner, but I'm glad I didn't have to worry about it. I keep my personal life private and I would have hated having to explain how I ended up abandoned at the hospital with no way to get home. I'm thankful enough that Jax hasn't asked. I think again about the fact that I need to do something to thank him for all his help. Flushing when my mind immediately goes in the gutter, I turn my thoughts to going home promising to think on it again later.

"Alright, ready?" Jax asks.

"Definitely."

Shifting my body in my chair makes me wince just a little as I feel pain in between my legs. I need to take some more motrin when I get home. Jax helps me buckle Lily into her car seat since it's hard for me to reach. He maneuvers the straps like a professional. The nurse checks the car verifying the car seat is present and then wishes me luck.

"Thanks again for getting the car seat. For taking me home. For everything. I really can't thank you enough."

"Yes, you can. I'm happy to help and a continuous thanks isn't necessary."

I nod and grab hold of the "oh shit" bar in his truck taking a deep breath before I try to maneuver into the seat. Before I can lift my leg, Jax is there. "I don't think so." Before I can ask what he means, he scoops me up and sets me into the seat. Giving him an appreciative smile, I buckle up as he closes the door.

Giving him my address, I watch him plug it into his GPS before he starts driving. Feeling my gaze on him, he looks at me when he stops at a stoplight and gives me a big smile. "Excited to get home?" When he smiles like that his dimples flash and it's truly a sight to behold. Hell the man is hot. My body gets goose bumps and I feel my nipples harden in lust. All I can do is nod at him then look away all the while telling myself how inappropriate I'm acting. Closing my eyes I still see him there. Blue eyes, dark hair, strong jaw with a sexy five o'clock shadow, and high cheekbones any actor or male model would covet. Once I get my hormones under control, I open my eyes and they automatically move in his direction, and once more take in his relaxed body. He's wearing a tight black t-shirt that showcases his built and lean frame to perfection. His biceps bulge a little as he turns the wheel and I see a tattoo peeking out under the sleeve at times with his movements. He rests one wrist on the wheel and another hand taps out a beat on the console between us. His whole demeanor is pretty content and relaxed considering he had very little sleep through the night and is likely as exhausted as I am.

Looking away quickly, I try to focus on the road instead of peeking at the man next to me. I think I could stare at him all day. I'm lusting after some guy I barely even know. Because make no mistake, this is definitely lust I'm feeling. He can't smile at me like that anymore. If he does, I won't be able to be responsible for my actions. A brief thought of jumping him and putting my lips on his at the next stop light crashes through my mind making me shake my head and clear my throat. I certainly have other things I should be focusing on right now, not to mention the fact that my so-called boyfriend abandoned Lily and me. Now is certainly not the time to go there with anyone else. What the hell is wrong with me?

Turning my thoughts to more serious matters, I think about how soon I need to get back to work. I have a couple weeks of paid time the diner was generous enough to offer me because they certainly didn't have to. They are just a little mom and pop place. It isn't like I get full paid benefits or can afford to take a leave of absence. I will take whatever I can get though. I'm anxious to spend as much time with Lily as possible before I need to go back. With Tyson in jail, it's more important now than ever. The little savings I had is dwindling more and more every day. We have an emergency fund too, but I'm determined not to dip into it if I can help it.

Thank goodness my sweet retired neighbor Audrey has offered to watch Lily for me when I return to work. She told me that she would be happy to watch the baby in exchange for helping her with some errands now and then. She's a sweet lady that lives in the townhouse next to ours and I've yet to ever see any family visit her. She has pictures of a daughter on her bookshelf, but I've never seen her actually show up, even when Audrey said she anticipated a visit. I don't ask questions because I don't want to bring up something that could be potentially painful, but she's amazing and I know she will be wonderful with Lily. I'm lucky to have someone.

My boss at the diner also offered to help whenever possible. Sometimes in the midst of chaos and feelings of loneliness I forget the people that are always quietly present in my life. Silent and steady like a winter snowfall they deserve to become a loud and consistent presence in my life and I intend to make that happen.

It isn't long before we're pulling into my gravel drive. There are townhomes all up and down this road. Since I'm located pretty close to the local college, I'm surrounded by a lot of college students. There are a few neighbors my age, and older like Audrey too. Once we're stopped I've barely gotten my seatbelt off before Jax is already opening the door for me. "Thank you," I murmur and he helps me ease out of my seat.

"I'll get Lily. It took me a minute to figure this thing out when I put it in the car, but it's actually pretty easy." He demonstrates his words by removing the car seat from the base and then unbuckling the base too. He follows me to my front door, waits for me to unlock it and then steps inside behind me. I catch a glimpse and see him standing there looking around while I place my things on the kitchen table. I approach him and gesture for him to place the seat down so I can remove Lily. She's still sleeping so I take her straight to her room and place her into the crib. Standing there smiling at the sweet picture she makes, I turn to find Jax in the doorway, taking in the room – and perhaps me and Lily.

He follows me back into the living room and I try to take in my home from his perspective. Mismatched, worn down furniture fills the space. Tyson and I went to several garage sales and second hand stores for every item. When we left California we didn't take much as our mom was screaming at us when she found us packing up, so we just grabbed what we could and took off. Each item we have we painstakingly picked out, cleaned up, and some of them we even sanded and repainted. I've not much in the way of knick knacks, but what I do have is books I've gotten from garage sales. A large bookshelf is the primary focus in the living room. What we have may not be brand new or even lightly used, but I think it looks homey enough.

Jax turns to me with a smile holding a framed picture of Tyson and me. "This is a good picture of the two of you. It's crazy how much the two of you look alike. I'm surprised I didn't know who you were for sure until you said your name."

"Yeah, the twin thing is weird."

He laughs. "I bet it's awesome too."

Laughing, I agree, "You're right about that." I look at him feeling unsure, "Would you like a drink or anything?"

"No thank you, I need to get going."

"Oh, of course," I feel so stupid. Lord knows he's spent more than a little time with me. I basically kidnapped his whole weekend from him. No doubt he has a life to get back to.

He steps to me and I hold my breath when his face comes closer to mine. Oh hell, is he going to kiss me? Do I want him to kiss me? Shit, does my breath smell okay? I feel his breath on my lips for a moment before he turns his head to the side and kisses me softly on my cheek. "Get some rest. No doubt you will sleep better now that you're home."

Letting out the breath I was holding I'm not sure if I feel disappointment or relief. That's certainly not the thing I need right now. "Thanks again for everything. You have been so amazing. I'm really glad you were in that emergency room, and... Oh my gosh! I didn't even ask! How did you get injured anyway? Are you okay? I'm so selfish!"

"No, you're not. I'm pretty sure you've had other more important things on your mind and this is just a cut from sparring with another fighter. No big deal."

"Still, I'm sorry. And again, thanks for everything. I'm so glad you offered to help me when I almost fell over from pain," I laugh at the sight that must have created.

"Me too." He hands me a card and I look at it. It's a card for the gym he owns. "On the other side is my cell number. Call me any time okay? If you need something, want help, or just want to talk… anything, okay?"

Nodding my head agreeing when truthfully I have no intention to call him, he seems happy with that. I go to the door and open it for him. "Thanks again."

"Bye, Rowan."

"Bye, Jax."

I close the door behind him and then put my head against the door and take a few breaths in and out for a moment. I jerk my head back when I hear a small thump on the other side. Part of me wants to open the door. I put my hand on the doorknob to turn it, but then a small cry comes from Lily's room and I turn away from the door to take care of my new baby and to figure out where I go from here.

CHAPTER SIX

Jax

Sweat pours down my face and back as I work the heavy bag in front of me over and over. I should be concentrating on my training, but I'm really only half assing it because all I can think about is Rowan and how she and Lily are doing. It's been a week and all I can think about is how she's managing all alone. Does she have everything she needs? Does she feel lonely? Is the baby keeping her up at night? Is she getting enough sleep - enough to eat? She hasn't called. Why hasn't she called?

"What the fuck is wrong with you, Jackson? You're punching like shit. An eight year girl punches harder than you are."

And that is why my dad is a fucking prick. Ignoring him, I continue to punch the bag, albeit a little harder now.

"Cole, why don't you get next to Jackson and show him how it's done?"

Gritting my teeth I ignore him and Cole's uncomfortable laugh that follows the question – well, actually order. I know that giving him a reaction is exactly what he wants, so I do my best to ignore him. He hates me. I can never remember a time in my life when my dad gave me props for a job well done or encouragement to do my best. It only got worse when my grandfather died a little over a year ago and willed me this damn gym, thus passing over his own son in the process. You would think that a man that didn't have a great relationship with his own father would do everything in his power to cultivate a good one with his own son, but no. Not my dad. At least the difference is that now, I can fucking fight and talk back. Not that that's kept him from hurling a punch or smack in my direction even as an adult.

All the guys deal with it but I know it puts them in an uncomfortable position – especially Cole. The only reason we keep him around is because he helps obtain sponsorships for each of us for our fights as well as organizes the fights themselves. He does a damn good job and I've convinced myself that dealing with his shit in the mean time is worth it. However, there are times, days and weeks where I daydream about firing his ass because I think the thing he hates the most is that no matter how you slice it, the old man works for me. I pay his fucking salary and so when he really gets under my skin I do my best to remember that, or point it out to him because then that makes his jealousy of the whole situation go to new heights. Just because I'm a son of a bitch and his reaction amuses me. Like father, like son, in that respect I guess.

"That's it, Cole! That's a fucking mean right hook boy! Look at that, Jackson. You could learn a thing or two."

And that's all it takes. I grab my towel, wipe my face, then turn and walk away.

"Get back here while I'm talking to you, boy!"

I give him the middle finger salute and start walking across the gym toward the locker rooms. On the way I see Britney, officially dubbed one of our gym hookers, trying to sink her talons into Levi. She and her friends Nikki and Sasha are here all the time. They are our MMA groupies. The guys pass them around like a druggie passes a joint and they could care less. I admit I've gotten it on with Britney a couple times, but once I realized she was making rounds, I decided it was best to keep my dick out of that waffle shack. Unfortunately, she doesn't get obvious signs I'm throwing down and keeps trying to get my attention. It's pathetic really.

Levi winks at me as I pass and Britney has his bottom lip between her teeth. She's looking at me while she does it clearly trying to get a reaction from me.

"Okay, Jax?" Looking over at Zane as I walk in the locker room I give him a nod, not sure how he heard my dad from in here. "Your old man's an asshole, dude."

"Yep," I agree as I keep walking to the showers. Grabbing a towel, I turn the water on and wait for it to warm up before yanking my shirt over my head and sliding my shorts and briefs down my legs. Stepping into the warm spray, I pray it helps melt the tension off of my body. Closing my eyes, Rowan's face is there and I sigh at the sight. I can't get this girl out of my mind. Every time I have a quiet moment she's there waiting for me.

Having needed to do something – anything – I made a decision and sent an email arranging something I felt unsure about. However, when I opened my email this morning and saw the response sitting there, I know I did the right thing. Ever since, I've been anxious for the appointment, so I kept as busy as I could to pass the time. I quickly wash my hair and body, then rinse and shut the water off. Toweling myself dry, I spin around to go to my locker to dress but stop short when I see Britney standing there, eye fucking the shit out of me.

"What the hell, Britney? What don't you get about this being the *men's* locker room?"

Her eyes continue their perusal and she runs her tongue along her bottom lip making me shudder in disgust. She mistakes my reaction for lust and saunters over to me running her hands up my chest until they wrap around my neck. "Let me help ease some of that built up tension for you, baby. You seem stressed out. I can make you feel so good. You know I can."

Unwrapping her hands from around me, I push her away gently but firmly by her upper arms, "How many times do I have to tell you I'm not interested? Get out of here now, or I'm going to start banning you from coming into the gym at all. Besides, you were just hanging all over Levi. Go bother him."

"You know I really want you though, baby."

"I'm not your baby, now get the hell out." I move past her to my locker and take my clean clothes out. Heading to the bathroom, I shut the stall so I can remove my towel in peace, and at the same time make a point.

"Asshole," I hear her mutter to herself, as if I care. I breathe a sigh of relief when I hear the door close behind her. I'm too nice to her and her dumb friends, but the fact is they have a lot of connections and they work them to bring a lot of people to our fights. Our MMA fights are always well attended, but the fight nights we put on here at the gym are always full of people they invite. A lot of them are girls hoping to get it on with a hot fighter. They can be as annoying as hell hanging on us all night hoping to get laid. I've always put up with it because I have a business to run, and money is money. If it means I have to put up with slutty horny women for an evening, so be it. Although lately, my views on the subject are changing – I'm not so sure it's worth it any longer. Besides, the gym has started to take on a life of its own and their referrals are no longer needed.

Once I'm changed I look for Zane in the gym. He has an extra key to the gym as does Levi, Ryder and Cole. I'd give one to Dylan too but he loses all kinds of random shit. I can always count on all of them to help me when need be. "Yo, Zane?"

He turns from the weights he's lifting, face flushed and grabs his towel to wipe his sweaty brow. "Sup?"

"Just thanking you again for closing up tonight if I'm not back later."

"Yeah, no problem. I have to head out in a bit for a quick errand, but Cole's covering."

I automatically tense at Cole's name wondering if that means my father will be here with him too. With me gone I don't want him to get into anything he shouldn't. I force myself to let it go because I can trust Cole, plus the other guys will be here to keep an eye out. I may not understand Cole's relationship with my dad, but it sure as hell isn't his fault my dad is using him to get to me.

"I'll be back to close, though."

"Great," I clap him on the back. "I appreciate it. I'm going to lock the office, but if you need anything, help yourself."

"See you later."

Making a quick stop in my office, I wait for the computer to quickly come to life, pull up the internet and jot down the directions I need. Grabbing my keys, I lock the office door behind me knowing the guys will unlock it if they need anything then head out to my truck. The drive to Florence where the jail is located takes me about fifty minutes since traffic is pretty light. Finding a parking spot takes a little time since it looks like I'm not the only one here for visiting time. I park in between two squad cars and make my way inside, walking through security before I reach the guy sitting behind a desk taking names.

"Hi, can I help you?"

"Hi, yes. I'm Jackson Stone here to visit Tyson Martin. I booked my appointment online per the requirements."

He taps on his computer for a minute, "Here you are. As you know, your visit was approved or you wouldn't be here. I just need you to sign your name on this form, please." I do so and hand it back to him. "Thank you. Here is a key to locker 15," he gestures down the hall towards the lockers lined up against the wall. "No personal belongings of any kind are allowed inside the visitation room. This includes your wallet, cell phone, keys, even lose change."

"Okay."

He looks at his watch, "You only have a couple minutes and they will start letting people in."

"Alright, thank you." I deposit my belongings in my locker removing everything from my pockets then lock it up. Taking a seat in the waiting area, I look at the people surrounding me. A few people have been randomly chosen to undergo additional security checks, but I'm apparently not one of them. There are spouses or girlfriends here with their children to see a loved one, older people possibly a parent here to see their child and men with briefcases that have attorney written all over them. One lady holding a picnic basket gives me a smile. I'm guessing her basket items were approved and I belatedly wonder if I should have brought something for Ty.

Finally, someone announces that visiting time is starting and we each take turns filing into the room where the prisoners are waiting for us. I look around the room and spot Ty quickly, his likeness to his sister makes me smile. It's just enough to see that they're twins but not too much to make it creepy like I'm lusting after a girl that looks like a guy. They have similarities but differences too.

He looks surprised, curious and maybe even a little happy to see me here. Smiling, I walk over and shake his hand and pat him on the shoulder. "Ty. Good to see you, man. Sorry it's under these circumstances."

"Jax, hi. How are you? I'm really surprised to see you. No offense, but what are you doing here?" He laughs at his own words, "Not that I'm not also happy to see you too. But how the hell did you know I'm here?"

We each take a seat across the table from one another before I answer his last question, "Rowan told me."

"Rowan?" An anxious look crosses his face, "Please tell me that means you've seen her recently. I've been trying to call her the last couple days and she hasn't been answering the phone. I'm trying not to worry, but it's hard."

"Yes, I just saw her a week ago."

"How? I mean where did you see her? How do you know each other? I never got around to telling her about your gym and the fighting."

"Well… I bumped into her at the hospital emergency room."

Immediately his whole body tenses, his fists clench and a look of alarm crosses his face? "The emergency room? Is she okay? The baby?"

"She's okay. She was in the emergency room because she was in labor with Lily."

"Lily? It's a girl?"

A smile comes automatically to my face. "Yes, a girl. She named her Lily Rayn."

He smiles; his face full of joy at the thought of his niece, but it quickly falls, "So she and Lily are okay? I don't understand where you come into this."

"Well like I said, I was in the emergency room," I gesture to my stitches, "and as I was leaving the hospital, Rowan was rising out of her seat. When she stood up to get some help, because she had been sitting there by herself for three hours, she doubled over. She was having a contraction and I offered to help her. Uh, she never let go of my hand after that. When she gave her name to the nurses, I knew why she looked so familiar, and I told her I know you." I look at the ground and blink a few times before looking at Tyson in the eyes. "She asked me to stay with her through the birth and I did. She told me she had no one else."

"What do you mean? Where was Jason?"

I look at him in confusion, "Jason?"

"The baby's father. Where the hell was he?" He's spitting the words through a jaw clenched so tight I swear I hear it grinding.

"She wasn't very forthright with information, but I got the feeling something bad happened. She was obviously troubled, scared and alone when I saw her. This Jason guy was never around. I even gave her a ride home from the hospital because she had no way to get there."

Tyson could start a fire with the heat in his eyes. He repeatedly taps the pinky finger of his right hand over and over on top of the table in agitation. My eyes keep dropping to his hand. "That son of a bitch must have done something to her. I knew he was no good. I knew it. And now here I am stuck in this hell hole and I can't do shit to help her."

"I think…" I hesitate not sure if I should share my suspicions but sigh and then decide to be honest. "Considering she didn't have a ride home, I got the feeling she was dumped there. I mean how else would she have gotten there? Unless she had taken a cab, but something tells me that's not the case."

Tyson stands immediately in his anger and looks like he's about to pace but a guard yells at him to sit down and he does so after a little hesitation and a glare at the guard for good measure. "I am going to kill him if he hurt her. Kill. Him."

"Look, I don't know what happened. She didn't open up to me about anything, like I said. I just know that when we talked about you it sounds like she doesn't get to talk to you often. I have no idea how your phone calls work here man, I could just tell when she talks about you how much she misses you." Before I can continue with the reason why I came, Ty interrupts.

"I miss her too." He looks down and puts his hands in his hair and pulls. When he looks back at me his jaw is tight and he clenches and unclenches his fists over and over. He appears to be working up to saying something so I stay silent and wait him out. "I'm so fucking angry at myself for getting locked up in this joint." He looks away for a beat and then looks in my eyes. "Rowan and I have never been separated for more than two days at most. She's my sister, yeah, but she's my best friend too and I take my job as her protector very seriously and here I am locked the fuck up and not able to be there for her when she really needs me. And why? Because I can't control my goddamn temper."

"Her protector? Why does she need a protector?"

"Every woman should be protected and kept safe, man. But Rowan and me? We didn't have a great childhood. Out dad split when he found out our mom was pregnant and let's just say my mom never let us forget it. She said stuff to both of us our whole lives about it being our fault, but Rowan got it worst of all. I protected her when I was around, but the second we knew we were going to leave as soon as we could, I started working more to save money. Anyway, our mom would say shit to Rowan about her not being deserving of love and how she'll always be alone. She did stuff that was really fucked up and unfortunately, it has really done a number on Row. She's doesn't trust people's motives, ever. I think even if Jason beat the shit out of her she would have made excuses for him because she wants to prove our mom wrong. If Jason did what I think he did, I have no doubt Row is thinking that our bitch of a mother was right and that this is exactly her fate."

"That explains why she didn't have a parent at the hospital with her." I'd like to say that I don't understand how a parent could treat a child that way but unfortunately, I understand that all too well.

"Yeah well her sorry ass boyfriend, Jason, should have been there. I don't know what's going on there, but I intend to find out."

"What was their relationship like? Serious?" The thought makes me want to punch something.

"He was a douche. I don't think Row's been honest with me about the way he treats her, but I picked up on stuff you know? Like how he never assisted her to stand, sit or anything when her belly started getting bigger. How he never put her first like opening a door for her, or letting her grab her food first when we made dinner. Just shit like that. He's a selfish prick and I have a feeling he was less than enthused when he found out Row was pregnant, but she would never tell me anything about it."

"You are now not the only one that would like to kill him." He nods in understanding. "Well when she told me you were here, I was going to visit you no matter what, but I thought you'd especially appreciate knowing you have a niece, especially if you hadn't found out yourself yet."

"I can't thank you enough for coming here." He looks down at the table for a minute and runs his hand over his face. "I need to ask you a favor regarding Rowan." Raising my eyebrows at him, I nod letting him know I'm listening. "Look, like I said, things haven't been easy for her and now if Jason's bailed I'm really worried about her. I know she's got to be stressed too with a new baby. Can you... I mean... would you mind keeping an eye on her until I get the hell out of this place? I'm counting down the days until I get out of here, but until then, I would feel so much better if I knew someone I know and trusted is keeping an eye on her."

"You got it, I'm happy to. Look, I'm just going to be honest. I like your sister, man. She's left an impression and for whatever reason I feel protective of her, and Lily, myself so even if you hadn't asked, I was already planning on looking out for them."

He stares at me for a minute, maybe trying to see if I'm sincere. I hold his look and don't back down. I've never been more serious about anything in my life. Ty smiles at me and cocks his head to the side, "Just don't hurt her, alright? I don't want to have to kick your ass down the line."

I laugh out loud at that. "Noted."

We chat about MMA stuff, the upcoming fights and how he can't wait to get out of there in a few months. Then, with another pat and handshake, I head out and go to the store to pick up some things for Rowan. I don't know what kind of stuff Lily might need so I just load up on baby stuff - diapers, pacifiers, wipes, powder, some type of ointment, and take a guess at formula brand although I have no clue if she's using it. I see a couple of cute stuffed animals and grab them too. I momentarily look at something called onesies and smile at some of the things they say and decide I need to order Lily one special for fighter fans. I even grab a couple of blankets. I have no clue about any of this shit, but hell, I would buy one of everything in this whole baby department if I could. I just want to help.

Trunk full of so much baby stuff that I'm questioning my sanity, I make my way to Rowan's apartment and find myself anxious to see her and Lily. Rowan's dark hair, hazel eyes and full lips flash in my mind and I realize I want more than to help. I want to get to know her… really know her. It's driven me crazy that I haven't been able to get her out of my mind, but I realize, I don't want to. I like her there.

CHAPTER SEVEN

Rowan

How does the world keep on turning when it's stopped for me? My world has become filled with nothing but darkness, loneliness, crying, staring at the walls, and feelings of hopelessness. All of these emotions are occasionally interrupted by the needs of a one-week-old little girl. She's my world, my heart, my *more* so why does it take so much effort and all of the energy I have to take care of her?

Basic household tasks have been ignored. Getting dressed is a chore that requires more than I can muster on most days. All I want to do is sleep or fall asleep since doing so seems to rarely come easy. I get lost in time staring out my bedroom window caught between repeated daydreams: in one, Tyson comes home and takes care of us; in another I miraculously come into a ton of money and all my stress and troubles instantly disappear; or my faceless Prince Charming shows up to sweep us off of our feet.

When I'm not lost in the movies in my mind, I'm amazed by the constant comings and goings outside my window. The window in my room faces a townhouse across the street that may as well be a bar. It's always hopping. Echoes of laughter make their way to me through my open window and somewhere inside of me I feel longing to feel as carefree unencumbered as they sound. I hate them. I hate that they can find happiness when I cannot. But what I hate most are the couples that stand outside wrapped up in each other's arms, lips locked and genuine joy transparent in every facial expression and body movement. Why are they deserving of love when I'm not?

I stupidly made the mistake of trying to call Jason again. For some crazy reason I really wanted to hear the sound of his voice. Maybe I even needed something to make me know that I'm not crazy. Other than the little girl that is a clear representative of the fact he exists - I have nothing else. The first day after I came home I burned all his pictures. Every remnant of anything he has ever given me - an Arizona Cardinals t-shirt, movie stubs I'd saved and a card he gave me for a long ago birthday - destroyed. I screamed at his pictures as if he could somehow hear my hateful, angry, pleading words through them. I cried rivers and scratched out the stupid smiling faces looking back at me. Smiles that I feel like I'll never make again. My screams woke Lily and it took me nearly an hour to get myself off of the floor to see what she needed. And only then it was because I was afraid of what the neighbors would think and how they might start complaining.

Everything just feels difficult. So overwhelming. So painfully and exhaustingly dark.

I've been sitting here for a while now, while Lily's been sleeping, staring out the window crying. Tears…they have their own mind now and come and go without invitation or notice. There is no logic in their appearance and it seems to take very little to make them stream down my face in rivers. Briefly I wonder if it's possible to cry yourself out of tears. Do they ever dry up? How do they keep coming? My mind will take hold of a simple thought or a memory and not let it go. It replays over and over and over in my mind until I'm certain it's going to make me insane if it comes just one more time. I've tried hitting my head against the wall –repeatedly at times - to see if I could shake the memories loose. But it doesn't work. Sometimes counting or distracting myself with one of my beloved books or watching some stupid TV show will help, if I'm extremely lucky. But it works only for a short time. Today my mother's cruel words seem to be locked in my mind and no matter what I do, they've decided to imprison themselves there, repeating themselves endlessly, and never wanting out.

"No one will ever love you."

Forcing myself to leave my chair by the window, I make my way to the bathroom while rubbing my red and swollen eyes. Taking a seat on the toilet lid for a minute trying to catch my breath, I smooth my hair behind my ears. Just the little walk from room to room exhausts me. Taking deep breaths I look in the shower and consider taking a bath thinking that the warm water will wrap around me and offer me a sense of comfort. Help me to keep from craving arms I wish were there to offer comfort instead, even though he doesn't deserve to ever touch me again. But it requires much too much effort for a potential hollow promise.

At my lowest, I packed Lily up in my car and went to Jason's place. I knocked on the door of his apartment, beat at the door and cried my heart out until a neighbor threatened to call the police. She told me she hadn't seen him for a while. I don't know if she was lying or not, but I gathered what I could of my pride and left. I've told myself I won't do that again. He clearly doesn't want anything to do with us and I refuse to allow myself to go there and try to beg him. Somehow I was able to drum up a modicum of self-respect.

Even though he left me, my craving for Jason is at an all time high even after my failed attempt to make contact with him. He may have been an asshole, but he was there. He offered me connection to another human being that I crave. When we had sex for a few moments at least, I felt loved, cared for. Wanted.

The razor in my shower captures my attention and for some reason I find myself unable to look away. Would anyone even notice? Would anyone even care? No. There's no one. Jason is gone. Tyson is gone. My mother doesn't even know where we are. I've never had a father. The girls at the diner might miss me, but probably only because they are counting on me to come back soon. I called them and told them I need more recovery time than I anticipated. They told me that's not a problem, but it is for me. I have almost no more money. I have to go back to work. Somehow. Some way. I have to find the energy to go back.

The razor calls my name again like a siren's song. All I have to do is break open the plastic and take the blade out. One deep quick slice on both wrists and this misery will be gone. With trembling fingers I pick it up. Lily deserves better, doesn't she? Better than some mother who can barely bring herself to take care of her. She's only going to end up hating me some day anyway. Wouldn't I just be doing her a favor? A daydream forms in the most remote part of my brain of a wonderful family, maybe a couple that had been trying to have a child for years and hasn't been able to. They would adopt her. She would be loved and cared for. She would have a mother and a father. A real family. A complete family. Maybe she would even have brothers and sisters one day. She would be normal. She would have something that I've failed to give her.

Running my finger over the blade I'm transfixed by the shiny steel. I prick myself with the blade and hiss at the bite of pain, but then I stare transfixed at the blood that falls down my finger.

She deserves better.

Cracking the razor with strength I hardly feel, I pull out the blade. I can barely hold it still in my fingers, they're shaking so bad. With as much steadiness as I can, I place the blade on the inside of my wrist and close my eyes. One quick slice. That's all. No one will even care. I won't have to endure this loneliness any longer. I picture everyone's relieved faces when I die. They won't have to bother with me any longer. They'll be happy I'm not here. Better. They'll be better off without me. I'll no longer be a burden to my brother, to my employer, to Lily.

Taking a deep breath, I press down and feel the small bite in my skin. A sudden, violent knock at the door of my apartment alarms me. With a cry I jerk the blade in surprise and cut myself a little. I barely feel it. Guiltily I throw the blade away and grab a towel to wrap around my wrist. Making my way to the door I look through the peephole to see who it is.

A gasp of surprise leaves my mouth when I see Jax standing there, arms full of bags, waiting for me to answer the door. I don't want to answer it. I'm just going to ignore it. But when he knocks again it startles me and I make a noise, likely alerting him to my presence because he calls out, "Rowan? It's me, Jax."

With a sigh, I unlock the deadbolt then open the door as far as the chain will allow. "Jax?" My voice sounds raspy. It hasn't been used in hours? Days? I don't even know. Jax's eyes widen when he sees me and it occurs to me how I must look to him. Unclean hair, likely sunken swollen red eyes with dark circles, and ratty clothes. I don't remove the chain and just stand there as Jax furrows his brow and takes a small step forward.

"Can I please come in, Rowan?"

"Now isn't really a good time."

He comes closer still, and his eyes drift behind me before they focus on me once again. "Is everything okay?"

"Everything is fine," I lie.

"I have some diapers, formula and a bunch of other stuff for you. I have no clue what kind of formula you're feeding Lily, if at all, but I thought maybe it would be helpful? I know you haven't called or messaged me at all, but I thought maybe I would just come by and check on you." He's talking fast. He senses I have no intention of opening the door for him so he's trying to finish his prepared speech. He's right to worry.

"Why?"

His brow furrows again, "What do you mean why?"

"Why do you care, Jax? I'm not your goddamn responsibility and I don't want your sympathy or charity. Just leave me alone. No one gives a shit without wanting something in return and you know what Jax? I have nothing left to fucking give. I'm all wrung out."

Closing the door, I ignore his insistent knocks and calls of my name. He tells me through the door that he doesn't want anything in return. He says he just wants to be my friend, to help and get to know me. I do my best to ignore him and walk to the bathroom again, but am interrupted by Lily crying. Going into her room, I look at her over the top of her crib. Her face is screwed up while she cries and something inside of me clenches at the sight. "Shh, Lily. It's okay," I say automatically and her little face relaxes at the sound of my voice. She opens her eyes and looks at me while her bottom lip pushes out with a little pout and she sniffles. Picking her up, I take her to the dresser that I use as a changing table and replace her wet diaper, then take her to make a bottle. I didn't have the energy to breastfeed. I know it's the right thing to do, but I let my milk dry up and chose formula instead.

The whole time she drinks she looks straight into my eyes and holds them. It's the first time she's really focused on me since she's been born. Usually her eyes look everywhere else, somewhat unclearly, or stay closed. I can't look away from her big blue eyes and tears start pouring down my face. I feel like she sees me, really sees me. This small little soul connecting with mine – it's indescribable how it makes me feel.

The towel falls away from my wrist and I see the cut there from the razor blade and it makes me shudder and bile rises in my throat. Shame floods me. What was I thinking? What was I about to do? She needs me. I dare to think that maybe she could even love me some day. As if she knows my thoughts her little hand wraps around my fingers that are holding the bottle to her mouth and it makes me cry harder. "I'm sorry," I whisper. "I love you so much."

Standing from the couch, I make my way to the front door and remove the chain, opening it. My eyes sweep the hallway looking for Jax, but he's gone and in his place are piles of items he's left at my door. Carefully stepping over them, I walk next door to Audrey's and knock. I'm not waiting long before she opens it and gasps when she takes in my appearance, "Rowan? Are you okay, honey?" Her concern somewhat eases when she sees my sweet content baby in my arms.

"No," I whisper, "I need help. Please help me."

CHAPTER EIGHT

Jax

It's been almost three months since I visited Ty in jail. Almost three months since the first time I tried to see Rowan and was turned away. Since she answered the door and was clearly unwell. Almost three long months of watching, worrying and waiting. Three months of quietly supporting Rowan even though she has no idea.

After trying a few more times to see Rowan and being left standing by myself in the hallway, I decided to back off and watch. And wait. I may have initially felt like a creepy stalker but one day when I saw Rowan going for a walk with an older lady, additional observation helped me realize the other lady was her neighbor. That's when I made my move. Following Audrey to the park one day when she was returning from an errand, I scared the shit out of her when I approached her. That was not a fun experience. Not just because I was desperate for any and all information about Rowan, needing verification that she was okay, but especially when Audrey threatened me with pepper spray. Quickly explaining myself Audrey relaxed, then she and I began a tenuous relationship – at least on her part. At my request, she gives Rowan supplies I purchase for Lily under the assumption that Audrey buys them, not me. Our friendship is unlikely, I suppose, but it's been working. It wasn't long before Audrey opened up with a little friendly conversation and she started feeding me the information that I had been craving. In all truth, I was probably more honest with Audrey about my concerns than I had intended to be, so I guess our opening up went both ways.

FIGHTING ENVY

After the way Rowan answered the door that day, I knew something was wrong. Really wrong. It was just a gut feeling and after promising Ty I would watch out for her, I wasn't about to back down. My protective feelings regarding her and Lily were as strong as ever. When I told Audrey about visiting Ty and how I was genuinely concerned, her eyes softened and then began our plan. I would bring over items for Rowan each week and deliver them to Audrey during our standing tea date. Just the thought almost makes me gag. I think her tea tastes like shit. She serves some lavender crap or something, but Audrey seems to enjoy the company and I like the information exchange, so I pretend it's the best damn tea I've ever had. On lucky days, I get a two for one – Lily's there too. The kid is cute and just gets cuter ever day.

Audrey told me the struggles Rowan went through – is still working through. She was hit hard with post partum depression and didn't understand what was happening to her and kept sinking deeper and deeper into a pit of despair. It astounded me what a difference only one week could make. I wanted nothing more than to break down her door and wrap her in my arms and never let her go.

Initially, knowing she was being cared for and that I wasn't wanted, I tried to work her out of my system. Talk about embarrassing. I picked up a girl at the bar and then was unable to follow through on what I initiated. Not cool. I was such an asshole to her too. I led her on, got her back to my place and on her knees. While she was sucking me off all I could picture was Rowan's face instead of the blonde doing her best in front of me. Realizing that I had just gotten off by pretending the blonde was Rowan freaked me out. Before thoughts of my reciprocating entered her mind, I tossed the blonde out on her ass. I didn't even remember her name - I just wanted a distraction. A total dick move, but all I wanted to do was shower and pretend it had never happened and choose not to evaluate those feelings too much. Besides, it was obvious. Rowan's under my skin and I want her.

Now, two and a half months later, Rowan's doing great according to Audrey and based on the little I've seen of her from afar, she looks fantastic. She's been on medication to help with the depression and looks to be on the tail end of that, which is good. Regular visits to her doctor and Audrey's help is making a world of difference. I've stayed away and given her time to adjust and get better, so today is the day. She's working at the diner this afternoon like she does most days and I'm going in. I almost asked one of the guys to come to lunch with me, but considering it's the first time she will see me since she shut the door in my face, I'm not sure how this is going to go. The least amount of witnesses to give me shit about a potentially bad face to face later, the better.

Casually making my way into Al's, I look around and locate Rowan behind the bar serving someone sitting there. I slide into a booth in what I already know is the section she's working and put a menu in front of my face. I slowly lower the menu and peek over the top when I hear laughter. Rowan is smiling and laughing at something some guy is saying to her. At least it's an older man, because otherwise I would feel the need to punch him in the face since he's made her smile and laugh instead of me. Damn she's beautiful. The way her face lights up and the smile reaches her eyes makes me smile too. It's contagious. Her hair is pulled up on her head in a bun thing and she's got a pencil stuck through it. Her cute little white apron is tied around her waist and when she walks out from behind the bar to serve another table, I see she's wearing a black button down dress. When she bends over to place their plates on the table, I suppress a groan. An image of bending her all the way over that table until her stomach is flat and her pert little ass is in the air as I fuck her from behind flashes through my mind and I'm instantly hard. Adjusting myself in my seat I return my attention to my menu and try to calm myself.

"Hi there, what can I get ya?" Her voice sounds like honey and I smirk to myself knowing I need to resign myself to the fact that this erection isn't going anywhere.

Lowering the menu, I give Rowan a hesitant smile. Her eyes widen and her mouth drops open in a silent o making me think of what I'd like to put there. Pushing that aside, I let my smile widen, "Fancy meeting you here, gorgeous." *Did I just say fancy? Smooth Stone, really smooth.*

"Jax," she whispers. "Shit. I mean what are you doing here?" My brow furrows, "I'm sorry that sounded bad. What I really mean is, hi."

I raise a brow at her and barely suppress my laugh at her surprise, "How are you, Rowan?"

I'm thrilled when she finally breaks into a smile and sits down across from me. "I'm glad you're here. I was hoping I would see you again. You must not have known I work here because after the way I treated you, I'm sure you wouldn't purposefully come near me."

"You really think something like that could keep me away?"

She looks like she isn't sure how to respond. "Well…regardless, I owe you an apology. I'm sorry I was such a bitch to you."

Raising my hand, I signal for her to stop talking. "Don't apologize. You're forgiven. So tell me how you are. How's Lily?"

The smile that curves her lips is so genuine and filled with happiness that it feels potent in the air around us. Pure love and adoration is all over her expression and I can see in one simple look how much she loves her child. "She's perfect. Just perfect. I find myself wondering a lot how the hell I'm someone's mom and then thanking god I am because she's amazing." Her whole face is lit up, her hands animated with her words, and her eyes sparkle. "Anyway, I know you said not to apologize, but I still feel bad. Truth is, I was suffering from post partum depression and didn't know it. I just wasn't myself."

"And now?"

"Now, I'm much, much better. Enough about Lily and me. How are you?"

"Hungry," I tease.

"Oh shit! I guess you did come in here to get some food."

"That's not the only reason."

She stares at me for a moment, maybe not sure if she heard me correctly, or wondering if perhaps I really did know she worked here all along. "Can I please get a water and the chef salad with the house dressing?"

She raises an eyebrow, "Salad? Not a cheeseburger or something?"

"Nope. I don't eat that shit when I'm training."

"You're training?"

"Yeah. There's a fight coming up."

"You'll have to tell me more about that later. I'm going to go get your water and salad. I'll be back in a minute."

I nod and smile, then watch her hips sway as she walks away. I'm not the only one either. A man across at the booth kitty corner to mine watches her when she walks by, even turning his head to get a better look. When he turns back around he happens to catch my gaze. I glare at him until he looks down at his food.

I can't help but watch Rowan through the window that let's one see into the kitchen. Nothing could have prepared me for seeing her face to face again. My whole body reacts to her in a way I've never felt before, and not only below my belt. Being near her makes my body heat up and my fingers twitch with the need to touch her. Somewhere. Anywhere.

When she comes back with my food, I can't help but smile to myself when she immediately sits down again. Maybe, just maybe, she's having the same reaction to me. "So, Tyson told me that you went to visit him. He said you told him about Lily being born, and my being alone."

I look at her warily not sure if she's upset about my interfering. I can't read the expression on her face and it makes me unsure. "I did," I drag out the word, my hesitance evident in the sound.

When she reaches out and grabs my hand, my breath hitches, and my cock swells in my pants, having a life of its own. Fuck. If she can do this with an innocent touch on my hand, what will she do to me when I get more? Because I am fucking determined to get more. I have to. My body craves her and it's worse than a body builder addicted to steroids. My life has been full of her the last three months even though she has no clue.

"At first I was a little pissed that you got involved in my business but Ty made me realize how stupid that was, so I want to say thank you. Again." I let out a breath in relief at her words not even aware I had been holding it. "When I think about you standing at my door with your arms full of things for me and Lily, I feel shitty. If I could go back and do that moment, well more like that day over, I would. Thanks for being so sweet. I mean… you hardly even know me and here you went out of your way to help me and I was nothing but a bitch to you."

"Really, it's okay. Stop beating yourself up. I could tell you weren't exactly yourself."

"Understatement of the year."

I give her shrug of my shoulders, "We all have moments we wish we could redo."

She gives my hand a squeeze and then pulls away, and I'm all too aware of its loss. "Well, thank you for understanding and also for going to see Tyson. He mentioned it was nice to see you."

"It was good to see him too."

"He's been there four and a half months now. I'm so ready for him to get out. I'm counting down the days. I can't wait."

"Have you taken Lily to see him?"

She laughs, "No. He's adamant about the fact that I should not bring his niece to see him in jail. He says he doesn't want her to see him like that. I told him she's not going to remember, but he doesn't care." She looks down and notices I've finished my water, "Let me get the pitcher of water and fill you up." She walks away to retrieve it and I finish the last few bites of my salad while contemplating how I'd like to see her again and if she feels the same way. I run my hand through my hair wanting to punch myself at the thoughts I'm having. If anyone could read my mind they'd tell me to man the hell up.

Rowan returns and fills up my glass, but not before checking in with a few other tables on the way over. When she reaches me, I decide to just go for it, "Rowan, would you like to go get coffee with me when you get off of work?"

She looks at me for a few moments before asking, "Why?"

"Why? What do you mean why? Because I'd like to spend some time with you and get to know you better."

Her eyes narrow a little and if I'm not mistaking she's tapping her foot. Is it in nervousness? "I can't. I have to pick up Lily."

"Some other time then?"

Again she pauses and looks at me as if she's looking for some answer to an unknown question. I can tell her mind is moving at a rapid pace and I would give anything to know what she's thinking right now. Her eyes focus back on me, "I'm busy. Sorry."

"But I didn't even say when."

She smiles in a way that can only be called saucy, "I know." She walks away and I'm left sitting there wondering what the hell just happened. She told me no? No one tells me no. At least not in a really long time. I close my mouth when I realize it's hanging open. She walks back with my check, "I'll be your cashier when you're ready." Watching her closely, I wonder if this is her way of dismissing me. Pulling my wallet out of my back pocket while keeping my eyes on her, I hand over my debit card without looking at the bill. "I'll be right back."

I stare at her the whole time she walks away and she looks up a few times catching my eyes on her. A soft smile curves her lips and all I want to do is have her look at me like that with her underneath me. She's torturing me and she doesn't even know it. Or maybe she does. When she brings my receipt back to sign, she has a coffee pot in her hand. "Here you go. It was great seeing you. I have to go fill up people's coffees. Did you need anything else?"

"Yes I need a lot of things and woman, *you* are going to give them to me. I'll be seeing you later."

Signing my name with a flourish and leaving her with an obscene tip, all I can think is game on. I'll do whatever I have to, to wear her down. When I look over my shoulder as I leave, I'm happy to note this time it's her that has her mouth hanging open.

CHAPTER NINE

Rowan

"You are such a pretty girl my sweet baby." I coo at Lily and she gives me an adoring smile as if she understands my words. Maybe she does, who knows? She makes sweet little sounds and I continue responding and prompting her while she wiggles around as I do my best to get her arms and legs pulled through her outfit. "Mommy has to go to work again. I'm sorry baby. If I could stay home with you all day, every day, I would in a hot second. Yes, I would."

She gives me another toothless smile and shakes her little fists around like she's telling me I should make that happen. "It's just the two of us and that means mommy has to work so I can make money to pay for our house, buy us food and keep you in formula and diapers." Standing her up she pushes on her little feet for a second before her knees collapse and I hold her under her arms, "Such a big girl! Yes you are!"

My heart bursts with love every time she gives me a smile and I swear her little eyes twinkle when she looks at me. Sometimes I get sad when I feel like I'm missing out on important moments with her, but then events occur that help me realize everything I experience with her is a first. Like the time I picked her up from Audrey's and as soon as Lily saw me she started squealing and squirming, letting me know that she recognized me. She was as excited to see me, as I was her and I cried. Like a big damn baby. It's daunting at times to have such a little person so completely dependent on me, but at the same time, the responsibility makes me feel wanted and useful. Needed. Loved. And those feelings are indescribable.

With Lily on my hip, I walk to the kitchen and place her in the highchair purchased at a garage sale for ten dollars. I couldn't believe my luck. It's so cute with a little yellow duck pattern on the cushioned seat. Lily loves to sit in it and watch me move around the kitchen. It supports her well and I love watching her little face as she takes in everything around her. Sighing at the thought, I quickly prepare a few bottles and put them in the refrigerator and then gather up the trash so I can take it outside on my way to the diner.

A knock on my door comes just on time and I open it to Audrey and give her a hug. "Hi, Audrey. Come on in." The day I walked to her front door and told her I needed help was the worst day of my life, but it was the best thing I could have done. Audrey has been a godsend. Not only did she help me with Lily almost every day, but she also drove me to the clinic to see a doctor and stayed with me while the doctor spoke to me about post partum depression. She even took me to the pharmacy to fill my prescription. While I was doing my best to get well and wait out the four to six weeks my doctor said it would take for my meds to kick in, Audrey was there picking up my slack. The changes in me at first were subtle. Smiling more. Laughing more often. Finding it easier to get up in the morning and having more energy each day. But then, I felt like myself again and it was an amazing feeling. I was very resistant to medicine at first because I was under the impression I would be some unfeeling drone, but that wasn't the case at all. The doctor helped me realize my health is important because without it, I can't take care of Lily at all. It was the right decision because now I'm able to function again which is good because my butt needs to work to support me and my girl.

"There are some bottles in the fridge for you. I should be back around five o'clock."

"No worries, honey. Like always if I'm not here when you get home, your sweet pea and I have just gone next door to my place.

I think I might start a new show on Netflix a friend was telling me about, so when Lily goes down for a nap we may go over there."

"That's fine with me, you know that. I can't thank you enough for watching her. Do you need an errand or anything done for you this week?"

"No honey, I'm fine. I'll let you know if something comes up."

"Okay, please do. No matter what it is. I want to thank you and give you something in return."

"Honey, her little smiles and baby noises are thank you enough. I love to do it. I'd just be alone otherwise."

I give Audrey a hug in thanks. "I'll see you later." She pats my back and gives me a squeeze in reply.

Walking to Lily, I give her a big smacking kiss on her cheek, making her giggle. "Bye little one. Mommy will see you later." She shakes her legs and fists and I take that as her goodbye and go on my way.

Thinking back to a few days ago when Jax came into the diner makes goose bumps break out onto my skin. Damn that man is good looking. Picturing him sitting in the booth, his dark hair kind of messy and his piercing eyes appearing to devour me, I wanted nothing more than to trip and fall onto his full lips. I would have apologized later if he didn't return the kiss, but I would have at least enjoyed a few seconds of heaven and been grateful for the brief taste. Just looking at him makes me clench my thighs in need – it's ridiculous. If things were different I would throw myself at him and hope to enjoy at least one night of his rocking my world – because he would I'm sure. Everything about him screams hot sex. It's been so long – too long – since I've had some male attention.

But that's not to be. I'm a mother now and Lily is my first priority. Always. Having a mother like I do only makes me more determined to be the exact opposite of what I've experienced. I want Lily to know without a doubt, every single day, that I love her. I want her to know that no one and nothing is more important to me and that our family may not be normal, but I'll do my best to make it up to her any way I can. I hope she doesn't resent me for the fact that she doesn't have a father. I know it won't be easy for her, but hopefully my love for her is enough to be both mother and father. I know I'm getting ahead of myself, but these are things I worry about. Does not having a father affect her now even though she's only a few months old? Does she feel his absence at such a young age? I can't remember my not having a father in my life ever affecting me in a really horrible way - I didn't know any different. The fear is still there for Lily regardless.

Sighing, I push the thoughts aside because I know there's nothing I can do about them right now, other than making sure she feels my love each and every day. Besides, what young, sexy, successful guy like Jax wants to be saddled down with a girl and her new baby? Plus, I may have lost most of my baby weight but I'm all too aware of the extra pounds I'm still carrying in my stomach, not to mention how my body just seems... softer and fuller that before. No doubt Jax has girls falling off of him on a daily basis. I can't compete with that. Yes, he asked me out for coffee, but I know it's most likely out of obligation to my brother.

Thinking of Tyson makes me feel guilty. He's been asking me each time we speak why the hell Jason isn't around. I keep putting his question off, changing the subject right away. I know I'll have to talk to him about it eventually, but not while he's in jail. He'll get angry and I don't want him reacting to it while he's there. Perhaps I'm not giving him enough credit, but he has a temper. I can see him needing to vent his frustration and taking it out on someone and earning himself more time in jail. No thanks.

The diner is hopping when I walk in and I rush to the employee room in the back, stow my purse in my locker, put on my apron and get my butt into action. "Hi doll," Nina the owner says. I turn to her and smile. "Good morning. Where do you want me to go?"

"You'll take my section so I can go into the office and place some orders and pay some invoices, honey. Just come get me if any of you need anything for any reason. I'll pop out here and there."

"Okay. Have fun." She snorts with a stifled laugh and walks off. She really is a great boss. She and her husband, Tim, own the diner and are really great with all of their staff. When I initially called to tell them I needed more time to recover from delivering Lily, they were great. When I sucked it up and came in to talk to them about my post partum diagnosis, they were so supportive I broke down and cried. Not that tears were a hard commodity for me, but their kindness astounded me. I think I scared Tim half to death, but Nina just patted her husband on the shoulder and gave me a look that said, ignore him. They gave me all the time off I needed and Nina stopped by more than once bringing me dishes of food from the diner. I was lucky to have them. Both of them.

An hour into my shift and we're slammed. Seeing out of the corner of my eye that new folks are sitting in my section, I grab the pot of coffee and head over. I stop short when I see Jax and another guy sitting in the booth. Jax is looking at his menu, but I know damn well he knows I'm standing here. There's a smirk playing on his lips that automatically makes me feel a combination of amusement and irritation. The man with him is sexy as hell, but isn't quite Jax's caliber. He's covered in tattoos and has a faux hawk. He's built just like Jax, but has his eyebrow and both ears pierced.

Placing one hand on my hip, I sit the coffee pot down onto their table loudly. "Well, well, well. Look who it is."

Jax looks up at me and smiles, but his friend looks at me in confusion. I stick my hand out for a shake, "Hi. My name is Rowan. And you are?"

Instantly amusement curves his lips and his brows lift in clear interest. "Well hello there, Rowan. My name is Zane. My friend here dragged me to breakfast and initially I was annoyed because I have shit to do, but all of the sudden, I'm not minding so much." He looks me up and down and I feel flustered at the attention. I'm not generally shy but hell, these boys are hot.

Glancing at Jax, I see he's scowling at my hand still in Zane's which makes me automatically pull away, then wonder why I did. "And Jax. What was it you said last time I saw you? Oh yes, I remember. Fancy meeting you here."

He smiles and I nearly swoon at the sight. Will I ever stop being bowled over by those eyes, and those dimples? I hope not. "Hi, Rowan. What can I say? I'm hungry. Again." And the way he's looking at me I don't think he's talking about food.

"And you chose this diner as opposed to all the other restaurants because…"

"Well I would think that's obvious." His brows lift and he's biting his bottom lip and I swear I stop breathing. "I love the food here."

My eyes narrow at him and I feel this strange urge to stomp my foot like a child having a tantrum. He's smiling in a way that tells me he knows that I was hoping he'd say he's here to see me. Damn him. I turn to Zane, who is curiously looking from me to Jax, and back again. Just to irritate Jax, I give Zane what I hope is a sultry smile and touch his arm. "Tell me something. Why the hell are you here with this guy?" I jerk my thumb towards Jax but don't look at him.

Zane smiles, "He said he'd pay."

I laugh. "Well I can't say I blame you then." Jax calls Zane a name under his breath that I pretend not to hear. "Coffee?" I ask and both say yes, but also request glasses of water. I fill up their mugs then go grab their waters telling them I'll be back to take their order soon.

While taking an order from another table and serving drinks to a third, I keep the corner of my eye on Jax. He and Zane look at their menus but talk the whole time. I can tell they must be good friends and I find myself curious to know more. How do they know each other? How long have they been friends? What is Jax's favorite food? How good of a kisser is he? *Wait, what?* I'm smiling at myself when I walk back up to their table and Jax returns my smile. My eyes involuntarily lower to his mouth and then back to his eyes again. I swear I see blatant want flash in his eyes as his tongue darts out to lick his lips and my eyes go there again. I bite my lip in response and I swear I hear a small groan from Jax.

Zane clears his throat and my eyes shoot to him in embarrassment, "Ready to order?"

"I sure am, sweetheart.

They both order eggs, turkey bacon, and fruit. "Okay. I'll be back soon with your order." I smile and tuck my pad into my apron pocket while I check on another table. As I'm walking back towards the kitchen I look over my shoulder at Jax's table, but look away quickly when I catch Jax's stare. When I almost run into another waitress I decide it's probably not smart to do that.

Just seated in my section is a family of four. A mother, father and two little girls. The mom and dad sit on one side of the table and the girls the other. My mind flashes to my sixteenth birthday and I push the thought away knowing it will do me no good. They're all looking at their menus, but the father keeps stealing kisses from his wife behind their menu. It's adorable and it also makes me sick to my stomach. The girls are cute and are coloring on their kid's menus and they all just look…perfect. That's how I always pictured my life to be when I had a child some day, which is seriously ironic considering my upbringing. I long for something normal. My child deserves to have a mother and a father that love her just like any other child. I find myself almost feeling angry and can barely bring myself to smile as I take their order. I try my hardest to shake it off, but it's hard.

When Jax and Zane's order is up, I walk their food over keeping my eyes on their plates. Once I set them down, Zane smiles up at me, "So, what do you say you and me get together some time outside of this place." I can't help but smile. He's got a goofy grin on his face and he's looking at Jax instead of me while waiting for my answer. When I chance a quick glance at Jax, he's glaring at me as if I somehow told Zane to ask me out.

Suppressing a smile I reply, "Well, what did you have in mind?" Jax's scowl deepens and I see the hand that's next to his plate clench into a fist. He's glaring at Zane now.

"Whatever you want sweetheart, although I'd prefer an activity that will make us sweat."

"Jesus, Zane." Jax curses and looks like he's ready to throw a punch.

I almost choke and then outright laugh when he says, "Dude, I was thinking we could go hike the Camelback mountain or something. What the hell were you thinking?"

"Can I get some extra napkins, please?" Jax asks me not answering Zane's question.

"Sure, I'll be right back."

Purposefully not answering Zane's question I walk away to grab his napkins, but look over my shoulder when I hear a loud smack. Zane's rubbing his head and cursing and I hear Jax spit, "Dude, that's Tyson's sister. Back the fuck off and eat your breakfast."

Zane says something in return but I can't hear him and I smile all the way to the back where I retrieve some napkins for them, my feelings about the family of four forgotten. What is wrong with me? Haven't I learned my lesson from the Jason shit? Why would I want to get involved with another man? Especially right now when my main priority is Lily. Shaking my head at myself I'm almost shocked at my own thoughts and realize that the truth is I have needs and I wouldn't mind at least a taste. If one of us walks away afterwards, that then so be it.

Who the hell am I? Or what the hell is it he's doing to me? I try to stay away from their table, only stopping by to refill their coffees and waters once. I feel Jax's eyes on me a lot, but I do my best to take care of my other tables and ignore them the best I can. When I leave the bill, Zane hops up out of his seat and gives me a hug, "Good to meet you Rowan. Maybe I'll see you around soon." Then he whispers, "I just like to fuck with Jax, it's fun." I smile at him as he leaves and when I turn back around Jax is fumbling with his wallet so I walk away giving him some privacy.

I'm humming and nodding my head to the music playing overhead when Jax approaches me with his bill. "Oh, thanks. You didn't have to bring it to me."

He just smiles. "Do you like this song?"

Nodding my head I wonder how long he stood there seeing me quietly singing along. "Yes. Do you?"

"Yes, very much and I just happen to have two tickets to see them this Friday night when they're in town." My mouth falls open because The Sinners are one of my favorite bands. "I have some friends that hooked me up."

"That's so cool, I bet it will be a lot of fun."

"I'm glad you think so. I'll pick you up at seven o'clock, Friday night. Wear something tight."

"Wait...what?"

He walks away from me backwards, eyes on me the whole time. With a final wink, he turns and walks out the door. Well shit. I guess I have a date.

CHAPTER TEN

Jax

"Did you seriously just ask me that, Gil?" Stepping off the treadmill finished with my five-mile run, I stare at my training coach like he's grown another head. Grabbing the towel Gil holds out to me, I mop the sweat from my face. He's pissing me off, and not just because he's pushing me harder than I want to be pushed today.

"Fucking right I did. You need to win this fight, Jax." He points at me as if it helps emphasize his point. "It would look shitty if the owner of an MMA gym can't even win his own fight."

"Whatever. First of all, that's not going to happen, so lighten the fuck up. Secondly, we aren't exactly hurting for business and I have plenty of trophies and plaques on the wall, asshole." I gesture to the wall where they're all displayed.

"So what you're cocky now? Don't need any more trophies? Then maybe you should just quit."

"That's not what I said or what I meant. Don't put words into my mouth."

"Doesn't matter. That's not the point anyway."

"Then what is? Why the hell would you ask me if I'm going to be ready for this fight? Have I ever not been ready?"

"Look, your head hasn't been in the game lately," he stops and spits his chewing tobacco into a cup. Nasty as hell habit but the man is sixty-seven years old. It isn't like the infamous Coach Gillespie is going to change his ways at this point. "You've been distracted and I think a reminder of what's what is in order."

"Oh well by all means, please remind me." The sarcasm is apparent in my tone, but I top it off with an eye roll just for good measure. Clearly, I don't care about looking childish.

"How about the fact that your prick of a father always makes sure to set up the meanest, toughest son of a bitch for you to fight? He puts Cole up against someone just tough enough to make him not look bad, but then always tries his hardest to see if he can get your ass kicked."

"That's nothing new, Gil, and you know it."

"I don't want him to win at his sick game."

"You and me both," I pat Gil on the back because I know in his own way he's just looking out for me. He's been my coach for a long time and I'm lucky to have him. I used to think that my dad would coach me, but that was before what I always chalked up to be his harsh tough love treatment, turned into clear hate. Looking at Gil, I promise, "I'll be ready, like always. I won't let him win."

"Then get your fucking head in the game, Jackson. Tonight, I want you back here after the gym closes for a sparring session. I'll see if Zane is available to spar with you since he's in your weight class too. Let's coordinate schedules and line up some more with him this week and next too, alright?"

Shit, he's not going to like this. "Sorry, Coach, but tonight's no good for me."

His face starts to turn so red that I think it may actually be purple. He takes some deep breaths in and out before asking, "What do you mean tonight's no good? I think I should just ignore that you said that because I don't believe my goddamn ears." For good measure he acts as if he's cleaning his ear out with his finger. I almost want to laugh at him. Almost. If I did, I'm positive he'd deck me. He may be older, but he's still got one hell of a left hook.

"Sorry, Gil. I've got tickets to a concert and a hot date that can't be cancelled." I give him a shit eating grin hoping it will break down his pissy attitude. It's not working.

"What the hell? What did I just say?"

"Just trust me. I'll be ready. One night isn't going to make a difference. Alright? I promise."

He shakes his head and walks away, mumbling under his breath about "punk ass disrespectful fighters" while I make my way to the back of the room where the punching bags hang. After wrapping my hands, I attack the speed bag doing my best to clear my mind of everything and concentrate on the asshole that's going down in the upcoming fight.

A few hours later, I'm showered and sitting in my office working on scheduling. Looking up as I take a drink from my water bottle, I see Gil making his way to my office. Hopefully he's also had time to cool off because I don't want another lecture. I understand his frustration with me, but there's no way I'm calling off my date with Rowan. For years I've lived and breathed this gym and my fights. I'm still all in, but dammit, it's nice to having something else to look forward to. Nice to have something that's just mine and has nothing to do with this place or training. It isn't like I suffer for companionship if I want it, but Rowan is different and now is my chance to get to know her more. Later is not an option.

Gil closes the door behind him when he walks in, "I've got the updated card for the fight and there's been changes. Your opponent has changed."

"Changed?"

"Yeah, I guess your previous opponent dropped out due to injury so you will be fighting, Lance 'The Hammer" Henderson."

Whistling low, I lean back and cross my arms over my chest, "He's tough."

"You're tougher."

Grinning at Gil's compliment I reply, "I guess we'll find out won't we?"

"We will. Cole, Levi and Zane are on the card too. Levi and Zane are both paired up well, and Cole's isn't too bad I guess, but he could have someone more difficult. Let's just say your dad is up to his usual tricks and it will be a quick fight."

"Well, that's expected."

"Otherwise, it should be a great card. I expect the venue will be packed."

"And where is it this time?"

"The Red Rock Casino, so the crowd will be large. The weigh-in will be in their large ballroom there too."

"Sounds good. Thanks for the update."

Gil opens the door back up and starts to leave then suddenly stops to face me again. "After your *special* date tonight, I expect one hundred and ten percent, Jackson Stone. I won't expect anything less."

"I wouldn't expect you to."

"I'm serious. No screwing around, no more interfering dates."

"You got it, Coach."

He flips me off and walks out of the room leaving me smiling after him.

Deciding to shower and change in the gym locker rooms was a bad idea. When I walk out ready to go pick up Rowan, all the guys are practicing and they all start giving me shit about the fact that I'm not. I should have just snuck out and gone home to change.

"Are you getting soft on us, Jax? Maybe that walk from the locker room was too much, and you should sit down." Levi yells to me.

I grab my cock, "Sit on this, asshole."

"Stop making fun of him boys," Zane adds. "You're going to hurt his wittle feewings."

"Maybe we should just call Lance and forfeit for you," Cole teases.

"Laugh it up boys. I'm off to go see a much prettier face than all of yours. See you tomorrow. Thanks for locking up, Zane."

They all laugh and Zane gives me a wave as I walk out the door. I anxiously make my way to Rowan's and find that I can barely contain my excitement. I seriously need to dial it down a notch before I knock on her door. Practically running up the walkway to her door, I laugh when I realize I didn't take my own advice. Pausing to collect myself, I take a deep breath before I knock. I only wait a few moments before the door opens and the sight before me makes the blood pound in my ears so loudly I'm sure she has to hear it.

Rowan's standing before me in black jeans so tight they should be a second skin. Her white flowing tank top is almost sheer and I can see her black bra through it. Her hair is down and flowing over her shoulders and her lips are crimson. She's playing with a long silver necklace and watches me as I take her in. Rubbing my jaw, I speak the only word that comes to mind. "Wow."

Her red painted lips part in a smile and all I can think about is how I want to see that lipstick smeared all over her lips because she's been doing naughty things with that mouth. "Well at least after bossing me around about when to be ready, you had the decency to show up on time."

I laugh at her sassiness and walk inside as she gestures me in. She closes the door behind us, "Let me just grab a few more things for Lily's diaper bag. My friend next door usually watches Lily for me and agreed to watch her tonight as well."

"Can I help with anything?"

She looks at me and smiles widely, "Yes, hold on."

She disappears down the hallway and when she comes back she's got Lily on her hip. Her beauty at the door pales in comparison to the way she looks now. The smile on her face as she looks at her baby girl is exquisite. Lily's smiling while she chews on her slobbery little hand simultaneously making noises of delight. She's adorable. "Jax do you remember Lily? Lily, this is Jax." As if Lily knows she was just introduced, she looks at me and gurgles with what I'd like to believe is recognition. She's spent many times in my lap while I drank tea with Audrey and I've even read her stories. "She likes you." I smile at her. "Do you mind holding her while I finish making a couple bottles?"

I think maybe she's expecting me to be nervous or scared over her request. Well, she's about to be surprised. I take Lily from her arms like a pro and bounce her in my arms. "Hi sweetheart. Aren't you just a gorgeous girl?" I talk excitedly to her and am delighted when she smiles at me in response. "You are such a pretty girl. Did you know that I was there the day you were born? Did your mommy tell you that story?"

Rowan stands there and stares at us for a moment and I can't decipher the look on her face as she takes us in. Maybe a cross between amusement, longing and lust. I'm no fool, I've heard that women think that men with babies are sexy. Smiling at Rowan I start swaying side to side. It almost seems instinctual. And hey, if it turns her on, bonus!

"Well don't you look extremely comfortable with a baby in your arms?"

"I should do it more often," I tell her staring into her eyes making it clear I want to be around more. That I *will* be around more. With a smile at Lily she walks into the kitchen and gathers the rest of what she needs. I walk Lily around the room and talk to her the whole time. "What did you do today? Was it a good one? I trained most of the day and I ate a salad and some fruit for lunch. My coach, Gil bossed me around and gave me a hard time and I did a little work in my office." I speak to her in baby talk and she makes sweet noises back to me like she understands what I'm saying. At one point she even goes on and on for a minute like she's seriously got some things to say to me, and it makes me laugh. Maybe she does, hell if I know.

"Okay, I'm ready," I turn and see Rowan standing with the diaper bag in her arms, and the door open. When I walk towards her she holds her arms open for Lily, but I tighten my arms around her soft little body. "I've got her." Rowan smiles and walks me out her front door and locks it behind us. Then we go over to Audrey's door and knock. When Audrey opens the door she looks from me to Rowan and back again.

"Hi, Rowan. Hi, Lily," Audrey holds her arms out for Lily and Lily reaches out to her. She opens her mouth I think to tell me hello also, but I'm grateful when Rowan beats her to the punch.

"Jax, this is my neighbor and good friend, Audrey. Audrey this is Jax. He's taking me to a concert tonight and is the reason I need a sitter."

Audrey looks at me, back to Rowan, then to me again. "I know who-"

I quickly stick my hand out, "Hi, Audrey. It's nice to meet you. Rowan says great things about you. Thank you for watching Lily so I can take her out tonight."

Audrey looks from my hand to me, then back again. She looks like she's trying not to smile or laugh maybe. I think she expected me to have told Rowan that I know her. Not a chance. I breathe a sigh of relief when she takes my hand. "Hi, Jax. It's very nice to meet you. You know, since I never have before."

Oh, Jesus. She's going to blow it. When she gives me an exaggerated wink, I peek a look at Rowan and blow out a sigh in relief when I see she's distracted by something in the diaper bag. "I made her a couple bottles, and there's enough diapers and wipes in here. If you end up wanting to come over, you know that's fine with me. Just use your key."

"Thanks honey, but I'll probably stay in the comfort of my own home unless for some reason Lily is restless and I think she'd be happier at home. Otherwise, you can just pick her up here. "

"That's fine of course, thank you so much."

"You just have fun, honey. Take your time. We'll be here."

"Okay. Call me if you need to okay? Don't hesitate."

"I won't. Go. Have fun. Lily will be fine."

Rowan kisses Lily softly on the cheek and then runs a hand over the top of her head, "Bye sweet baby of mine."

Rowan turns to me and I offer my arm. We walk to the passenger side of my truck, I open the door and help her up. "Is it hard to leave her?" I ask before closing her door.

She looks down at me and smiles as if she's relieved that I understand. "I keep expecting it to get easier. I mean I know it will eventually but it hasn't yet."

"She'll be good. Audrey's great. I mean… you know… she seems really nice."

"Yeah, she is and Lily loves her."

"Thanks for coming with me tonight."

"It isn't like you gave me much of a choice," she teases. I smile and close the passenger door, then walk to my side and let myself in. After I buckle up, I respond to her comment.

"Nope. I didn't give you a choice because I knew you would overthink things too much. Why? You don't like being bossed around?"

She smiles at me with a grin that can only be called mischievous, "I wouldn't say that exactly."

"What do you mean?"

"Let's just say there's a place where being bossed around is pretty hot."

"A place?"

"Yes. The bedroom," she says with a wink.

Holy. Fuck. She did not just say that. My eyes hold hers until she bites her lip and looks down. She makes me want to drag her out of this truck and bring her back to her house, slam the door behind us and then fuck her against it. A vision of her completely naked with her legs wrapped around my waist as I pound into her, flashes into my mind. I run my hands down my legs and adjust myself before starting the truck and clearing my throat. I can't get a handle on this girl. She makes me crazy.

"Well...I look forward to putting that to the test."

She smirks and I chuckle at the sight. This is going to be a fun night.

CHAPTER ELEVEN

Rowan

It's ridiculous how giddy I feel about being on a date with this man. I spent a couple hours getting ready. Straightening my long dark hair, carefully applying makeup around my eyes for a perfect smoky look and going through my closet seeking the perfect clothes to wear. All like a crazy woman being set free. It was important to me to look good for him.

While I got ready, Lily was sitting in her bouncer seat, eyes wide no doubt wondering how the hell she ended up with me as her mother. Each outfit, I would pose for her and ask her what she thought. She was a captive audience and spoke to me in her little baby chatter the whole time. I loved it. When I tried on the outfit I felt was the one, her jabbers made me decide she must have agreed. The bonus was when I held her and she didn't spit up on the choice. I don't want to even think about how many shirts I can go through in a day right now and how I've come to loathe doing laundry.

Turning my thoughts from Lily back to my handsome date, I ask, "How was your day?" I feel nervous and unsure about what I should talk about. I feel like my life revolves around my child and I have nothing to offer. It would be awful if we had an awkward silence situation.

He looks at me briefly and raises a brow, before turning his attention back to the road, "It was great honey, how was yours?"

"Ha. Ha. I'll have you know I'm no stranger to sarcasm. I'm being serious. I heard you tell Lily that you practiced today. Is that typical? Do you train every day? You know what I do. I work at the diner and take care of Lily. Bam. The end. What does your day usually entail?"

He chuckles at my description, "I doubt your day is as simple as all that, but my day was fine. I spent most of it practicing with my coach and being lectured by him. Yes, I generally practice every day – it's just become part of my daily routine. I feel strange if I don't. After that, I did some boring paperwork that needed done for the gym. Nothing too exciting about my day - that is until I finally left to pick you up. This is easily the best part of my day."

My lips curve upwards in response to his comment. "What do you mean you were lectured?"

"Oh my coach, his name is Gil, he always gets into lecture mode when a fight gets closer."

"How soon is it?"

"It's in a couple weeks."

"Wow, that's soon. Are you nervous?"

"Nah. It's just a job. I mean, I love it, don't get me wrong, but it's also what I do for a living aside from owning the gym. I've been competing for a long time and while I still get nervous before a fight, it also feels right. I don't know how to explain it, it's just that I know it's what I'm supposed to be doing. It's in my blood."

"What do you mean?"

"Well, professional fighting runs in my family. My grandfather was involved in the MMA as a coach. When I was in high school, I was on the wrestling team – and I loved it. I did some boxing and mixed martial arts on the side because my grandfather and father taught me, but wrestling was my focus for a while. Especially when I received a small scholarship to wrestle in college. When I graduated, I began doing MMA full time and started fighting professionally through connections my grandfather had. I've been doing it ever since."

"Did your dad fight too?"

"He did. He was injured, took a bad hit to one of his eyes that messed up his sight and he had to retire."

"Oh my god, that's scary."

"That's not a typical injury. It was kind of a crazy fluke, but it made him angry and bitter."

"Do your father and grandfather come to your fights?"

"My father does because he helps organize our sponsors. He has a lot of connections from his days as a fighter. Plus, he's taken a personal interest in one of our fighters, Cole."

"What do you mean by personal interest?"

"He's backed him personally, meaning he's one of Cole's sponsors along with other invested companies."

"Is he one of your sponsors too?"

"No."

I look at him with a clear question in my eyes, but he doesn't expand on his statement. "And your grandfather? He watches your fights?"

"No. My grandfather passed away."

"Oh, I'm so sorry for your loss. Was it recently?"

"It was a little more than a year ago. When he passed away, he left me the gym in his will."

I'm surprised by how forthcoming he's being about something so private. "He left you the gym? Wow. What an amazing gift."

"Yeah. It was a big surprise. He would make comments here and there about when I ran things I needed to remember this or that, but I never took him seriously. My dad, needless to say, has never been happy about it. But that's a whole other story. We don't have a great relationship in case my telling you about his support of another fighter, and lack of support for me, didn't make it clear enough."

"Ah. Well, I know more about difficult parental relationships than you think."

He reaches over and takes my hand and brings it to his thigh,

"Maybe some day we can compare notes." I just laugh at his comment and in a bold move, place my hand on his thigh giving it a squeeze. Feeling the hard muscle underneath makes me want to touch more of him. "Will you come to watch me fight? I bet you'd be my good luck charm."

"I would love to come."

"Yeah?"

"Definitely. Just give me the details as soon as you know them so I can be sure to request the time off of work. I'll also arrange for Audrey to watch Lily."

"You've got it. I have it all written down in my office, I'll get it to you. In fact, why don't you come to the gym? You can watch me train, or work out yourself if you want, or just hang out with me. You can bring Lily. There's always plenty of us around and we will all help and keep an eye on her."

"Plenty of you?"

"Yeah. There's a lot of fighters that work out at the gym, all ages. We even have kids classes during the week, but I was specifically referring to a group of my friends that I'm with all the time. We've all been friends a long time, and all fight and train together. I'll introduce you to them. You already met Zane."

"Oh yes, Zane." He gives me a look and I laugh. I'm honored he wants to introduce me to his friends. I mean, meeting the friends - isn't that serious? "I'd like that. Tell me about them."

"Nothing much to tell really. They're all good guys. I've known Zane the longest because we grew up in the same neighborhood and met when we were eight years old. The other guys – Levi, Cole, Ryder and Dylan – Zane and I have been friends with since high school."

"That's really cool."

"Yeah, we all even went to college together. Just locally to Arizona State University, but that's the main crew. There are some other fighters that train at the gym too of course, but the six of us are all professional. The others either do it for keeping in shape, or to compete in our gym fight night events."

"Wow, well, I look forward to meeting them. I think it's great you've all been friends so long."

"Do you have friends from your childhood that you keep in touch with?"

"No. I had a couple good friends when I was in high school, but Tyson and I moved away as soon as we could and that meant leaving them behind. We tried to keep in contact initially, but then life got in the way."

"That's too bad, but sometimes we all have to sacrifice things for our ultimate happiness. We don't see it at the time, but later things like that always become clear."

"That's an interesting way of looking at it. Unfortunately, my friends were sacrificed for my happiness I guess, because getting out of California wasn't an option for Tyson and me, it was a necessity."

"Why is that?"

Before I think twice about it I find myself wanting to be honest, needing to tell the truth instead of the watered down version I usually share when asked. "Our mom has problems and she always blamed Tyson and me for all of them. We were always her crutch, her targets - the people to blame for her self-defined horrible life. It didn't matter what we did, or how much we tried to provide her everything and anything she ever wanted, she always found fault. We were the reason she was single and a poor provider, a poor mother, and everything else that she lacked. We were young when we first started dreaming of the day we would escape her. When we were sixteen, we told each other repeatedly that as soon as we were eighteen we would leave. And we made it happen. The day after our eighteenth birthday, we got the hell out."

His brow furrows and he gives my hand a squeeze letting me

know he's paying attention although his focus remains on the road. "Wow. You are both so brave."

"No we aren't. We are just two people who knew that in order to survive we had to escape our history or face a life of low esteem and defeat since we were constantly told by someone who hated us that we were worthless. We refused to believe her, continually tried to support each other, and wanted the chance to determine our own destinies."

"She sounds like she was very cruel and hateful."

With a deep sigh, I look at him quickly, then look back at the road before us. "She was – and likely still is. She blamed our birth on the fact that our dad left her."

"What?"

Laughing without humor I explain, "She's told us since I can remember that the Martin women are cursed. Her grandmother and mother all had men that left them. My amazing father left when she told him she was pregnant. She's blamed us ever since and I grew up hearing about our family curse and how I would always be alone and unworthy of love."

"Fuck. You don't believe that shit right?"

Smiling weakly, I shake my head, "No, of course not," I lie trying to both sound convincing and persuade myself, but catch a quick glimpse of Jax's expression that says he's not quite sure he believes me.

"Does she know where you are?"

"No. The night we left, she was on her way to getting significantly drunk. Not atypical. She caught us packing and initially screamed at us. Eventually, her drinking became much more important and she left us alone to lose herself in it, and we walked out and never looked back."

"Wow."

It's my turn to chuckle at his reaction. "Yeah. I guess in a way I should thank her."

"Thank her? Why?"

"Well, despite her hatred and carnage, she's made me even more determined to be the mother to Lily that she never was to me." I shrug my shoulders not knowing what else to say.

"Well hell, some date I am. All I've done is bring you down with this conversation. We're supposed to be having fun."

Laughing I give his thigh a squeeze again, "I haven't been out for fun in ages, or had adult interaction like this for a long time, other than with Tyson on the phone and Audrey. We could go to the golden arches for dinner and I'd be happy. As long as I had adult conversation on the side with my cheeseburger."

He smiles wide, making his dimples wink at me and I find myself smiling wide in return. As we pull into the parking lot to the concert venue, he unbuckles his seatbelt and places a soft kiss on my cheek. It makes me shiver and break out in goose bumps all over my body. My nipples harden and my back arches a little in response. "Let's go have a good time. Yeah?"

"Sounds good," I whisper having trouble finding my voice. He grins at me knowingly. "Wait here."

He walks around to my side of the car and helps me down, then holds my hand all the way inside. He maneuvers us through the crowd after we each get a beer and I'm astonished when I realize where our seats are. "The front row?"

He smirks, "I told you I have connections."

"Yeah, but holy hell. I've never been in the front row before!"

He laughs at my enthusiasm and takes a sip of his eight dollar beer. "Only the best for you, babe."

I like the way the word babe sounds coming from his lips. Especially when he's saying it to me. Jason called me baby sometimes and I had always hated it. Forcing that asshole from my thoughts, I wrap my arm through Jax's and place my head on his shoulder. "Thank you. I'm glad you invited, er told, me to come."

He laughs, "Me too."

When The Sinners come out to perform, Jax brings my body in front of his own and wraps his arms around my waist after we discard our beers. He sways us to the music when it's slow and grinds his hips into mine when we dance to the fast songs. His lips are at my ear and each breath he takes ruffles the hair at my neck. The band is amazing, but my attention has become completely focused on the feeling of his body against mine. Every brush, every bump, every caress is magnified so much that I want to turn in his arms and kiss the hell out of him. I want to push my ass back into his hips in invitation. I want to take one of his hands and place it on my breast, while I push the other down between my legs begging him to help me find release. My breaths come in pants; my need and want for him so strong I can feel it pounding in my chest and ringing in my ears.

A small voice in the back of my mind tells me that it's too soon. It says he will walk away like Jason did, that this is stupid and I'll end up broken in the end, but I don't care. What is life without taking risks? I don't want my mother's hateful words or Jason's hateful actions to influence the rest of my life. I realize that these emotions are like a fucking teeter-totter. Some days I can see the foolishness in believing my mother's words, but others I think maybe she was right. It's a headache at times, but I hope that someday I'll be able to let that teeter-totter stay dipped down on only one side – the right side.

Pushing aside my feelings of unworthiness, I let myself simply feel. I feel the way he runs his fingers up and down my arm. I feel the way his chest vibrates against my back as he hums along to the songs. I feel the need in my heart to be a woman lusting after a man, refusing to ask myself what the ulterior motive is. For once, I don't want to let my past dictate my future. So when I feel his lips graze my neck, I close my eyes and lose myself in the feeling and I wrap my arms tighter around his.

When the concert is over, Jax turns me around in his arms and smiles down at me. Looking at him, my lips itch with the need to kiss him. Yelling to be heard over the screaming he asks, "Did you love it?"

Smiling so big my jaw aches I nod my head, "So much!"

"I have a surprise for you."

Before I can say a word, Jax takes my hand and pulls me behind him. We make our way to the side of the stage and he pulls something from his pocket and shows it to a security guard standing there. To my utter astonishment we are let by and Jax leads me to the back of the stage, down some stairs, and inside a large room. Looking around I see some other people loitering around. There are couches, chairs, a bar and a bunch of food set up on a table. I look at him questioningly. "What's all this?"

"Oh nothing, it's just that you're going to meet the band."

"Shut up!"

He laughs and pulls me into his arms. "How am I doing for our first date?"

"How are you ever going to top this?" I tease.

He laughs and pulls me over to the table of food. "Hungry?" I nod and we fill our plates and find seats talking all the while about the concert, our favorite songs and what other concerts we'd like to attend.

When the band finally comes through the doors, I feel nerves flutter in my stomach. Jax stands and starts to pull me along, but I find that I can't move. He turns around and looks at me in confusion, "What's wrong?"

"I've never met a celebrity before."

He laughs and cups the side of my face, "You are so adorable, do you know that?"

"Don't make fun of me."

He holds his hands up in a gesture of retreat, "I'm not, I swear. I promise it's not a big deal. Those guys are just like you and me –

what's that saying? Oh yeah, they put their pants on one leg at a time just like us. Personally, I prefer to say that they poop and fart just like the rest of us."

"Oh my god!" I look around to make sure no one heard him. "I don't want to talk about that!"

"Hey, it's the truth." He keeps laughing at my embarrassment but then says seriously, "You have nothing to be nervous about. The only difference is that they know how to play musical instruments and sing, and we don't."

"Yes, and they have thousands of fans screaming their name on a nightly basis."

"Well yeah, that too. Trust me though, it's really no big deal."

Before he can continue my eyes widen when I see Simon, the lead guitarist, tap Jax on the shoulder. Jax turns around and smiles, "Hey, man."

"Hey, Jax. How's it going?" They do some weird dude handshake thing and clap each other on the back. I just stare in awe.

"Good. Really good. Great concert tonight."

"Thanks. How's the training going? Have a fight coming up?"

I stand there astonished and can't believe they're talking about Jax's upcoming fight. He told me he had a connection to the band - that sneak! He didn't tell me that his connection is because he knows the band. I can't freaking believe it. I mean, holy hell, Simon called him by name! *Don't freak out, don't freak out. You will not hyperventilate and make a fool of yourself!* When Jax turns to me and introduces me to Simon, it takes everything I have not to faint. "Simon, I'd like you to meet my girl, Rowan. She's a big fan."

"Hi, Rowan. Nice to meet you."

"You too." I answer softly making Jax chuckle and I give him a glare. "I really enjoyed the show."

"Thanks. Glad you guys could make it. Wish I could come and watch this guy fight in a couple weeks. That's way more exciting."

"Wish you could make it too, man. That would be awesome. You'll just have to make another one when you can."

"Sounds like a plan."

As they are talking the drummer Tyler comes up and greets Jax too and once again my mouth drops open. Does he know all of them? Before Jax can introduce me to him, Tyler notices me standing a little behind Jax. He pushes Jax out of the way, "Well, well, well, hello there little darling. I'm so sorry I was wasting my time on this guy when you were obviously waiting to meet me." He winks and I giggle. I freaking giggle. His eyes flick over my frame, resting for a beat at my breasts, before they meet mine again. "What's your name, gorgeous?"

Before I can respond, Jax shoves him back and answers for me, "This is *my* Rowan, so back the fuck off Tyler."

Looking at Jax in astonishment my mouth hangs open at his possessiveness. I can't decide if I want to laugh at this showing of testosterone or if I'm totally turned on. He looks back at me clearly daring me to argue with him. Instead, I hold my hand out to Tyler, "Hi, it's nice to meet you. Great show."

Instead of shaking my hand, Tyler takes it and leaves a lingering kiss. "You're pushing it, T," Simon says making Tyler glance at Jax and then laugh.

"Aw, I just like fucking with ya."

Jax visibly relaxes, but doesn't quit glaring at Tyler, "Whatever. I've heard plenty about your man whore shit. My girl will probably catch something just from touching your hand. Anyone have any hand sanitizer?" Jax calls out making me giggle again. He looks at me and winks making my stomach flip in excitement and I can't keep the grin off my face.

We hang around for a little while and I meet Brian and Chester, the other two band members. They are all really cool and I laugh most of the time at Tyler's antics as he floats from woman to woman.

He compliments all of them, touches them, poses for pictures and I even hear him blatantly ask a woman if she wants to go back to his hotel room later. He's pure entertainment.

When we're walking to his truck later, I squeeze Jax's hand the whole time and practically bounce on my toes. "That was so much fun. Thank you so much. I can't believe I actually met the band! They are really nice and the concert was great. I also can't believe they gave me all this stuff."

My arms are loaded down with a signed t-shirt, a hat, keychain, stickers, posters, souvenir cup, even a foam finger which made me laugh out loud. I thought they only had them at sporting events. I was wrong. Jax scowls at me, "I think Tyler definitely likes you. He just kept giving you more and more stuff."

"Maybe. But I only have eyes for one guy."

He smiles and his dimples pop out as if they're grateful to escape their hiding place. "Oh yeah?"

"Yeah. Simon is definitely more my type."

Jax stops and stares at me in amusement, then I dodge his reach and run down the aisle toward the truck laughing all the way while he chases me.

CHAPTER TWELVE

Jax

I can't take my eyes off of her. Not wanting the night to end I'm glad when she agrees to get something to eat saying she's hungry too. We had little appetizers at the after party, but it wasn't much. Deciding on a simple pizza joint since they're open late, we sit across from each other at a corner booth and I keep contemplating whether or not to join her on her side, or if that would be too pushy. I've never given two thoughts to a girl the way I do Rowan.

"I really had a lot of fun with you at the concert." Her eyes glow with excitement and happiness and right then and there, I promise myself that I will do my best to always put that shine in her eyes. "Thank you so much for a great time."

"There's no one else I would have rather gone with. I'm glad you enjoyed yourself. I had a great time too."

"I more than enjoyed myself. The music was great, but the company is even better. And I still can't believe you actually know The Sinners and we went backstage. Why didn't you tell me you know them?"

"Because I didn't want to sound like a pretentious douche."

She laughs throwing her head back and it makes me want to put my lips on her neck – kiss my way to the back of her ear, the down further making my way to her breasts. "I don't think it's possible for you to sound like that."

I momentarily forget what we're discussing. Oh right. Pretentions douche. "Yeah well, I didn't want to take the chance."

We order a simple pepperoni pizza, drinks, and a salad. I may allow myself one slice of pizza, but that's it. When our food arrives and she begins eating, I have a hard time taking my eyes off of her. The way her mouth surrounds the food when she takes a bite. She chews her food slowly with a soft smile on her face, telling me she enjoys the taste. Everything this woman does is sexy. I don't stand a chance. More than anything I want to put my mouth on hers. Who am I kidding? I want to put my mouth all over her. My eyes quickly drop to her cleavage again. The light in the restaurant highlights the black lace under the white perfectly. I can't help but imagine her naked breasts in the palms of my hands. I imagine myself sucking on her pretty pink nipples, bringing them to a hard point. I can even imagine the melody the sound of her moans will make – they would be music to my ears. Adjusting myself to the tightening in my pants, I quickly look up again and try to remove the images from my head. Both heads.

Instead, my mind goes to how it felt to hold her in my arms tonight, her body moving against mine to the music. Exercising restraint was not easy. All I could think about was grabbing her hand, leading her to the closest bathroom or hell, a closet, and taking her up against the wall until I had her screaming my name. It's like she's some kind of witch who's cast a spell over me, because I am completely caught up in her magic. The magic of her smile, her laugh, her body, her touch. I want more. I crave it.

There's something about her. I'm not sure when it happened. I don't know if it was when she grabbed hold of me at the hospital needing support from someone, or if it was when she asked me not to leave her. Maybe it was when I went over to her house that sad day. When she opened the door, I saw how broken she was. Her face had been so full of pain. All I know is that I want nothing more than to be the person to put her back together, one devastatingly jagged piece at a time. She's gotten under my skin, branding herself like a tattoo, and keeping an eye on her these past few months has only embedded her deeper. She's mine. She just doesn't know it yet.

"Rowan?"

She wipes her lips with a napkin and I want to be that damn napkin, "Yes?"

I hesitate not wanting to ruin her good mood, but my curiosity, worry and hell my competitive nature, wins out. "Will you tell me why you were alone at the hospital?"

Her body stiffens and she looks down at her plate. She licks her lips making me think her mouth went dry at the question. She's silent and her eyes hold feelings I can't decipher and it makes me feel like I should say more. "Look, the reason I'm asking is because I like you. I *really* like you and I just want to make sure there isn't anyone else standing in my way. Maybe this is fast for you, maybe you don't feel the same way, maybe you're just humoring me and this has been the worst date ever and you won't want to see me again after this. I hope that's not the case, but what I do know is that I don't do things half way." I put my napkin on the table and run my hand through my hair then look straight into her muddy green and brown eyes. "When I want something, I take it. And make no mistake, Rowan, I want you."

Her eyes widen, but they hold mine unblinking. For a horrifying moment, I'm afraid I pushed too far – revealed too much. Given what Tyson told me, she was with this Jason dude for a little while, so I know it hasn't been long since her relationship with him ended. Suddenly, I wish I could reverse time and swallow my words, but then, she reaches her hand out and takes mine. My whole body reacts to her simple touch and when she gasps quietly and pulls her hand back as if it were burned, I know it's because she feels it too. "I feel the same way about you. I like you and would really like to see you again. I promise I'll tell you more about Jason another time, but let me at least say that you don't need to worry about him. I don't even know where he is. And now that's all I want to say about it tonight, okay? This has been the best date I've ever had and I don't want to ruin it with thoughts of him."

I can't help it, I smile, "The best date you've ever had, huh?"

She smiles and it's like the sun is suddenly shining in the middle of the night. "Definitely."

"For me too."

"And just for the record?" She has a sly smile on her face and I raise my eyebrows and give her a nod. "There is absolutely no one in the way."

The wolfish grin that I give her at those words can't be contained and it makes her smile bigger in return. "There's something else I need to make clear."

Her eyes glimmer and her hand is once again on mine. "Tell me."

"I don't share. You like me, I like you – there's no room for anyone else."

Her brows lower and she pulls her hand from mine making me frown, "But Lily…"

I reach back for her hand and wait until her eyes look in mine, "I'm not talking about her. She's yours and therefore she's part of this too, as far as I'm concerned the two of you are a package deal and it's one hell of a package. I'm talking about another man, Rowan. I am not okay with you dating anyone else while you're dating me. I won't share you."

"Oh." Not breaking our eye contact, she leans forward, "There is no one to share me with, and I don't play those kinds of games. And just so you are also clear…"

"Tell me," I reply mimicking her words.

"I won't share you either."

"You won't have to. Ever."

We stare into one another's eyes and the sexual tension between us is so potent I'm sure everyone around us can feel it too. I revel in the feeling. The swelling in my pants, the tightening of my muscles, the way the hair rises on my arms and neck. My fingers ache to touch her. Thoughts of her naked and writhing under me float through my mind and I adjust myself suddenly uncomfortable. When she lets go of my hand to take another bite of pizza, she unknowingly breaks the spell and I'm thankful. She may not have shared everything I'd like to know just yet, but this is a step forward in the right direction. I need to keep reminding myself to move slow and follow her lead.

After we finish our pizza we start heading back to her place. I make random conversation on the way to her place asking her cliché things like her favorite color, movie, flower, and food. Truth is I just like hearing the sound of her voice. It pisses me off that I can't keep my eyes on her and have to pay attention to the road. When we get to her place, I pull into the drive and turn off the car, then hurry to her side of the truck helping her out, "Thank you," she murmurs.

Taking her arm, we walk straight to Audrey's door and knock quietly so we don't wake Lily. Audrey answers after a minute giving us a tired smile. She holds a sleeping Lily in her arms. While Rowan takes the bag from Audrey and gets filled in about Lily's evening, I reach out and take Lily from Audrey's arms. Rowan looks at me in surprise.

"I've got her," I whisper.

Her soft little body is against mine and I can feel her exhales against my neck as I hold her close. Without a thought I gently rub her back, nod a thank you to Audrey, then follow Rowan through her front door. She immediately goes to the kitchen and washes out the bottles from the bag and begins making new ones. While she does so, I pace the floor with Lily, rocking her in my arms. Once again I take in the place she shares with Ty. While all the furniture is oddly matched pieces as far as design, each has been painted and coordinates perfectly. It's so utterly Rowan in its homey yet perfectly bright, yet simple, way. It screams Rowan's taste and I love it.

While glancing out the front window as I rock Lily, I feel arms come around me from behind and Rowan rests her head against my back. The comfortable gesture also feels intimate and I revel in the feeling. "Sorry, I had to make some bottles for later. She still gets up during the night sometimes. She's so close to sleeping all the way through though. I can't wait for that to happen. Although I'll probably wake up in a panic when it does and wonder why she hasn't woken me," she says with a laugh.

I frown, "Is that normal?"

"What?"

"For her to wake up during the night like that."

She laughs softly, "Yes. It always takes babies a little while to sleep through the night and not wake up hungry or with a wet diaper. I'm lucky she's already doing so well."

I don't like the thought or Rowan always having to get up with her and doing everything on her own. Turning around and leaning down to Rowan's level, I smile when she runs a hand over Lily's head. "Give her a kiss and then I'll put her to bed."

She gives her a soft kiss and whispers, "I love you baby girl." My heart constricts in my chest at the look of love on her face and in her eyes.

Without a word I walk to Lily's room and place her in her crib. She lets out a soft little breath and moves her lips in a sucking motion before quitting. She's a gorgeous little girl. With her mama's nose and lips and those long lashes of hers, I already know she's going to be a heart breaker one day. Placing a blanket gently over her legs, I leave the room and find Rowan straightening up in the kitchen.

When she sees me she smiles, 'Thanks for doing that."

"I'm happy to. She's a doll you know. You are going to have trouble when she's older."

"Don't I know it. Luckily she should have her Uncle Tyson around to keep all the boys in line." She laughs then walks over to me, pressing her body against mine in a hug. Her body fits perfectly to mine and when her hips brush against the tops of my legs all I can think about is how I want to spread her legs open with my knee and kiss and touch her while she writhes against me. I have to hold myself back from picking her up and walking her into her bedroom. Or better yet, I can lift her onto the kitchen counter, step between her thighs and take her right there. Of course, there's always the kitchen table. I could lay her on it, spread her creamy thighs and have a feast that has nothing to do with food. Fuck. A cold shower is seriously calling my name when I get home. Instead of doing any of those things, I place my arms around her and squeeze her to my chest, placing a kiss on her forehead. "I had a great time tonight. I want to see you again soon."

"Me too." She buries her face into my chest and inhales. Is she… smelling me? I have to suppress a groan at the thought.

"Are you working this weekend?"

"No, I have it off actually. I'm usually lucky enough to work Monday through Friday. They schedule the college girls on the weekends."

"Come to the gym tomorrow some time. You can bring Lily too. Just come and see me."

She pulls away and looks into my eyes giving me a smile, "I'd like that. I still have your card with the address."

"Good. Did you plug my number into your phone?"

She stares at me blankly and I take that as a no. Pulling my phone from my pocket, I ask for her number then call her. When I hear her phone ring I say, "There. Now I have your number and you have mine. I will see you tomorrow. Any time. I'll be there early."

"Okay," she agrees softly, "I will see you then."

Cupping her cheek, I run my thumb over it feeling her smooth skin, then give her a soft, "Bye." Forcing myself to leave, not wanting to push her too far, I open her front door and walk out closing the door behind me. Leaning against the door my whole body hurts with the need to get back and touch itself to her. My whole body vibrates with the need to reconnect with hers. Running my hand through my hair I take deep breaths and try to get myself under control. Turning around I put a hand on either side of the door and hang my head down. All I can picture are her lips, her eyes, her flowing hair, her body. It's like she's my own personal temptress, personally sent to be my undoing.

Before I can think twice I knock on the door. She must be standing close by because she opens the door quickly. Before she can say a word I crush my mouth to hers. She gasps in surprise and I swallow the sound, taking advantage of her open mouth by swooping my tongue inside. Her taste makes me groan – so sweet. I clench my hands in her hair and use it to tilt her head to the side, ravaging her lips with my own, holding myself back from the bruising kiss I'd like to give her. Holding back the need to possess her and brand her as mine. Her moans mix with mine and it's the sweetest symphony I've ever heard. I put everything I'm feeling into the kiss but can't yet say. That I want her. That I think about her all the time. That while I may not understand it, the fact is she's already mine and I'm hers. When we pull apart she's gasping for air, her breaths rapid, her lips wet with our passion. I kiss the corners of her mouth, right and then left. "Good night, Rowan."

Giving her forehead a lingering kiss, I turn on my heel and walk away making my way back to my truck.

CHAPTER THIRTEEN

Rowan

All I've been able to think about is that kiss. The way his lips devoured mine, his need and want coming to life in the sound of his groan, the feeling of complete and utter domination in just one simple kiss. I want another - many others. But, I also want more. If one kiss made me feel that amazing, what would it be like sleeping with him? I already know the answer– explosive – and I want that feeling. More than that, I need it.

Lying in my bed enjoying the quiet before Lily wakes up again, I watch the sun rising in the sky through my window painting the sky the color of cotton candy and spun gold. Reliving the night before, the only word I can use to describe it is perfect.

I like you. I really like you.

His words resonating in my mind make me smile. I really like him too and I love the way I feel when I'm with him. I keep thinking about the way he took Lily from Audrey's arms like it was no big deal. But it was. It's a big deal, to me at least. I had to keep myself from tackling him right there and ripping his clothes off in pure lust. Lily's small little body against his big chest – completely drool-worthy - it's astounding I didn't embarrass myself, and orgasm right there on the spot.

The doubt creeps in slowly like an animal stalking its prey. It always does. It asks me why I'm bothering because he's just going to leave. It tells me not to get my hopes up, or to wish too hard for mere companionship. It tells me not to consider even for one moment that I could be considered worthy of his attention, let alone him, because

I never will be. And horribly, as if to provide validation, it reminds me that Jason left and taunts me with the likelihood that Jax will too. But I refuse to let those things get the best of me. Squeezing my eyes shut and clenching my fists, I picture my mom in my mind and remember how unhappy, bitter, and cruel she was. I remind myself that allowing these thoughts to creep in, I'll ultimately end up just like her. That helps me push the thoughts aside, and when Lily begins to cry, that makes it easier to do so.

"Hi sweet girl," I say when I look at her over the side of her crib. She smiles when she sees me, and my unhappy thoughts melt away. How does she do that? After I change her and feed her, I decide to get us both ready to go see Jax at the gym. I feel happy at the slightest thought of seeing him.

A couple of hours later we are both ready and I've got Lily's diaper bag completely packed for any possibility. I'm just about to walk out the door when my phone rings. Placing Lily's car seat and bag down, I dig my phone out of my purse in case Jax is calling and there's a change in plans. When I see the number for the jail, I pick it up immediately.

"Hello?"

"You have a collect call from....Tyson." I hear his voice stating his name and it automatically makes me eager to hear more of his voice. I miss him. "Do you accept the charges?"

"Yes."

The line clicks a couple times before I hear, "Rowan?"

"Tyson! Hi!"

"Hi sweet girl! It's so great to hear your voice. How are you?"

"I'm good. Lily and I were just on our way to go see Jax."

"Oh yeah? How is my niece doing? God Rowan, I can't wait to finally meet her."

"She's doing great, Uncle Tyson. She's almost sleeping through the night, in fact, she almost did last night and she's putting anything she can get her hands on into her mouth. She's adorable."

"Of course she is. She's yours."

"Aw, well aren't you sweet?"

"You said you're heading to see Jax, huh? That going well?"

"Yeah it is. I like him but…"

"But what?"

"You know what," I sigh.

"Listen up. Jax is a good guy. Stop letting stupid shit our mom said fuck up a good thing. Don't let her win."

Sighing, I don't respond to his comment, "I am so ready for you to get home."

"Well about that… I have some good news and besides checking in, it's the reason I'm calling."

"What is it?"

"It looks like I'm going to get out of here early. I mean I know it's not that much since I'm due to get out in a month anyway, but I'll take it. And, it looks like it will be really soon. Like, in a week or less kind of soon."

"Oh my gosh, really?"

"Yep. My attorney met with me yesterday and he said he was contacted by the jail and they are just waiting for approval to come through. He said I should know for sure later today or tomorrow and they will let me use the phone again so that I can arrange for transportation."

"That's great! I'll be sure to keep my phone handy so I don't miss your call."

"Thanks. I can't wait to get the hell out of here. Aside from giving you and my niece a hug, I want a feast when I get out of here. This man wants some meat!"

Laughing, I respond, "Good to know. I'll be sure to go to the grocery store."

"Okay, sounds good. I miss you, Row. Can't wait to see you."

"I miss you too."

"Also...when I get home, be prepared to have that talk you keep putting off."

Knowing he's talking about Jason, I agree because I know he's been patient with me and it's time to give him some answers. "We'll talk after you get home and settled in, okay?"

"Yes we will. Alright, my time's about up, but really quick, how are you doing financially? Is everything okay?"

"It's fine. I'm back to work and making ends meet. It's a little tight now with Lily, but I'm making do."

"You've been taking my part of the rent out of our savings, right?"

"Yes."

"Take money from the emergency fund if you need to. Don't struggle when you don't have to. Promise me, Row."

"Okay, I promise. Besides, you're getting out soon, so stop worrying."

"I'll never not worry about you. It's a big brother's job."

"You're older by two minutes."

"Exactly," he laughs, "Alright, I'll talk to you soon. Tell Jax I said hello. Love you."

"Love you too."

We hang up and my heart aches with the missing of him. This is the longest we've ever been separated and I don't care for it. He can't get released and home fast enough, although I'm dreading talking to him about Jason. I'm embarrassed that I let myself be with such an asshole. Not for the first time since his abandonment I wish I had been the one to leave him. When he was so awful to me when he found out I was pregnant and then after – never taking an interest in anything relating to the pregnancy, I should have left long ago. Instead I clung to some stupid notion that things would change. How very wrong I was given that he didn't even stick around to meet our daughter. I can definitely admit I wasn't expecting that.

Briefly I've wondered if I'm jumping into something too fast with Jax, but Tyson has insisted each time we talk that Jax is a great guy and somehow that calms the hesitation, self-doubt and fear lingering inside of me.

Ensuring that Lily is buckled securely in her car seat, I make sure she's settled then punch the address for the gym into the GPS on my phone. I'm happy to see it's only about twenty minutes away.

Ready for the short drive, I turn the radio up and sing along to the songs. Lily makes little noises along with me and I can't help but laugh thinking it's her way of singing along. The drive goes quickly and before I know it we've arrived.

Pulling into the gym parking lot, my nerves set in. I didn't text Jax to tell him we were on the way and now I'm wondering if I should have. Feeling a bit uncertain but admittedly excited to see him, I unbuckle Lily, grab our bags and head inside before I can change my mind. Opening the glass entrance door, I immediately notice the large reception desk in the front and the girl sitting behind it. She's cute and talking on the phone so she doesn't greet us right away except to cast me a smile. Waiting, I look around and observe all the men that are working out. There's a few lifting free weights with loud grunts of exertion in one far corner and a couple more running on the treadmill opposite of the others. Turning my head to view the other side of the gym, I scan all the punching bags and men hitting them so hard the thwack's echo around the room. There's two guys sparring in a large off-center ring and I can see them dodging one another their focus intent, while a few people appear to be working at what looks like a juice bar on the other side. There's also a large cage like thing ---the kind that fights are held in, I think, recalling something I've seen on TV, but no one is in it right now. I've never been in a gym quite like this before and in fact this is my first visit to an MMA facility, so I try to absorb everything quickly. I'm surprised at the sheer size of the place and am quite impressed that Jax runs all of this. There's even a gift shop off of the reception area and I decide to take a peek inside while waiting for the receptionist to finish up. I see gloves, water bottles, t-shirts, shorts, energy drinks and more. Wow. Color me impressed. I expected to see a ring, cage, and weights, sure, but not everything else. It's pretty amazing.

"Hello. Welcome to XTreme Fitness Center. How can I help you?"

"Hi," I reply somewhat shyly. "I'm looking for Jax?"

"Oh sure. Can I tell him who's here to see him?"

"Yes, of course. My name is Rowan."

She picks up a phone and repeats my name to the person on the other end. "He'll be right out."

No more than thirty seconds later, Jax walks out of a door to the right of where I'm standing. His arrival surprises me since I never saw that door. He makes his way over to me with a huge smile on his face. When he reaches me, he leans down and gives me a light kiss on my lips, "Hi, gorgeous."

"Hi, yourself."

His thumb brushes my cheek. "I'm so glad you came." Then he does something that will forever make me his. He leans down and unbuckles Lily from her car seat. He struggles a bit getting the straps off of her arms, but he doesn't let that bother him. When he lifts her out, he places a kiss on the tip of her nose, "Hi, sweet girl. Thanks for coming to visit me with your mommy."

Lily reaches out and grabs his nose and Jax laughs. He picks up her seat, moves her to one arm like a pro and says, "Come with me to my office."

"Okay."

I follow him back the way he came and out of the corner of my eye I notice a few guys that stop what they're doing and watch us walk by. When we reach his office I release a breath I didn't even know I was holding. I'm nervous to meet his friends.

When we walk into his office, it's massive. He has a large desk, a bookshelf and I'm shocked to see the other items in the room. "A bouncer and toys?"

I swear the tips of his cheeks turn red, "I want Lily to be comfortable when you guys come to visit, so I grabbed this stuff from the store this morning."

He places Lily in the bouncer seat and buckles her in. Pressing a button, it makes a bar above the seat light up and play music. Lily instantly starts kicking her arms and legs in joy and swats at the mobiles hanging in front of her.

When Jax turns around to look at me, he opens his mouth to say something, but I swallow the words with my mouth because I've lunged at him and am kissing him with everything I have. His initial surprise disappears quickly and he kisses me back with equal passion. My hands clutch handfuls of his shirt and I'm standing on my toes to reach him. Our mouths move in sync, tongues twirling and tasting. I pull back and place one more kiss on his lips. "Thank you."

"I will go to the store right now and buy one of everything I see if this is the reaction I'll receive."

I laugh with joy and feel my cheeks flush in embarrassment at my enthusiasm. I guess I did pretty much tackle him with my lips. "It means a lot to me that you thought of her like this."

"Of course I did. It's not a big deal."

"Please don't downplay it. It's a big deal to me. Okay?"

"Okay. Then you're welcome."

He leans forward and takes my lips in another kiss, but before we can get too carried away, there's a knock on the door. He sighs, "I knew this was going to happen."

"What?"

"I hope you're ready to meet the guys, babe, because behind that door, they're all standing there ready to meet you."

I look at the door and feel my eyes widen and Jax chuckles. "What? How do you know?"

"I just know."

"Buy why?"

"It's the first time I've ever brought a girl here." I stare at him and he shrugs, "They're curious the nosy bastards." He keeps grumbling all the way to the door and when he pulls it open, five sets of eyes look past him and at me. I have to force myself not to shrink back from their gazes.

Giving a hesitant wave, I murmur, "Uh, hi."

That's all it takes. They all come bounding into the office pushing one another out of the way like little puppies, while making snide remarks to one another about moving so they can meet me. I take a step back, mouth opening in surprise as I take them all in. It's like a freaking hot guy festival right in front of me and I'm the only one that bought a ticket. *Please don't drool, Rowan. Please don't drool.*

I recognize Zane and he walks forward and gives me a hug. His frame envelops mine and he holds me for a touch too long, "Good to see you again, Rowan."

"Hi."

"Get the fuck off of her now, Zane."

I can feel the vibrations of Zane's chuckle against my cheek and I cant help but smile as he pulls away. Giving Jax a quick smile my focus is taken from him when a guy that can only be described as a walking advertisement for a surfer boy walks up to me. He has bright green eyes and blonde hair that's long on top, but short on the sides and he's shirtless, so I try really hard to not take in his ripped chest. But it's hard – oh so hard. Pun intended – the dude's ripped. "Hi beautiful, I'm Levi. Do you have your phone with you?"

"My phone?" I look at him in confusion but nod my head yes.

"Let me give you my number, doll, so you can call me up when you come to your senses and dump this guy," he jerks his thumb at Jax.

"Shut up, Levi."

I can't help but giggle, "Hi, Levi. Sounds like a plan." I teasingly whisper back at him making him beam and Jax narrow his eyes.

Pushing him out of the way is a guy with a shaved head except for a strip of spiked hair that runs down the center. They're all covered in tattoos from what I can tell, but he seems to have many more than the rest. His arms are covered in them, and while he has a v-neck shirt on, there are tattoos peeking out the top. His eyes are a light blue, and his dark eyebrows make them pop. An earring winks at me out of his left ear and his full lips curve upwards in a sexy as sin grin. "Hello there, beautiful." Without another word he gives me a kiss on the cheek and I admit it, I gasp softly. His sexuality is as potent as the smell of cologne in the air.

Jax of course interrupts, "Okay, that's enough, Ryder."

With a laugh, Ryder backs up and I smile a little wobbly at him, "Nice to meet you."

He winks, "I know."

"Hi!" I turn away from Ryder and take in the red haired, soul patched, freckled blue- eyed guy who stands before me. He's shorter than the rest of the guys, but by no means is he lost in the crowd. "My name is Dylan."

"Hi, Dylan. It's nice to meet you."

"You too."

He's super cute. I kind of want to pinch his cheeks, which wouldn't be appropriate at all.

Just behind Dylan is a guy with dark hair, and eyes so dark they look black. His ears stick out just a smidge, but they make him look almost… charming. He could certainly rival Ryder with his tattoos and when he gives me a shy smile and wave, I find myself automatically returning it. "Hey, I'm Cole."

That's all he says and then he looks at Jax as if making sure that it was okay to do so. "Nice to meet you, Cole."

Not wanting to be ignored, Lily chooses that moment to fuss from her seat. Before I can get her, Jax is there, unbuckling her from her seat. He holds her in his arms and gives her a couple bounces making her, and me, smile. I wonder if this feeling I get when I see her with him, like I'm suddenly goo, will ever stop. "Guys, this is Lily. Lily, these are the guys."

Jax holds her proudly and I wish I had my phone in my hand so I could videotape the reaction from these men. That's the only way anyone would believe me later. These tough, covered in tattoos fighters all turn to big softies as they coo at and talk baby talk to Lily. She gives them all big gummy smiles and bats her lashes. I swear she's flirting with them.

"She's so cute."

"Look at her little smile."

"She's beautiful like her mama."

I find myself beaming at all of them, and when I look at Jax, I find that he's already looking back at me. I hold his stare and try to articulate everything I'm feeling into my eyes. I don't think I've ever been more attracted to him than in this moment. His eyes narrow a little as if he knows what I'm thinking and then his lips curve up into a smirk. "Okay guys, get out of here. I think you've overwhelmed Rowan and Lily enough for now."

With grumbles and waves goodbye, they all file out of the office. Jax places Lily back in her chair and gives her a bottle when she fusses. She takes it to her mouth and sucks happily, eyes partially closing in happiness.

When Jax turns to me, I practically fall into his arms eager to get my mouth on his. When I do, we both let out simultaneous groans. My hands move over his chest and I feel the hard muscle underneath. Wrapping my hands around his waist, I pull him closer to me and explore his mouth with my tongue, feeling my lips firm against his and reveling in the feeling of my whole body pressing against his in need. My core throbs with want and the feeling makes me feel ravenous. Jax pulls back from me, "Whoa," he says making me smile.

"Yes, whoa."

"Babe, if you keep kissing me like that, I'm going to strip you bare and take you right here on the couch. But I don't think that would be appropriate in front of the little lady."

"You're right about that. Not sure I want her to have an anatomy lesson quite yet."

"Come on, let's get Lily and I'll give you a tour of the place and then let me take you out to eat."

"Okay, that sounds good."

He places another soft kiss on my mouth, and when I pull away I feel the possibility for what could happen between us when I see the promise sparkling in his eyes.

CHAPTER FOURTEEN

Jax

The days leading up to the fight have passed quickly. I've seen Rowan almost every day and the few times I haven't, I think about her so much she may as well be standing in the room with me. I don't know what it is – I've wanted her from the moment I saw her and that feeling hasn't diminished at all. It only grows more each day.

The last couple weeks have been an exercise in restraint, that's for sure. Just thinking about Rowan makes my body tremble with need. I've been careful not to push her too far as not to scare her away. Truth is, she rocks my world with just her kisses. Each time I kiss her in return, I throw all my passion and my all-consuming thoughts of her into every stroke of my tongue and each movement of my lips. I only hope that she feels the same spark I do each and every time. Spark is too mild; it's sheer fireworks.

My attraction to her is much more than sex. She's smart, funny, kind, loving and so sassy that I want to spank her ass and see what she would do. Taking it slow has been the right thing. I want to make sure the douche before me is well out of her mind and heart before we go there, but I'm not sure how much longer I can take this. I'm about to explode. Cold showers and jacking off like a horny high school kid has become the norm for me. It's been that or choosing to be a walking erection twenty-four seven.

Stepping out of yet another cold shower, I'm thankful that this one is not to cool my hormones, but rather to clear my head. Focus on this day is needed because it's going to be a brutal one. It's weigh-in day, which normally wouldn't be a big deal, except for those of us that are over our weight limit for our fight class. And as of right now, that includes me. That means working out like crazy in order to lose the last few pounds before pre-fight weigh-ins occur tonight. No one wants to have issues in front of the fans and MMA coordinators. Audrey is watching Lily the next two nights so Rowan can stay with me for the weekend. She insisted on being here to support and cheer me on. And I'm really glad. I'm not sure how Coach Gil is going to feel about it considering he will say it's a distraction, but he can deal. I want her here.

Putting on shorts, t-shirt, socks and my running shoes, I walk out of the locker room and into the gym where Gil and the other guys are hanging out waiting to begin – not that they couldn't start without me. I'm pretty sure they're delaying as long as possible. Given how much I'm about to sweat, a shower was probably stupid, but it certainly felt like it would help. I'm ready to get this show on the road.

"Alright, motherfuckers, let's do this."

"About time, Jackson. I don't want to stand here all damn day," Gil grumbles.

"Cool it old man, my shower was only fifteen minutes tops."

He gives me a grin and holds out my sauna suit with glee in his eyes.

"I think you enjoy this a little too much you sadistic prick."

He just continues smiling while I slide my arms into the long sleeves of the suit jacket and push my hands past the gathered fabric at my wrists that's supposed to keep heat from leaving my body. Zipping up the front, I then step into the pants and push my feet past the same gatherings at the ankles. Made to keep heat enclosed so that I sweat like a pig, I'm ready to sweat off the pounds.

We all weighed ourselves earlier in the locker room wearing only our briefs to see how much weight we had to lose. I only have three pounds to drop, and so does Ryder, but Levi has five and Cole six. All of us must have overindulged a bit the last few weeks, or we've just gained too much muscle weight. Either way, it needs to come off so we aren't disqualified.

"Start off on the treadmill boys," Coach Gil bosses. "Five miles starting now."

We all shuffle our way to the machines and start running. Shortly, our competitiveness takes over and we race to see who can finish the miles first. Boys will be boys I guess. After the treadmills we lift weights, sit in the sauna, jump rope and run again. Then we start all over. Between each set, we strip, weigh ourselves to see our progress, then put the sweat soaked suits back on and keep going. It's a tedious process and the exhaustion starts to make us crazy.

"I think I'm going to hook up with Nikki tonight," Levi announces. We're all practically lying down in the sauna, too tired to sit upright any longer.

"Why? You into STD roulette or something?" Ryder asks.

"Oh please, we all know you've gone there yourself," Cole points out.

"True story, but as you know, I hit it and quit it. No girl is worth getting all of this," he grabs his junk, "more than once," Ryder says.

"And what you do isn't STD roulette? You're just as bad," I say. He just shrugs in response. "You can't tell me that there's never once been a girl that you wanted to be with more than once," I push.

"Nope. I don't need or want any chick getting attached to me. I don't do relationships. And I always wrap it before I tap it, so no roulette here."

"God, it's like a conversation full of the worst sexual references known to man," Cole says.

"What about Rowan, Jax?" Levi asks. "You hit that yet?"

I lift my head and glare at him, "None of your fucking business."

"That's a no," he snorts.

"Fuck off, Levi. Rowan isn't just some fighter groupie chick or one night stand. Don't talk about her like that."

"Whoa, sounds like someone's got it bad," Ryder adds.

"If I had a girl that looks like that to sink into every night, I'd probably have it bad too," Cole replies.

"You all better shut the fuck up or I'll beat your asses."

Possessiveness runs through my veins and I want to cut off their dicks and rip their tongues out for speaking about Rowan with sexual innuendo. She's totally off limits to them – in every way that implies - and I intend to keep that very clear. Taking deep breaths I do my best to ignore all of them and they eventually move on to a discussion about the best sex they've had with groupies and a few non-groupies as well. Tuning them out, I try to distract myself and push the feeling that I'm going to die out of my mind. It's hot and every minute that passes it gets harder to breathe. Thoughts of Rowan and Lily enter my mind and like a soothing balm, they immediately help calm me.

When Gil tells us it's time to get out of the sauna, we all practically crawl on our hands and knees to the scales.

"Thank bloody Christ," Ryder says when he sees he's dropped his three pounds. I second that emotion when I see I'm down my three as well and start ripping off my suit. I stifle a laugh, mostly, when Cole and Levi curse up a storm, aware they haven't made their weight yet and plod their way back to the treadmills with significant effort.

Once Ryder and I get our suits off, we immediately grab towels to wipe off our saturated faces and make our way to the treadmills to encourage Levi and Cole. If you can call it that.

"You can run faster than that, you pussies," Ryder hollers.

"You're never going to make weight at this pace, assholes. Pick up the stride," I add.

"At this rate, you're both going to get your asses kicked tomorrow," Ryder helpfully adds.

"Fuck you!" Cole and Levi yell at the same time making Ryder, Gil and me laugh.

We may joke, but this shit isn't easy and encouraging each other helps even if we don't admit it. We're a team after all.

It takes a couple hours for them to drop their pounds. We all head to the showers and clean up. Afterwards, we go our separate ways, knowing we'll see each other later at the weigh-in. Energy recharged, I practically run to my car, texting Rowan that I'm on my way, excited to pick her up. I've definitely found a second wind and feel wired up and ready to start the weekend. Now to put that vitality to good use. When I pull up to her townhouse and turn off the ignition, I'm barely out of the car before she appears before me, "Hey, I was just getting ready to come up to the door."

"No need. When you texted I decided to keep an eye out."

I like to think maybe she's just as excited to see me as I am her. Taking her in my arms, I give her a brief kiss and open the truck door for her. When I see she has an overnight bag hanging from her hand, I want to fist pump the air. I asked her to stay over for the weekend, but wasn't sure if she would take me up on it. "So, you're going to stay?"

She bites her lip and looks at me almost shyly, the effect making me want to take her up against my car right now in front of anyone and everyone. "Yes."

"Are you sure you're okay with that? I know it's probably hard to leave Lily."

Her face falls for just a moment and I want to kick myself in the ass for bringing it up and wiping off the smile she had. "It really is. But, Audrey helped convince me that time to myself is really important too. I have her number, she has mine, Lily loves Audrey and she will be okay."

"Yes, she will. We will call and text to check on her a lot, okay?"

Her face lights up again and I feel relief. Putting her bag in the car, I close the door behind her then hustle to my side, start the truck and begin the short drive to my place.

She looks at me and smiles, "How was the work out?"

"It sucked, but produced positive results. We're all down to our required weight and ready for the weigh-in tonight."

"That's good. And that's in a few hours?"

"Right. I thought we could go to my place and hang out for a bit until we have to leave and head over. The fight is being held at the Arizona Red Rock Casino, as is the weigh-in tonight. After I'm done, I thought we could have dinner at the casino if you'd like before we go back to my place, or we can get carry out and take it home. Whatever you want to do, we can play it by ear. I just can't eat beforehand because I can't run the risk of gaining back the weight I lost."

"I understand and your plans sound good to me."

When we reach my place, I feel excited when I let her in the door. My condo isn't anything amazing, but it feels good having her in my personal space. As soon as we walk inside, she lingers in the living room looking around. "It's not anything special," I tell her self consciously, "kind of plain."

"It looks great. Give me a tour?"

"Sure," I smile and grab her arm. "As you can see, this is the living room." I glance around and note the dark wood bookshelves, black leather couches and big screen TV, trying to see things through her eyes, and find myself feeling thankful I've cleaned and dusted recently. "The kitchen is through here." Her eyes skim the dark cherry cabinets, marble countertops, and the stainless steel appliances that are so shiny they look new. Taking her down the hall, I show her the first bedroom on the right, which is the master suite with bath. She peeks in through the doorway and pauses as though she's taking a mental picture, capturing the dark mahogany king size bed, the grey and black bedding and black leather furniture. Not wanting to make her uncomfortable and give away how much I want to take her into the room and rip her clothes off, I show her the other bathroom and two bedrooms on the south side. "This room is a guest room. When I bought the house I knew I needed to have an extra room for guests in case one of the guys ever needs to crash, and this room I use as a home office."

She walks into the room and seems to be inspecting it. I'm curious what she thinks. This room is my office slash man-cave - a shrine to my wrestling and MMA career. Shelves holding awards and medals are on one wall and a big couch and desk take up the majority of the room. Hanging on the wall are dozens of photos of me fighting, posing with other fighters, with the guys, at competitions and at the gym. She walks closer to get a better look of the photos and her gaze stops on one and holds. It's one of my favorites and the central point of all of the photos. I walk up behind her, "That's me with my grandfather."

"The one that left you the gym?"

"Yes, his name was Steven and I called him Pops." I look at the two of us sitting together on the edge of a boxing ring, him likely giving me tips and me taking in everything he had to say.

"How did he pass away?"

Staring at the photo, my heart feels heavy and I swallow the thickness that's suddenly in my throat. His loss is still palpable. "He had a heart attack. They rushed him to emergency and through tests saw he had artery blockages and needed to do emergency bypass surgery. He died on the table."

"Oh no, I'm so sorry."

Turning her in my arms and smiling at her, I tuck the hair that's fallen forward behind her ear. Smiling sadly, I brush her cheek with the back of my hand. "Thank you. I'm sorry too. I miss him. It would be easy to lose myself in the grief, but he wouldn't want that for me, so I choose to remember the good times, like those represented in this picture."

"How long has he been gone?"

"A little more than a year. I've had the gym pretty much since then though in retrospect I was running a lot of things long before he passed. I thought my father would fight the ownership since he was so angry, but he didn't. He chooses to wallow in his bitterness and anger. I tried to do anything to make him not hate me initially, but then I realized it was his problem, not mine, and decided to focus on maintaining the gym my grandfather loved. I love it too. Maybe even more now that he's gone."

"That's a healthy way to look at it. I don't think that's an easy thing for people to do."

"No, it isn't. I learned that I can't move forward with my life when I let things in my past hold me back. Only a fool carries other people's envy, insecurities, and troubles into their future, ya know? And that's exactly what my dad is – envious."

"My mom had that problem too."

I stand still, not wanting to move, or do anything that will make her clam up and quit talking. I know how hard these memories are for her. I was surprised the first time she spoke so freely about her mother, and thought perhaps it was a one-time thing. Whether she ever brought her up again or not, my goal has been to help her move past the pain of her mother's words, any way I can. I will never bring it up until or unless she wants to talk about it, but I can certainly use other situations to help send a message that pertains to her mother too. I know very well what it's like to carry that kind of pain in your life. Parents can seriously fuck you up.

"She would have her good and sober moments and would be happy until something would set her off. It didn't take much. Often it would be seeing a couple with their children. A 'normal family' as she would say. She would see a man, a father, lovingly interacting with his wife and children and she'd start in and wouldn't stop. She'd lose her mind, initially letting me know how that should be her and usually resort to interesting name-calling. She'd wrap it up by telling me not to ever expect having such a life because the women in our family are cursed."

"You mentioned the curse before. It sounds like she truly believed it."

"Yes. She said repeatedly that all the Martin women are cursed. That any man we care for and are ever with will inevitably leave. That we are destined to be unloved and alone."

How does a mother say that to her own child? "You told me when I asked before that you don't believe it's true. Is that really how you feel? I'm not saying you lied to me, I just know that telling yourself you know she was wrong and actually believing it, are two very different things."

"Honestly? Sometimes. Sometimes I believe that it isn't true. Other times, I'm not so sure. . When Jason…well…let's just say that at times I do believe her, yes. But then I had Lily, and even though it's not the same thing, for the first time in a long time, I feel hope." Again at the mention of her baby her eyes light up and chase away the fog that old ghosts had placed there and the tension in her body eases and ebbs. She's beautiful and she doesn't even know it. "Lily makes her whole entire theory die. She loves me. And I love her and that's all that matters. With Lily I know that love is possible – a forever kind of love." I walk to her and cup her face and kiss her lips softly. "You deserve to be loved, Rowan. Not just by your daughter, but by anyone else that's lucky enough to know you. Don't ever let her win. By giving in to her words and making them your own, you give her power. She sounds like a woman that let herself become bitter by her circumstances, instead of choosing to allow them to make her stronger. You are the epitome of strong. Don't let her touch you."

"Why?"

"Why what?" I ask.

"Why would you care?"

I look at her brows lowered in confusion, "What's not to care about? Why wouldn't I care?"

Her eyes soften and she smiles, prompting me to say, "I want to ask you a question now."

"Okay."

"Why do you always ask why? This isn't the first time you've asked me that."

"In my experience, no one ever does something without wanting something in return. There's always an ulterior motive. Other than with my brother, other people and relationships in my life have been harvested to satisfy some need or desire or issue for the other person. I guess I'm trying to learn from my mistakes. And asking why and being up front to understand the intention seems like a good step in accomplishing that. "

Tucking her hair behind her ear, I speak earnestly, "Not everyone does something to get something in return, or from selfish motives. They do it because that's a part of who they are. They actually want to be loving, to be caring, to want more for the other person. By asking why or assuming the worst, or in not letting them give to you, you're denying them an opportunity to give you a gift. And I guess themselves too – though not a selfish gift. It's the most basic, loving, caring human emotion, the need to do a good deed or good work or to show love. Why does everything have to require an concealed motive?"

She just shrugs, but I can see the wheels turning in her mind. While I don't understand her need to always ask, I can see that the answer sooths something in her and I'm glad. She reaches up and puts her hands on either side of my face. Rising to her toes, her moth descends to mine and she places a soft kiss on my lips, lingering there, eyes open and watching me. I stare back, letting her see the want and desire in my eyes and when she pulls back inch-by-inch, I can see the feelings reflecting back at me. "Thank you," she murmurs.

Nodding my head, I take a deep breath and pull her with a little tug on her hand to the couch. "Would you like to watch a movie or something until it's time for us to go."

She shakes her head no and as I'm about to ask her what she'd like to do instead, she surprises me by staring at me for a moment, and then pushing me back onto the couch and straddling me. "Can I ask you a question?" I nod my head, words failing at the moment as her most intimate parts press firmly and tightly against my own. "Do you feel whatever this is between us? This… connection?"

"Yes," I whisper.

"I've never felt this way before," she says quietly as if it's a confession she's afraid to say too loudly, as if doing so will make it disappear.

"Babe, me either. Why do you think I've been so persistent with you?"

She smiles and instead of saying more with words, she uses her body. Plunging her tongue into my mouth, I'm both shocked and delighted. Her seemingly incongruous words and actions confuse and amaze me. This is not at all what I expected. But I'm certainly not going to argue. Though, I gather my wits and begin to suggest that perhaps we should slow down, when she suddenly pulls away, "For once, I don't want to ask myself why. I just want to lose myself in the answer I already know. And the answer is, that I want you, Jax. Instead of watching a movie right now, I have something else in mind and just to be clear, I do have an agenda."

Her words make me growl and I smash my lips to hers. Her hands grasp my shoulders and I can feel her nails digging into shirt. I put my hands on her hips and pull her flush against mine. She starts grinding her core against my cock and the friction makes me insane. Ripping my mouth from hers, I stare into her eyes, "As much as I'd like to take you to my room right now and introduce myself to every single part of your body, I reluctantly must acknowledge that there isn't nearly enough time for me to have my way with you thoroughly." The whole time I'm talking, she's running her nails up and down my chest and it's making me crazy. I want to let my eyes roll to the back of my head and just enjoy the sensation. Oh, what the fuck. Leaning forward, I remove her shirt over her head and hiss when I take in her lace covered tits. Leaning forward, I take a nipple into my mouth through the lace and revel in the sound of her gasps and moans.

"I thought you said there isn't enough time for sex."

"There isn't enough time for that, but there is enough time for me to make *you* feel good. Let me take care of you."

Without waiting for her to reply, I unzip her jeans and shove my hand down the front of her panties. Feeling her slippery folds, I insert a finger into her wet center. She responds by putting her mouth on mine and gasping into my mouth. She grinds her hips against mine so hard and so fast it's as if she can't control the primal urge she has to come. I insert another finger and smile against her mouth when she gasps. "Oh god, Jax. That feels so good. Please, don't stop."

"I'm not going to stop, babe." I turn my hand and press my thumb hard against her clit and as soon as I do, I can feel her walls suck my fingers like a vacuum. She pumps her hips up and down, fucking my fingers until she let's go with a cry. "That's it. Come for me."

"Oh god, I'm coming! I'm coming!"

I continue to stroke her until she comes down and then collapses against me. I rain kisses all over her face, "That was so hot, babe. Watching your eyes darken, seeing your face as you let go. Utterly beautiful. I'm so hard for you."

"Let me take care of that." She tries to unzip my jeans, but I push her hands away gently and hold them in my own. "No babe. That was all about you."

"But, I want to return the favor."

"You will. But later when we have unlimited time, okay? For now, let me hold you and we can watch a little TV, chat or whatever you want to do before we have to leave, okay?"

"Okay." She gives me another kiss and then, sighing and silently applauding my self-restraint, I help her put her shirt back on and straighten her clothes. "Jax, will you just… hold me?"

"Yes, please." I pull her into my arms and tuck her into my side. She places her head on my shoulder and I turn the TV on and start flipping channels. I'm so incredibly hard and I can't help but wince at the pain when I adjust myself, but it's so worth it. Having her here, feeling her in my arms, recalling the cries on her lips, I run my fingers through her hair and once again wish that my responsibilities for the night were over so I could just bury myself in her and get lost. Interestingly, I find that I have the question of why on my own lips. Why did it take so long for fate to deliver this creature to me?

CHAPTER FIFTEEN

Rowan

Leaving Jax's house is not an easy thing to do – my whole body is in complete protest. After just a small taste of him, I want more, so much more. Thoughts of going back to his bedroom so we can continue what began on the couch, consume my mind. But, after the tour, talk and make out session, we have to get ready and be on our way so he can get to the weigh-in on time.

When we arrive at the casino, Jax insists on walking me all the way to my seat in the front row. Several people call out to him and wish him luck, and several women scream his name as we pass. Their cries and yells to him startle me. He nods to some, but ignores others completely. "Okay, here's your seat, babe. Just enjoy the chaos and when this is done, I'll be right back here to get you, okay?"

"Okay," I nod with a smile and sit down.

"Remember what I said. This will be a little rowdy and crazy, but basically it's just an opportunity for press and fans to take photos and for fighters to trash talk one another. Don't let it worry you or anything, it's all meant to be a build up to add excitement to the fight."

"I'll be fine. Don't worry about me. Just do your thing. I'm excited to be here with you."

"I'm happy you're here too. It's just I know this is your first fight and I don't want you to worry about anything, or worse, never want to come back."

Standing from my seat, I put my hand on his chest, "Hey, stop worrying. I'm excited, okay? This will be fun! It will take more than a little catcalling and rowdiness to upset me. In fact, I have those exact things planned for later." I lean forward and give him a kiss that I meant to be quick, but when he puts his hands on my hips, pulls me closer, then opens his mouth under mine, I quickly forget where we are and lose myself in everything except him. He ravages my lips with his and kisses me so hard, it's almost bruising. It feels like a possessive branding in front of everyone and I'm completely okay with this. I know for a fact I will never get enough of this man. I feel his kiss in my whole body – my scalp tingles, lips burn, my nipples harden, my pussy pulses and my toes curl in my shoes. I've never felt this way before – it's completely consuming.

When someone clears their throat, it brings us back down to earth and breaks us apart. We stand nose to nose for a minute, his eyes full of promises for later, before he gives me one more kiss on the lips and pulls away. Behind him, an older man is giving him a combination of an irritated look and an amused smirk. Jax sighs, "Just a second, Gil."

"I've been standing here and it's already been a lot longer than a second, boy."

Rolling his eyes, Jax tucks my hair behind my ear, "Don't forget, I'll meet you right here."

"I won't forget."

Nodding, he turns to the man behind us, "Gil, this is Rowan. Rowan, this is my coach, and the almost daily pain in my ass, Gillespie."

"Everyone calls me Gil," he tells me, voice sounding like gravel.

Feeling embarrassed that we were so carried away in front of him, I give him a shy smile and a wave, "Hi, Gil. It's nice to meet you."

"Hi, darlin', it's nice to meet you too. Please excuse me, but I need to get my fighter backstage."

"Oh, of course."

With another smile, Jax kisses my forehead and walks away. Sitting in my seat, I take in the view as he walks away from me with Gil at his side. Before he reaches his destination, a sultry blonde with legs that go on for miles encased in super short shorts and boobs so big they're busting out of her tank top, approaches him. My eyes narrow as I see her slide her hands up Jax's chest, and I feel a curl of jealousy almost choke me. Watching closely at Jax's reaction, I let out a sigh of relief when I see him remove her hands, shake his head and walk away. She's left standing there with an annoyed smile on her face and I do my best not to stand up and point at her while laughing evilly. I'm glad he remembers our 'I don't share' chat.

Fans, fighter entourages, and press continue to crowd the room and while nothing is happening on stage yet, I hear multiple clicks from the shutters of more cameras than I can count. I'm seated in the front row waiting for the weigh-in to start, and my mind goes back to my conversation with Jax earlier. The things he said about not everyone having an ulterior motive and telling me that I deserve love, made me need to be close to him badly. I can't hold myself back any longer – denying my need and want for him is no longer possible. It feels disingenuous. No one's ever said those things to me and my reaction to his words feels visceral. Sure, Tyson has always told me similar things, but he's my brother. Something about a man like Jax saying them is…well…different. It's almost as if my soul stood up and took notice to his words and branded them there making me believe he's right. He makes me feel hope.

Pushing the thoughts aside for now, promising myself I'll evaluate them more later, I take in the stage in front of me. There are a few people on stage as well as a couple scantily clad girls in bikinis. I'm not exactly sure what their roles are and I have no idea where they fit into the events Jax outlined, but they look happy to be there as they talk in animated fashion to each other. There's a large scale right in the center that's so big everyone in the room will be able to see the results. Jax told me each fighter in the card and their opponent are called by the announcer, and they each come to the stage, disrobe to their skivvies, then step on the scale in front of the MMA commissioner, president of the fighting organization and all the spectators. Once they confirm the fighter's weight, they stand with their opponent and get their photos taken.

I did a little research about MMA fighting this week because I don't want to be completely ignorant about something that is a part of Jax's life. What I read explained that the weigh-in is done to make sure the fighters are within their weight class, but that this is also a way to get fans enthusiastic about the fights. Each weight class has a minimum and maximum weight. If the fighter is beyond the maximum for their specific weight class, they're not allowed to fight and get disqualified, sort of, even before the fight begins.

As more people take the stage, a man that walks to the microphone and taps it making sure it's live, before speaking, captures my attention. "Ladies and Gentleman, thank you for joining us for tonight's pre-fight weigh-in. Before we get started I'd like to thank all of our sponsors and the Arizona Red Rock Casino for hosting us. Now, let's get started! First up is our welterweight division."

Two fighters are announced and they come forward from back stage and smile and perform for the crowd. An entourage accompanies them, and I assume their coach must be one of the members, but I'm not sure. Then, as each fighter is announced once again individually, they begin to disrobe, handing each article of clothing to a member of their entourage. Once they're wearing nothing but their briefs, they walk forward and stand still on the scale. Their weights are announced and documented by a panel of people sitting in front of them, then the opponents face one another in a fighting stance, pictures are taken, they shake hands, then exit the stage.

When Jax's friend Levi is announced, I can't help but clap my hands and cheer for him. His enthusiasm is apparent and he is a good entertainer, sauntering out and flexing his muscles for the crowd. After he strips, he winks at the crowd and some chicks in the crowd reward him by screaming his name. Cameras snap and click when he steps on the scale. "One hundred and sixty-six pounds for Levi 'The Bounty' Hunter!" Levi pauses, flexes again and then waits patiently while his opponent is also weighed, casting smiles at the crowd. Once he's finished, they stand and face each other in a fighter's stance while cameras shoot and film.

The next category is middleweight, which is Jax's category. He told me that it's up to one hundred and eighty-five pounds. I recognize his friend Cole, and when he comes out it's the same song and dance as those before him. There's a man that looks an awful lot like Jax that goes on stage with Cole and cheers him on, even egging on the crowd about how great Cole is and that Cole 'Rampage' Russell is going to "kick ass and take names". It seems a bit over the top and he's certainly louder and crazier than those before him have been. In fact, Cole's posture seems to be that of someone who is embarrassed and I can't help but wonder what that's all about.

Finally, they call Jax's name and his opponent. Jax's opponent Lance 'The Hammer' Henderson goes to the scale first and I can't help but feel a little nervous looking at him. He's ripped and maintains poses and a stance that highlight that fact, but he doesn't even crack a smile the whole time. They call out his weight – one hundred and eighty four pounds - then he flexes and growls at the crowd again before walking to the side. "Next up, let me hear you make a little noise for Lance's opponent, Jackson 'Hands of' Stooooooooone," the announcer drags out his name and the crowd goes crazy. Maybe it's just me but it seems like he gets a bigger and louder reaction than those before him. There are women screaming their bloody heads off such that I feel possession and a mild irritation at them runs through me. Part of me wants to walk right up there and put my mouth all over him making it clear that he's mine. *God, possessive much Rowan?*

My eyes never leave him as I watch him take his shorts, t-shirt, shoes and socks off. This is the first time I've gotten a good look at his body and I fucking hate I have to share it with everyone else in the room. My eyes rake his frame and my mouth waters at his pure perfection. His body is tight and toned, his abs stand out and he has that mouth-watering v at his hip bones that goes down and disappears in his briefs. My fingers twitch and my body shudders at the sight. I want to run my hands all over him and trace the tribal tattoo that covers his upper left arm and chest with my tongue. When Jax steps on the mechanical scale he turns to the crowd and his eyes find mine. He gives me a smirk as if he knows I'm salivating over the sight of him. My grin reaches epic proportions at that look and I pay close attention as the announcer calls out the one hundred and eighty-five pounds exactly that Jax weighs. He flexes for the crowd and smiles his dimple panty-dropping smile and my body flushes with want when he winks at me. Walking to his opponent, they face each other and take the fighting position. His opponent is stone faced but Jax has a light smile on his face like he refuses to take all of this too seriously.

Then, they're off the stage and I sit back in my seat trying to calm my rapid breathing. Sitting through the rest of the weight card, I lose myself to the chaos around me. I can't help but laugh when I realize the bikini-clad women on the stage, do nothing but stand there and clap. It seems silly to me but what the hell do I know? Before long, Jax is standing in front of me with a wide smile and heat in his eyes. "You ready, babe?"

"Yes, I'm *more* than ready," I reply almost breathlessly. Jax looks at me and heat flashes in his eyes.

"Let's go," he replies, his voice gravelly with his desire.

Before we can make it out of the door, Jax's friends are in front of us. There are fans surrounding them trying to get their attention, but all of them are focused on us. "What are we doing now, Jax?" Levis asks with a grin on his face.

"*We* aren't doing anything. Rowan and I are going to get something to eat and bring it back to my place. I don't know, or care, what you all are doing."

"What do you mean? It's tradition that all of us go out for a big dinner of pasta after a weigh-in since we can gain all that weight back we worked so incredibly hard to lose. You know this is what makes that pain worth it. Besides, we all need the carbs before our fight," Cole says.

"Are you seriously breaking tradition, man?" Ryder asks.

"You all sound like a bunch of pussies. Go do whatever the hell you want. I'm going out with my girl."

The look of sadness, poutiness and disappointment that takes over their faces is probably orchestrated, but it works on me never the less. "Jax, I don't mind going out with everyone, I don't want to get in the way of your tradition."

"Yeah, Jax. She doesn't mind and she doesn't want to get in the way of tradition," Levi adds with a smile getting a nasty look from Jax in return.

"You are not getting in the way of anything. They're just being assholes."

"It's okay," I smile, "really."

Walking up behind Ryder, Levi and Cole are Jax's other friends – Zane and Dylan- who must have been in the crowd watching the weigh-in. Zane, catching the tail end of the conversation says, "Yeah, Jax. She doesn't mind."

"Maybe I mind," Jax growls. He looks at me and I shrug my shoulders making it clear that I don't care either way. With a big sigh Jax gives in, "Fine. *Just* dinner. Afterwards you all are not coming to my place, so don't even think about it, let alone try it."

"What? But we always come over and..." Levi starts and Jax growls at him making him laugh knowing he's pushing it. "Fine, we get it."

We all make our way out of the casino and Dylan calls back, "See you there!"

Jax walks me to the truck his jaw ticking the whole time. He helps me inside and once he's next to me, he turns to me and sighs in exasperation. "I'm sorry about them – they're a bunch of children. Now that we are out of sight and earshot are you sure you're okay with this? This is not at all what I had in mind for us tonight and I am completely fine with ditching them."

Raising my brow I ask, "What did you have in mind?"

Leaning so close to me that air can hardly pass between us, "Dinner just the two of us, and then dessert in my bed."

His eyes are liquid fire and my thighs clench in response. "Well," I whisper, "I really am okay with dinner with your friends, and I'm even more okay with dessert afterwards. Besides," I smile and feel my lips brush his with the action, "It's just dinner, right? And it sounds like this is tradition. No use in flirting with the gods."

"Fuck that. We can make new traditions," he grumbles.

"How about we make a new tradition after dinner?" He immediately touches his tongue to my lips and gives my bottom lip a soft swipe. I open my mouth in a silent moan and he seizes the opportunity and kisses me so intensely and thoroughly I'm gasping when he pulls away.

"I'm holding you to that." Without another word he starts the truck and drives us to the restaurant. I try to catch my breath the whole way.

Dinner is an experience. The guys are funny and enjoy playing off of one another's antics. Making fun of each other and seeing who can tell the better story is a matter of course. After teasing me because I've never attended a fight before, I ask them what their first fight was like. They then take turns telling stories on each other and I just take it all in. I laugh and find myself more entertained than I have been since I can remember. "Oh god, the best one is when Dylan got in the ring for the first time," Zane teases.

"Shut the fuck up guys," Dylan is not especially amused. They all laugh.

"Why?" I can't help but ask.

"His eyes were so big it was like he was standing on stage in front of a crowd for the first time getting ready to sing Ave Maria or some shit," Ryder adds.

"I seriously thought he was going to piss his pants," Cole laughs out loud.

"When the ref announced fight on, and they started circling one another, instead of Dylan looking for a way in to get in the first jab, he began running in circles. The guy he was fighting practically had to chase him around the cage instead," Levi explains.

"I just didn't want to make it easy on him. Shut up. I've told you that before," Dylan argues.

They all laugh including Jax and the sound makes me get shivers. "What happened?"

They spill on a few more of the fight antics and then all look at Dylan and his face flushes as he sums it up, "I got my ass kicked."

I try really hard not to laugh but fail when all the guys lose it. "It's okay," Jax says, "he's come a long way since then."

"What about you, Rowan?" Dylan asks.

"What do you mean?" I smile, "I've never fought."

"Ha! No, tell us about you," Dylan says wanting the focus off of him I think.

Jax tucks me tighter into his side while taking a bite of his garlic bread. We've all got heaping bowls of spaghetti or fettuccine and are sitting at a huge table in a little hole in the wall Italian place I've never been to. "What do you want to know?"

"We want to know everything," Ryder purrs and winks at me.

"Don't make me kick your ass," Jax says making Ryder and the other guys laugh at his possessiveness.

"There's really not much to tell," I shrug my shoulders having no clue what to even say.

"Somehow I doubt that," Zane says. "You seem to have completely enthralled our boy here so we can't help but feel intrigued."

"Leave her alone. She doesn't have to tell any of you shit," Jax says at the same time I say, "Well, ask away."

Cole goes first, "Are you an Arizona native?"

"No. My brother Tyson and I moved here five years ago after we turned eighteen."

"Where are you from?" Cole asks.

"California."

"Speaking of Ty, where the hell has he been?" Dylan asks.

"None of your bus-" Jax starts in but I just shrug my shoulders and say, "Jail."

This brings on a whole slew of questions, many about Tyson, and I answer them all. "He's supposed to hopefully get out this week and I can't wait. We've never been separated longer than a couple days."

"He's a really nice guy and was shaping up to be one hell of a fighter," Ryder says in all seriousness. "Is it cool having a twin?"

I shrug, "Yeah, I guess. I don't really think about him as my twin. He's just my brother. He annoys me because he says he's my big brother because he was born two minutes before me."

They chuckle and Levi asks, "Have you guys always gotten along?"

"Yes. He's my best friend."

As quickly as the interview began, it ends and the conversation turns to the fight tomorrow and I enjoy listening to them talk about their predictions and strategy. As much shit as they give each other, it's obvious that they're all really good friends and care about and support each other. I find myself reveling in their friendship, but also feeling envious of it at the same time. What they have is special and I wish I had a group of girl friends as close as these guys are.

I'm pulled from my thoughts when the conversation turns to social media, a topic that interests me. "One guy said that Lance always blasts out his fights on social media and has developed a massive following on Facebook. I guess some of his fans will even travel all over the place to attend his fights. Maybe that's something we should look into?" Jax asks the guys and they all stare back at him blankly.

I can't help but butt in, "You guys don't already have fan pages? Like individually, or what about for the gym as a whole?"

They all stare at me, then at each other. "No, not for business, just personal," Cole says and they all agree.

"We don't really know a whole lot about the business side of it," Zane says.

"Speak for yourself. I have a personal Facebook page and I just use that to share all my fighting details. The ladies who are friends with me like to know where I'm going to be," Ryder says.

I can't help but roll my eyes. "Why does that not surprise me?" All the guys laugh, including Ryder.

"You guys should really have individual fan pages, including you Ryder, and start a conversation with your fans. Plus, haven't you ever heard of tweeting?"

"Tw-whating?" Levis asks.

"It's a social media site that let's you send out messages to all your fan following in one hundred and forty characters or less. You guys all need Facebook accounts and Twitter accounts. Plus, Jax, you should totally have a business page for the gym as well as a blog attached to your website if you don't already."

He clears his throat, "I don't have a website yet."

"What? Really? Well we need to fix that. Plus, for the blog each of you could take turns writing about work out routines, or exercise suggestions for specific body part focus, for example how to get ripped abs. Plus you could even take it further and talk about the importance of a good diet. Recipe sharing would be huge. I'm sure you all have a specific diet you maintain during training and smoothies you enjoy. That kind of thing. Jax, you could even sell the items you have in your store on your website too."

I finally come to a pause and realize I have been on a bit of a diatribe. I look at the faces around me to gather their appraisal of my unsolicited opinion. All the guys stare at me – mostly with blank faces and some have mouths a bit agape - and then they simultaneously start asking questions. The air I didn't know I was holding, suddenly escapes in a deep exhale, and I smile as Levi begins.

"You really think people would follow me?"

"I bet people would really like my triple berry bulk up shake special." – Cole.

"What a really great way to bring in more business to the gym. Why haven't I thought of this before?" – Jax.

"I'd be game for writing about exercise routines for the stomach, glutes, biceps, that kind of thing." – Zane.

"Think of all the new chicks that will discover me if I start tweeting and blogging too." – Ryder.

Laughing at all of them, I look to Jax for his thoughts. "How do you know so much about all of this?" All the guys look at me waiting for my answer.

"Well, I've always had an interest in social media marketing. I've taken a couple classes when I could afford them and even helped the diner get a business page started too. It's helped increase their pie sales during the holidays," I state proudly. "I guess I just have a knack for it," I shrug my shoulders.

"Would you be willing to help us with this? I would pay you for your services," Jax says making me frown.

"I will help you, but I don't want your money."

"Rowan, I have a marketing budget that I never use. I can and will pay you just like I would any other professional I'd hire to help do marketing for the gym."

"I, for one, would love your help too. I don't know anything about social media, but if it can help my career as well as help out the gym too, I'd be willing to hire you as well," Zane adds.

All the other guys chime in with more of the same and I feel overwhelmed and put on the spot, but a bit happy that I may add value to this group. "Okay, if you're sure. I'd love to help. Give me a few days to start laying the foundation for each of your pages and then I will contact each of you for the specific information I need from you. Sound cool?"

They all nod their agreement and I see something in Jax's eyes that tells me he's excited about this and that he has more to say on the subject later.

We all finish up our dinner and I'm surprised when all the guys give me hugs as they prepare to leave. Ryder holds on a little too long forcing Jax to pry him off of me, "You're seriously pushing it asshole," Jax says with a grumble, which makes me laugh. Levi and Cole whine a few times about not having their traditional hang out tonight. Apparently the night before a fight they binge watch old fighting movies or keep ESPN on a constant loop. Jax unceremoniously tells them all to get over it and before long, we are on our way back to his place.

I think about the dinner on the drive. A quick rewind of the conversation makes me smile, but I am especially pleased when I think about Jax. Throughout, Jax never stopped touching me. Whether it was a brush of his arm against mine, his hand on my thigh, his arm around my shoulder, or the kisses he placed on my head. He's very touchy and my body is constantly in tune with his.

We're barely through the door of his house before my body feels like it's going to explode with need. Without giving him a chance to do more than close the door and lock it behind him, I pounce. Throwing my arms around his neck and putting my mouth on his I kiss him with all the pent up longing from the night. He takes my lips with a groan of his own and slowly walks backwards with me all the way to his bedroom while we shed clothes along the way.

CHAPTER SIXTEEN

Jax

As soon as I get her past my bedroom door, I grab her ass and lift. She automatically wraps her legs around my hips and I walk us further into my room. Arriving at the side of my bed, I lower her down in the center, making sure the pile of pillows at the top cradles her head. Running my hands down her legs until I reach her shoes, I slip them off and drop them to the floor. All I've been able to think about since we left earlier tonight is getting her back here and naked underneath me. I'm tired of sharing her with everyone else and had to keep the impatience off my face when the guys were passing her around for hugs. I wanted to snatch her back from them and roar, "MINE". I'm not sure where all this possessiveness is coming from, but I've never felt anything like it before her. I don't care if those fools are my friends.

Seeing her right where I want her makes me want to hurry up and get her screaming my name. "God. I want you."

"I want you too," she hesitates, "but Jax?" Her voice is full of something I don't quite understand. I try to give her the attention she needs through my lust-hazed mind.

"Babe, what's wrong? Is this too fast?"

"No!" She practically yells, then smiles and lowers her voice, "It's just, well, you know I just had a baby not that long ago."

"I know," I'm not sure what she's getting at and I put on my best puzzled face since I'm full of confusion.

"It's just," she looks away in embarrassment.

"Hey, don't do that." I reach out and take her chin, turning her to face me, "You can tell me anything. What's wrong?"

Her face flushes at the top of her cheekbones, "My body…"

"Shit, is it too soon? Will I hurt you? I'm so sorry, I didn't even stop to consider that."

"No, no, nothing like that. It's just, I'm still carrying a little extra weight, and-"

Suddenly her worries are crystal clear and I realize the look in her eyes I couldn't decipher is insecurity. Placing myself over her, balancing my weight on my elbows I lock my eyes with hers. "Babe, you are absolutely gorgeous. I am so turned on by you, I don't think my dick has ever been this hard." Her cheeks pinken further but she smiles and I can already see the worry melting away. "If you're carrying a few extra pounds, I sure as hell don't see them. All I see is a sexually curvy goddess that I can't wait to explore with my hands, mouth and eyes. You are beautiful, in every fucking way. Do you understand?"

She nods her head and without another word, molds her lips to mine. She pours her reply into the movement of her mouth and in response I sweep my tongue inside and twirl it with hers. When she moans, my dick leaps in my pants and it's all I can do not to start ripping her clothes off right the fuck now. It's crazy what she does to me with just a sound – the feeling is electric.

Ripping my mouth from hers, I pull back from her a little so I can take her shirt off and gaze down at the lace covered tits before me thankful I get to give them more attention this time around. God was very good to her in the tits department and I immediately bite her nipple through the lace then lavish it with my tongue soothing the pain. Rowan arches her back and moans running her hands through my hair grabbing handfuls. I slide my tongue from her nipple, to the edge of her bra and trace along the cup, then move down to the valley between her breasts, making my way to the other giving it the same treatment.

She grinds her hips against mine and I feel her hands making their way down my sides until she's pulling my shirt from the waist of my shorts. I back up a little so she can pull it over my head and when our stomachs touch, skin to skin, we both exhale. I put my mouth on hers once more and trace her lips with my tongue while I reach my hands behind her back and unclasp her bra. Throwing it onto the floor to join the increasing pile, I pull away and look down. "Fucking beautiful," I murmur and then circle her nipples with my tongue.

"Jax," she whispers, "don't stop." Not fucking likely I think as she pushes my head into her further with her need and desire.

Kissing my way down her tight abdomen I wonder where the hell she's supposed to be hiding those extra pounds. She's crazy. I swirl my tongue around her belly and when I reach the button of her jeans, I waste no time undoing them and sliding them down her legs. She's naked before me in nothing but a scrap of lace that can barely be considered panties. Without hesitation I bend down and lick her through the lace. She practically jack knifes off the bed making me chuckle. "Like that, do you?" Her response isn't audibly decipherable.

Pulling the scrap of lace down her legs I throw it over my shoulder making her laugh and then she quiets as I push her thighs apart exposing her completely. Looking up at her, our eyes connect and I see the pure lust shining in hers. She's biting her lip in anticipation and the sight makes me crazy. "I'm going to taste you now," I announce. Then, slowly, keeping my eyes locked with hers, I reach my tongue out and lick her clit. Her hazel eyes turn a deep brown as they fill with her lust and she steadies herself on her elbows so she can watch me fuck her with my mouth. Giving her firm licks from her opening up to her clit, I work magic with my tongue, while stealing looks at her throughout. Her chest is rising and falling rapidly and my cock is straining so hard against the front of my pants I probably have a zipper imprint. Closing my eyes, I savor her taste and the sound of her sweet little gasps of pleasure.

"Oh god, Jax, please… I want to come. Please don't stop."

Opening my eyes again to look at her, I keep them there as I put one finger inside of her at the same time I take her clit in my mouth and suck hard. Her head falls back on her shoulders and I can feel her pussy tightening around my fingers as she lets herself go and shatters. I keep the suction on her clit while pumping her with my fingers at the same time prolonging her enjoyment.

When she's spent and gasping trying to gain control of her breathing, I rip my pants and briefs down my body, grab a condom out of the back pocket of my jeans, rip it open with my teeth and roll it on. Climbing on top of her body, I look down at her. She looks up at me with a smile that screams satisfaction and I want to bang my chest with male pride. When her eyes drop to my lips I know she sees them glistening with her wetness. Very slowly she lifts her head up and licks my mouth clean tasting herself on me and making me groan with need.

Opening her thighs further so I can settle between them, she pulls away from my mouth. "I need to feel you inside of me. Now."

"Me too babe. Fuck, me too." I take my cock in my hand and rub it along her opening and then with one strong thrust enter her with a groan and bury my face in her neck. She gasps and moans in return and immediately starts grinding her hips into mine meeting me thrust for thrust. I slowly pull out before sliding back in, once, then twice, taking it slow until she surprises me by grabbing hold of my ass and slamming me down to meet her.

"Oh, Jesus," I groan. "I'm not going to last long if you keep doing that."

I look down at her and she gives me an evil grin before she digs her nails into my ass and does it again. "Fuck!" I groan. "I can't hold it."

"Don't. Fuck me. I want you to fuck me."

That's it. I'm a goner. I push into her over and over and feel her fall off the edge again with a loud groan. Her walls squeeze the hell out of me and with a loud groan of my own, I pump my release into her, then collapse being careful not to crush her with my weight.

Lifting up I give her a quick kiss on the lips and then get off of her to make my way to the bathroom. Disposing of the condom, I warm up a washcloth and go back to the bed and help her clean up. After I put the cloth in the hamper, I join her in bed and pull her into my arms. We're quiet for a minute just catching our breaths and reveling in what just happened. I knew before this, but I really am gone. Completely gone. Totally enraptured by her. She owns me body and soul. When she folds her arms on top of my chest and places her chin on top of them she looks down at me with a smile. Returning it, I push her hair behind her ear and stare into her eyes trying to tell her the things I'm not ready to let leave my mouth just yet.

"Jax, that was…"

I interrupt her, "The best fucking sex of my life. Did you feel it again too? The connection? The fireworks?"

"I felt them. I feel them. All the time. With you."

"Me too," I confess.

"And that was the best sex of my life too." She leans forward and kisses me and I tuck her head under my chin, smiling at her words. The last thought I remember having is how right she feels in my arms and how I always want to have her there.

CHAPTER SEVENTEEN

Rowan

When I wake up, an automatic smile comes to my lips. Last night was... it was absolutely amazing. I wasn't lying to Jax when I told him it was the best sex I've ever had. I've never, ever felt the way he made me feel last night – certainly not with Jason. Out of nowhere, a twinge of sadness enters my gut and I wish I had come to my senses with Jason much sooner. I had no idea I was missing out on true passion. I was never able to just let go the way I was able to with Jax. Moreover, I've never felt like I could be myself – my true self – unconditionally and without judgment – like I can with him. Certainly, while I regret parts of my relationship with Jason, without it, I would never have had Lily. And I can't imagine my life without her. Suddenly, it feels like a weight has been lifted off of my heart. The clarity in that thought gives me peace for the first time with the whole situation. I feel a sense of closure and I feel lighter. I now know the purpose for that relationship.

With a happy sigh, I roll over to face Jax excited about a new day together, and realize the bed is empty making me frown. Sitting up, my eyes instantly see the cup of coffee sitting on the bedside table and I wonder if the smell broke through my unconsciousness until it woke me. Sitting next to the coffee is a red rose and a note. Picking it up I take in Jax's small and messy writing, "Went for some breakfast supplies, or maybe it would be considered brunch at this point. Will be back soon – miss me while I'm gone."

Smiling I sit up, and am happy to see Jax had the forethought to bring my overnight bag into the bedroom. Completely contented and relaxed, we fell asleep and I never changed into pajamas. Taking out my clothes and toiletry bag, I grab my cup of coffee carrying it into the bathroom. Searching for a towel, I find one in the linen closet behind the door and start the water. While waiting for the water to get to the right temp, I sip my coffee and enjoy its sweetness. Jax added the perfect amount of sugar and cream. I have no idea how he guessed the way I like it. I sigh wistfully and think about the night before. Jax's hands on my body, his lips on mine, and the thoughts make me let out a big happy sigh. I feel so relaxed this morning and when I realize it's because I'm happy, genuinely one hundred percent happy, my smile is so wide my cheeks ache with the effort.

Stepping into the shower I realize I didn't think to bring my own shampoo or body wash. Checking out Jax's products, opening them and absorbing the smell that is uniquely his, I don't waste any time pouring his shampoo into my open palm and lathering up my hair. It smells divine. After rinsing it out, I pick up his body wash and smell it too. It feels like a guilty pleasure or something and as I pour it into my hand I rub my hands together and lather them up then begin rubbing them all over my body. "Mmm, now this is one hell of a sight I could easily get used to." His voice is unexpected and I scream so loud I'm sure the neighbors will call the police while I cover as much as my body with my arms as possible.

Jax's arms instantly surround me as he laughs. Trying to school his face to look sorry while I teasingly glare at him, he fails miserably and starts laughing. I push him away and cross my arms to glare an extra moment for good measure, which only makes him laugh harder. My lips keep curving up into a smile and it takes effort to straighten them out each time. When he controls himself he manages to speak, "I'm so sorry. I didn't mean to scare you. I thought you heard me." He wraps his arms around me again and I uncross my arms and put them around his neck instead. He's smiling down at me and his dimples make my knees feel weak. My amusement quickly turns to lust when he shifts and his naked, wet body rubs against mine. This hot, wet, beautiful man is naked in the shower with me. I'm sure as hell going to take advantage of this. Moving my mouth closer to his, I grasp a handful of his hair, "Uh, next time at least make some noise by shutting a door or clearing your throat would you?"

He laughs and lets go of me to grab his body wash from the shelf to pour some into his hands and picks up where I left off, rubbing them all over my body. He takes his time and makes sure every single inch of me is thoroughly clean. My whole body is vibrating afterwards and I bite my lip trying to keep myself from moaning like a lust-crazed idiot, but damn.

Remembering that I brought a washcloth into the shower with me, I pick it up then take the body wash and pour some into it. "My turn," I smile up into his face and feel my insides clench when he gives me a sexy smirk.

Starting with his shoulders I smooth the washcloth over their broadness, washing from one side to the other. Moving my way down his chest and over his pecs, I can't help but use my other hand to trace his tattoo with the tip of my finger. When that's not enough, I lean forward and use my tongue instead feeling satisfaction at keeping my promise to myself about doing this very thing. He groans his approval and when I've finished, I move back and continue my washing.

Next, I move toward his abs and make a show of scrubbing each one making him chuckle. The sound is deep and gravely and makes my core throb with need. To distract myself I jokingly pretend to use his abs as a washboard with the washcloth making him laugh and me giggle. Following the v line at his hips I lick my lips when I finally reach his impressive erection. Standing tall and proud, his want of me so blatant, it causes me to want to lose control. Looking into his eyes, I see him looking back at me, eyes hooded and staring. Making sure I rinse him thoroughly, when I'm finished, I immediately drop to my knees, wanting to show my appreciation for how he made me feel last night and to return the favor. When I look up at him again, his eyes are wide and I can't help the smile that comes to my lips. Keeping my eyes on his, I lean forward and place the tip of his cock into my mouth making him hiss in pleasure and anticipation.

Swirling my tongue over him I grab the base of his cock and push him down my throat, inch by inch until I hear him groan and his hands clench into my hair. "Oh god. Just like that, babe. Feels so good."

Finding a good rhythm, I make sure my hand moves down, as my head comes up, and then when my head goes down, my hand comes up his shaft. Suck, swirl, slide. Suck, swirl, slide. He groans again and at the tail end of it I feel his precum explode in my mouth leaving a musky taste that sets my blood on fire. The sounds he's making instigates a surge of wetness between my thighs and when I open my eyes to look at him, I groan myself when I see his head thrown back in complete abandon lost in nothing but feeling. After a few more strokes he begins pumping his hips with my movements and I feel his thumb brush my cheek. Reaching one hand to massage his balls, I continue pumping with the other, completely lost in the feeling of passion and something I can't yet define. When I feel his hands suddenly under my arms and he yanks me up his body, I let out a squeak.

"I need to be inside you, right now."

Without another word he pushes me up against the shower wall and slams his body against mine. His hands are under my ass and he lifts me so that I wrap my legs around his waist. Gripping handfuls of my hair, he tilts my head to the side and plunges his tongue in and out of my mouth brutally kissing me - his passion out of control. Reaching between our bodies he grabs himself and enters me with a deep thrust. We groan in tandem and I can already feel my orgasm starting to unravel deep in my tummy. He moves in and out, sighing my name with his movements.

When he reaches between us once again and whispers, "Come for me, baby," then presses a thumb to my clit, I come undone as if I was just waiting for permission to do so. "Oh god, yes!" I yell and Jax quickly follows me, but at the last second pulls out and spills his release onto the shower floor letting the water wash his pleasure away.

He turns back to me and kisses me, then looks at me with worry, "I'm sorry. I realized at the last minute that I didn't even put on a condom, I was so caught up in the moment."

"It's okay, I'm on the pill. Plus when I found out I was pregnant with Lily, the OB tests for everything under the sun because it could create complications, so I know I'm clean."

"I get tested regularly because of the physicals and other tests we have for fighting, so I'm clean too. I've never had sex without a condom – ever. I just lost myself with you."

"I did too," I confess, "It's okay. I'm okay with us forgoing condoms in the future too if you are."

He smiles at me and nods. He steps out of the shower, then turns to help me out too. Grabbing my towel he wraps it around me, then gets one for himself and wraps it around his waist. Teasingly I smile at him, "I thought you said you were making me brunch."

He laughs, "I was about to, but when I heard you in the shower when I got back from the store, suddenly the need to get clean was really overpowering."

Laughing with him, he pulls me into his room. "Oh wait, I have my clothes in the bathroom."

"Let's save those for later. We have a while before we have to be anywhere so let's just be comfortable." He pulls out one of his t-shirts from his dresser drawer and hands it to me. "Cool with you?"

With a smile I slip it over my head, "Absolutely."

He throws on a t-shirt himself and some boxers, while I grab some undies and slip them on, then we walk out to the kitchen together. "Do you like eggs and bacon?" Jax asks.

"I do, very much. There really isn't any breakfast food that I don't like. It's pretty much my favorite kind of food."

"It is?"

"Yep, I mean what's not to like? Eggs, bacon, waffles, pancakes, breakfast potatoes, toast with jam, biscuits, crepes, I could go on and on. Plus don't even get me started about having cereal for dinner."

With a laugh Jax walks to a cabinet in his kitchen and opens it. Sitting there are about five boxes of different kinds of cereal. "Oh that's it. Now I know meeting you was kismet. I mean, what are the chances that you'd love cereal as much as I do?" Reaching for one, I pull out the frosted wheat cereal and hold it up, "This is one of my favorites."

"Mine too," he tells me with a smile.

Standing side by side we make breakfast together and I realize that I have a smile on my face the whole time- I can't stop – it's ridiculous. "We are so freaking domestic. Look at us."

He looks at me and his eyes take in my t-shirt clad body, bare feet and the spatula in my hand. "Oh, I'm looking, and I'm liking what I see."

I swat him with the spatula on the butt, "Me too."

We make a freaking feast and sit at his table and eat all of it. I rub my very full tummy, "I probably have a food baby."

"A food baby?" He raises and eyebrow and looks at me like I'm nuts.

"Yeah, it's that little poof you get after you eat a lot making you look like you're pregnant. A food baby."

"That's kind of gross."

Laughing I agree, "I know. So, are you nervous for your fight? Oh wait, you said you don't get nervous, huh?"

"Not really too often anymore, no. Like I said before, it's just a job, but it happens to be a job I love. It wasn't always that way though, I used to get so nervous I'd throw up before a fight."

"Oh, I bet I'd be the same way. So your calm, cool, and collected attitude took time to come by?"

"I guess you could say that." He rubs his chin as thoughts run through his mind and over his face, "Remember how I told you that my dad was angry at me when my grandfather left me the gym when he died?" I nod letting him know I do remember. "Well angry is an understatement. Instead of talking to me like an adult about his feelings or hell, even taking me to court to contest the will like I figured he would, he decided to retaliate instead."

Oh, god. My stomach drops with his words and I'm afraid I'll end up throwing up all the food I just ate. Stories where parents are less than loving to their children always bother me because of what I've endured from my own mother. I swallow hard before asking, "Retaliate how?" I can't help but ask, although I'm not sure I want to hear the answer.

"Well, even though I knew he was angry and that he thought not only that my Pops was delusional, but that I wouldn't be able to hack it, I was determined to be the bigger person. I jumped right in and started managing the gym, implementing some changes that I thought would improve and upgrade things and I also used some ideas that were conceived during talks with my grandfather. He always said I had great ideas, so I decided to implement them. One thing I kept the same though was having my dad manage our fighting sponsorships and the organization and arranging all of our fights. For all his many faults, he is really good at his job, I'll give him that. He'd already been doing it for years for my grandfather, and his contacts and knowledge is extensive. That doesn't mean that a determined person couldn't learn the job and take his place, but why mess with a good thing, ya know? But what I wasn't expecting was for him to start taking a personal interest in the training of fighters at my gym and for him to use them in order to get to me."

"Use them? What do you mean?"

"My father started approaching fighters behind my back and the backs of their coaches and tried to obtain their business. Meaning, he told them that he could coach them. Most people were kind and thanked him but declined, others like Zane couldn't believe he had the balls to even ask and told him so."

"Good for him. That's a loyal friend you have there."

"He's definitely that. It took time, but eventually my father got his first taker. Louie 'Lightening' Gates had just fired his coach due to a conflict of interest of some kind and my father stepped in at the perfect time and Louie agreed to a partnership. My father began training him and of course he did it t the gym. He was sure to train him at times I was there working and he was so fucking loud about it." He shakes his head at the memories. "He'd go on and on about how great of a fighter Louie was, and that he was the best damn fighter he'd ever seen. The worst though was when I trained at the same time as Louie was with my father. My father would make derogatory comments about my training, comparing me to Louie of course, and spouting off all the ways that he was better than me."

"Did Gil ever do something about it?"

He laughs, "He took a swing at my father once over it, but paying it attention only made it worse. Gil encouraged me to not say anything, but my dad got off on it and wouldn't let it go. He'd keep egging it on and my anger would build. He said getting in the cage with Louie would prove once and for all who was better. I'd ignore him and he'd call me a chicken shit and laugh. He'd say it was because I knew Louie would kick my as in a heartbeat."

"What an asshole. Uh sorry-"

He gives me a sad smile and nods, "Definitely. He made me angry, but truthfully, he also made me sad. Yes, my father would train Louie, but he would also give him pep talks, tell him how great he was, pat him on the back and smile at him in a way he'd never smiled at me. I watched my father have a relationship with another fighter that I always dreamed about."

"Oh, Jax. I'm so sorry."

"Me too. He still does it. Louie may be gone, but Cole has become his next target. Poor Cole wasn't able to say no and found himself with my father as his trainer. It's okay though; I don't let it bother me anymore. I've managed to overcome the feelings he found great fun in generating and realized that if I responded in the manner he provoked, I was merely giving him power over me. I absolutely refuse to let him do that to me any longer. When I got to that point, his words meant nothing to me anymore. Not if I didn't let them."

I can't help but compare my own situation to his. I think of my mother and the words that she always used against me. My mind is spinning with Jax's words and the harsh words of my mother that I fight every day. "How? How did you get past it?"

"Well, it wasn't pretty. Unfortunately, the anger and resentment continued to build up inside of me until it exploded one day at the gym and I did something that it took me a really long time to forgive." I stay quiet knowing he'll continue if and when he's ready and willing. "One day my father kept pushing and pushing. By this point he'd learned which buttons of mine worked the best and enjoyed pissing me off and making me feel invisible in his eyes. Like I meant absolutely nothing to him. Something inside of me just… snapped. I couldn't take it anymore. I refused. And then, I attacked Louie." He grimaces at the memory and runs his hand through his hair.

"I was really angry at my father, but took my anger out on Louie instead. While I was hitting Louie with jab after jab, it was my father's face I was seeing in my mind. I used my fists to fight against the rage my father made me feel. You see, fighting has never been about anger issues for me. I don't fight because I have some deep seeded need to beat the shit out of people, and it's not because it meets some deranged need inside of me that I have to hurt people. Those are all typical fighter stereotypes that all fighters have heard. But in that moment, that purely disgusting moment when I lost myself, I was fighting for all of those reasons."

Moving to him, I take his hand in mine, "It's your father's fault. He pushed you too far. Anyone would crack after dealing with that time and time again."

"That's what I told myself at first too, but I'm responsible for my actions, not my father. I let his words have power over me and affect me in ways that Louie certainly didn't deserve. It took four guys to pull me off of him. For a horrible moment I felt extremely victorious. I watched him bleeding and hurting on the mat and I turned to my father to throw it in his face. I wanted to shout at him and ask him what he thought about me now, and in one instant, one fucking instant all those feelings came crashing down. I realized that I played right into my father's jealousy and I did exactly what he was hoping I would do. When my eyes met his, I knew. I just fucking knew that it was what he was manipulating me to do all along."

"How? How did you know?"

"Because he was smiling."

Jax's story humbles me and after we clean the kitchen we are both quiet and contemplative. "Since we have a while before I have to be at the casino for the fight, I thought we could just relax and take it easy. That's what I usually do before a fight. I listen to music or watch movies that motivate me."

"That sounds good to me, what did you have in mind?"

"Well, since you are brand new to this whole fighting thing, I thought that today would be the perfect time to begin your initiation into the fighting world, movie style."

"Movie style?"

"Yep. Today we shall break your fighter movie cherry with the movie, *Bloodsport*." He pulls the DVD off of his shelf and puts it into his DVD player with a big smile. Once it starts, he grabs the remote and joins me on the couch.

"Sounds good, Jackson 'Hands of' Stooooooone," he groans in embarrassment at my teasing. "Let's get started."

He laughs and curls up next to me on the couch and we sink into one another and enjoy the show.

CHAPTER EIGHTEEN

I don't think I've ever enjoyed myself so much before a fight. When I woke up this morning I had a beautiful girl in my arms. Before getting up, I enjoyed watching her sleep in my arms for a long time. How could I not? She looked so perfect and peaceful lying there. Waking up with a girl is a new experience for me. Rowan and I haven't discussed our past involvements yet, maybe we never will, but one thing she would find out about me is that relationships are something I've never done before. The hit a sleaze and leave kind of relationship has always been my style. Eventually, I forced myself to get out of bed, make coffee and get my butt to the store so I could provide nourishment for my girl.

What happened in the shower was unexpected and a complete bonus. Technically, I really shouldn't have sex before a fight. The loss of testosterone, use of energy and all that shit probably isn't smart. Ah well, I will gladly take a few extra jabs in the face tonight in exchange, because that was all kinds of fucking worth it.

What is this girl doing to me? I find myself telling her things I've never told anyone. I also find myself wanting her in a way I've never wanted anyone and the thought of losing her isn't an option. I don't ever want to let her go. I'm pretty sure I was lost in her from the moment I saw her in that hospital emergency room. Our souls crashed into each other that day, and it was all over after that.

Sitting on the couch with her in my arms while we watch *Bloodsport* is fun. She keeps asking so many questions about the movie versus real life and I'm really enjoying myself. Teaching her about the sport my life is so wrapped up in is really cool. Especially because she seems genuinely interested. Which reminds me...

"Rowan, one thing that I want to talk to you about in all seriousness before I forget is that I really would love it if you would help me with the social media like we discussed at dinner last night."

She turns to me, "I'll help you. I'll help all of you like I said, I'm happy to. But, it's the paying me part that I don't like."

"Babe. I told you that if I was hiring someone else to help me they would get paid for their time, so I'm going to pay you just like I would anyone else."

She shakes her head making me frown. "I don't like it. Not at all."

"Then take the money and use it for another social media class. Put it in the bank. Open a college fund for Lily. I don't care, but you are taking it and that's all I have to say about that." I cross my arms and try to look stern.

Her full lips curve upwards and I see her eyes soften. "Okay. I would love to help you." She immediately jumps up and leaves the room. When she returns she has her laptop in her arms and it makes me laugh.

"You brought that with you? I'm not sure if I should laugh or feel offended that you thought you would need your computer to keep you entertained."

She laughs and I love the sound, "Yeah, I know it's silly but it's kind of my pride and joy. I bought it refurbished and got a great deal. My whole life is in this thing and I pretty much bring it with me whenever I go too far from home and certainly if I go to stay overnight."

"You go elsewhere over night often?"

Her face falls and she immediately looks uncomfortable, "Well... not anymore." It dawns on me that she is talking about the ex and I'm not interested in this conversation. At all. "Anyways, I'm glad I have it. Let's do a few social media things now, if you're game."

"Sure."

We spend a couple hours together making a Facebook profile for me as a public figure, which is really weird. We then start one for the gym. She asks me questions about the business, and about me, in order to formulate bios that won't make me sound stupid. When we're done she and I both feel great about what she has created so quickly and easily.

I check out the time on my phone, "Babe, we need to get ready to go, but can you promise me something really quick?"

"Yeah sure"

"When Levi, Cole and Ryder are done fighting, they will come sit with you. Dylan and Zane will already be there and will be sitting with you too. Will you please stay seated with them during my fight?"

"Okay, but why?"

"The fights themselves can get pretty crazy and it will make me feel better if I know you're with the guys and I don't have to worry about your safety."

"I can take care of myself, Jax. I have for a long time."

"First of all, I'm not suggesting you can't take care of yourself. If anyone knows how self reliant and strong you are, it's me. Second, you may have always taken care of yourself, but I'm here now and I consider it an honor to take care of my girl. And tonight, this is one of the ways I can demonstrate that I trust my friends to take care of you, okay?"

She gives me a kiss on the lips and whispers, "Okay, I understand. I'm excited for my first fight!"

We begin getting ready and it surprises me how much I enjoy watching her do such mundane things like her hair and makeup. Feeling like I'm going to have to hand in my man card any moment, I leave the room and wait for her to get dressed. When she finally walks out of the room, my jaw drops to the floor. She's wearing a jean skirt that makes me seriously question its ability to cover her ass, a ribbed low cut red tank and sandals. "You can't fucking wear that," I blurt out and cross my arms doing my best to close my mouth.

She looks down at herself and then at me in confusion, "What's wrong with this?"

"Babe. I'm supposed to be concentrating on the fight, not worrying about fighting guys off of you."

"Oh please. You're being ridiculous."

Sighing, I shake my head and make a note to have a serious talk with the guys. They'll have to keep a sharp eye on her, but not too sharp. Fuck, she makes me crazy. In a good way. Gesturing for her to walk in front of me out the door, I check out her legs and ass. It takes a physical effort to keep myself from jumping her again. I want her milky white skin under my hands, my mouth and my teeth. Doing my best to suppress a groan at the thought, I help her into my truck.

When we arrive at the casino, I have to get my butt backstage and into the dressing room so I can listen to my music, the advice from Gil and just zone out until I'm up.

Turning to Rowan, I cup her face, "Listen babe, I know I already asked you to stay with the guys during my fight, but please stay with them when it's over too. I'll have to meet with the fight doctor afterwards to get cleared, and clean up. I'll either come and get you, or most likely they'll bring you to me afterward. Regardless, just stay with them, okay? I'll panic if I can't find you in the crowd."

"Don't worry about me. I promise I will stay with them. Now go. I'm the last thing you need to focus on. Do what you need to do and I will see you afterward. You just worry about kicking some ass, okay?"

"Okay, oh and I almost forgot," I pull out Rowan's VIP pass and hand it over. She barely spares it a glance before putting it around her neck. Zane walks up behind her and I give him a nod. "Zane, a moment?"

He nods and we step aside, "If anyone touches my girl tonight in an inappropriate way, I'm going to hold you personally responsible. I know she's dressed to kill, but fuck man, if I see anyone coming onto her or touching her or just near her, I won't be able to concentrate. You and the boys keep an eye on her, yeah?"

"You know it."

"Thanks."

Walking back to Rowan, I smile, "Have fun watching the fights. I wish I could sit with you to watch them and take in your reactions, but we will another time for sure."

"Sounds great. Now go!" She reaches up and gives me a kiss that has good luck screaming all the way through it. I let the moment take me over and lose myself in the kiss. I grip her hips closer to mine and nibble on her bottom lip before I let her go. There are catcalls around us, but I ignore them. Fuck if I care that they know she's mine.

"I'll see you later, okay babe?"

"Okay, good luck. Kick some ass!"

I make my way to the back nodding and shaking hands with people on the way. When I get to the dressing room, Gil is already there chatting it up with some other coach and nods at me in hello. Putting my ear buds into my ears, I quickly text a message to all the guys but Zane, threatening bodily harm if anything happens to my girl. Then, I pull up the hood of my sweatshirt and clear my mind of everything except the fight ahead and the music blaring in my ears.

CHAPTER NINETEEN

Rowan

The crowd is crazy. Our seats are in the front row and I have Zane on one side of me, Dylan on the other. As each fighter makes their way to the cage, they pass right in front of us, which is pretty cool. My knee bounces up and down and I even pull my nails out of my mouth a few times finding myself biting them in nervous anticipation of Jax's fight. We've already sat through a few fights, including Levi's. He was pretty entertaining when he fought, I must admit. Jumping around like his feet were on fire, I don't think his opponent knew what the hell he was going to do next. I'm not sure if Levi won due to incredible strategy, or because his opponent was confused and dizzy as hell and gave up.

Levi hasn't joined our group yet, but Zane said he should be out any time. Cole is up now and the guys cheer super loud when he's announced. We watch as he starts making his way down the aisle towards the cage and when he passes in front of us we all pat him on the back and cheer him on. Cole nods his head at us and keeps his serious demeanor as he steps into the cage, walks to the corner, and removes his t-shirt and sweatpants. Once again, the man that I now know is Jax's father, and Cole's coach, is right there alongside him. Anger stirs in my belly when I remember the story Jax shared with me about his father. He's whispering in Cole's ear and looks like he's talking really fast. Cole is nodding at whatever he's saying.

"Zane?"

"Yeah, doll?"

"What's Jax's dad's name?"

He looks at me wide-eyed, maybe surprised I know who Jax's dad even is before he answers, "Jerry." I nod and look back at the cage. Each fighter is standing in their corner until the referee tells them to come forward. He gives a brief reminder of the rules and then signals the beginning of the fight. They barely take a step toward one another before Jerry is already yelling at Cole. "Get in there and take it to him!"

"Give him a chance before you start yelling, douchebag," Zane mutters and I absently nod my head. I don't know much about this, but I was thinking the same thing.

Each fighter seems to be dancing on their toes trying to feel each other out. Cole tries a punch and kick combination that isn't successful. Before he can catch a breath his opponent, Gene Francois, tries the same combination, but he doesn't land it either. Zane and Dylan are pretty quiet next to me. We're all standing but they seem to be taking it all in. When Cole dives for Gene's knees the crowd starts yelling in excitement.

"Why's he doing that?" I ask Zane.

"He was going for a takedown, but he missed. He wasn't doing very well standing up so he wanted to try and take the fight to the ground. Plus, fighter's that do the most take downs tend to be scored better by the judges."

After failing to land the take down, Cole throws a wild punch that completely misses. Through the first round it seems like Cole and Gene are evenly matched as far as the punches and kicks they've landed. When round one comes to an end, we all shout and cheer for Cole offering our encouragement. Jerry is immediately shouting in Cole's ear when he reaches his corner. Cole nods at his coach's words and drinks water trying to catch his breath, until the bell sounds for round two.

"Come on, Cole!" Dylan yells.

"You got this!" Zane adds.

"Get your ass in there and stop being so soft!" Jerry screams making the guys curse under their breath. I can't help but glare at Jerry even though he has no clue – it just makes me feel better.

Round two is more of the same except right before the bell rings Gene takes Cole to the ground. When round three begins, both fighters are showing signs of fatigue, but their fists stay high. Cole comes out more aggressive at the beginning, but eventually gets taken to the ground once again. Each of them fights for position, rolling around the floor. One minute Cole is on top, and then Gene. It all looks pretty wild to me, but everyone is cheering and screaming around me, including the guys this time. Neither one of them manages to top the other before the bell rings, indicating the end of the fight. They each go to their corners and sit.

"Ladies and gentleman, we go to the judges score cards."

"Okay guys, since neither of them was the obvious winner by tap out or knock out," they both smile at me and I roll my eyes. "Shut up. I read about this a little. Anyway, just tell me what's happening?"

Dylan laughs then says, "The judges are submitting who they think won each round and the fighter that takes the most rounds wins."

"And what makes a fighter win a round?" I ask.

"The judges evaluate each round based on mixed martial arts techniques like effective striking and effective grappling and aggressiveness. They each sit at various positions around the cage and based upon their evaluations choose who wins the round in their opinion."

"Okay, got it." We all wait on pins and needles for the judge's decision. I check out Cole while we're waiting. He appears to be doing okay. He's got a couple knots on his face, one under his nose and another on his forehead, but nothing too serious.

"Ladies and gentleman all three judges score the fight 28-29,

29-28, 29-28, declaring the winner by unanimous decision, Gene Francois."

Cole and Gene walk to the middle and shake each other's hands and do a guy hug back pat thing, then Gene celebrates with his team and is interviewed while Cole and his team make their way out of the cage. Cole's head is down as he makes his way past us and I can hear Jerry in his ear, "How many fucking times have we been over that? You're going to end up being a sorry sack of shit like my son. I expect better from you. If you can't get your shit together then stop wasting my fucking time."

My mouth falls open and I immediately look at the guys around me to see if they heard the same thing I did. By their body language they sure as hell did. Dylan's fists are clenched and Zane's jaw ticks in anger. We watch them until they disappear not saying a word, but the silence is heavy.

"Zane, why does Cole let Jerry coach him? I just don't see how he's benefitting from the arrangement."

"I don't know, doll. We've all tried talking to him about it and we don't get any answers from him. We've all kind of given up on him because he's an adult and makes his own decisions."

Shaking my head in confusion, I do my best to push it aside because I'm excited and nervous again about Jax's fight. "Is it time yet?"

"Time for what?" Dylan asks me.

"For Jax's fight."

Dylan looks at Zane in silent communication before looking back at me. I turn to Zane waiting for him to answer. "What did Jax tell you about the fight tonight?"

"What do you mean? He didn't say much other than how he wants me to stay with you guys because he worries about my safety which seems silly, but I agreed to stay put."

Before he can continue, Levi joins our group with a wide smile. We all congratulate him on his win and laugh at his antics. He's crazy excited, but feels bad for Cole's loss which he caught before making his way to us. When I see that Ryder is up next I can't help but sigh in disappointment. "So, I guess that answers that," I say.

"Answers what?" Levi says.

"Oh nothing, I was just wondering if Jax was up next, but I guess not."

"Of course he's not. He's headlining, so he fights last," Levi says.

Zane and Dylan give him a dirty look, but I ignore them. "Headlining? What does that mean?"

Zane shakes his head at Levi but answers, "It means that he's the main event of the night?"

"The main event?" I ask shocked. "Why didn't he tell me?"

"Jax isn't really a bragging kind of guy. Plus, he probably didn't want you to freak out when you realized that all of these people are basically here to watch him fight," Dylan tells me proudly.

"Holy hell," I reply. My mind is swirling with this information. I mean, the place is freaking packed. I can't believe that they are all here to watch Jax. A feeling of complete pride fills my chest and heart. He should have told me.

"Didn't you know, girl? Your boyfriend is the shit!" Levi laughs.

My heart flutters and I don't know if it's from the realization that Jax is much better at this than he let on, or the fact that Levi used the word 'boyfriend'. I think it's a toss up. I look around the room, but this time, I *really* look. There are people wearing t-shirts with Jax's name on them, and there's even some that are holding up signs for him even though he hasn't made an appearance yet.

"Zane. Where the hell do they get those t-shirts? I want one. Why the hell didn't he give me one?"

With a big smile, Zane whispers something in Levi's ear and Levi smiles and disappears. Before Zane can answer me, Ryder is announced and starts making his way to the cage, shadow boxing the whole way. Not surprisingly he plays up to all the ladies on his way. He smiles and winks at them over and over while they scream his name. I'm pretty sure I even saw one woman lift up her shirt to flash him when he walked by. Of course Zane and Dylan are laughing their asses off and they are making me giggle too. Truth is, I'm really getting into this and I start cheering really loudly for Ryder. He was too busy flirting to pay us attention when he walked by, but he looks over at us from the cage and winks before he gets the signal that the fight is starting.

Ryder's fight is great. They go all three rounds and right when the bell would have rung and required a judge's decision, Ryder gets his opponent in a hold that he can't escape from and he taps out making him the winner. We all cheer and scream in excitement.

"Hey, Rowan, here you go." I look over and see Levi standing next to me holding out a t-shirt. I smile, unfold it, and check out the front. It's black and cut to fall slightly off the shoulder. It says, 'Never Dethrone Stone' in large lettering and the back has all his sponsors listed.

"Levi, thank you! This is awesome. I'll pay you back." I turn to grab my bag but they all stop me.

"No big, Row," Levi says. "They didn't charge me." I grin and put the t-shirt on over my tank and model it for the boys.

"Well…what do you think?" They all whistle and catcall making me giggle.

"Jax is going to love it," Zane promises.

When the lights flash and music starts to play we know it's time for the fight to start. My stomach rolls with nerves and excitement and I bounce on my toes. First out is Jax's opponent, Lance 'The Hammer' Henderson. He makes his way to the octagon from the opposite end of the arena and it's all kinds of pomp and circumstance. He even has chicks in bikinis walking with him, which I don't even understand. When he gets in the cage and starts disrobing, I check him out trying to see how he will measure up against Jax and I feel a little nervous by all his rippling muscles. Taking a deep breath and pushing the worry away, I shift my focus to Jax when music starts playing again announcing his arrival. I get chills when *ACDC's Thunderstruck* starts playing. Necks are craning to try and get a look at Jax coming out the door and I can't see a thing. Zane moves me to stand in front of him so I have a clear look up the aisle. As soon as *ACDC* belts the first "Thunder" Jax starts making his way down the aisle nice and slow, punching his arms the whole time.

The way he makes me feel in this moment is difficult to describe. The whole room is screaming for him, clapping and yelling his name, but I suddenly feel as if I'm in a tunnel and become aware of every move Jax makes. There's a complete adrenaline rush and I get caught up in the excitement. A burst of pride fills my chest, which isn't all that surprising, but what I don't expect is the desire stirring deep in my belly and between my legs. I'm almost embarrassed to feel that I am turned the hell on. My nipples are hard under my shirt and wetness pools between my thighs.

Gasping when unexpectedly Jax stands before me, I stare up into his shining eyes. Levi, Dylan, Zane and Cole, who has now joined us, smack him on the back and wish him luck. He nods acknowledging their words but doesn't remove his eyes from mine. "Jax, what are you doing?"

He smirks and when he does it's as if my lady town is completely connected to that look. It clenches so hard in response to it that I'm surprised I don't explode in pleasure right then and there. "Nice shirt, babe."

I smile widely, "You like it?" I smooth my hands down my sides and give him a little wiggle, completely flirting with my man.

He winks, "I'll show you how much I like it later." The guys hoot and holler and before I can respond with the sassy comment on my lips, he pulls me to him and plants his mouth on mine. He thrusts his tongue into my mouth and kisses me so thoroughly I almost feel like we're naked in front of the whole crowd. When he pulls away he looks at me, "For luck." He smiles and then walks away entering the octagon.

Standing there completely kissed stupid, women behind me start screaming their displeasure.

"What the hell does she have that I don't?"

"Oh my god, the things that I would do to have his mouth on mine."

"Look over here Jax so I can show you my tits."

Wow. Classy. Without a thought I turn around and grin, "Eat your heart out ladies."

I don't even know how or if they respond because all the guys start laughing so hard it drowns out their noise. They all surround me, and my attention returns to Jax, who's standing just outside the cage, in time to watch him remove his shirt, shorts and shoes. He hands them all to one of his entourage and starts shaking out his arms while he shuffles from foot to foot. Someone starts rubbing stuff all over his face and an official starts patting him down. "I meant to ask when I saw this earlier, but what are they putting on his face and what are they looking for when they pat the fighter's down?"

"They're putting petroleum jelly on his face. It's to help reduce and prevent cutting," Levi replies.

"And they pat the fighters down on their arms and legs, and even look behind their ears, to see if a fighter is greased. Using a slippery moisturizer, oil or something like that on the body is illegal. It's easier to slip out of submissions," Cole adds.

"Okay, got it," I reply.

After they're done, Coach Gil holds Jax's mouth guard to his face. After he puts it in he walks to the cage and into his respective corner. He's not too far from where I'm standing and I'm startled when he turns to face me completely and smiles wide, showing me the guard. "What's that say?" I hear Dylan ask next to me.

Zane laughs, "That's awesome. You see that Row?"

I'm already laughing at the gesture and in response blow Jax a kiss. He's written ROW on the front of his mouth guard and the possessive gesture is a turn on. Is there anything this man does that doesn't turn me on? Hell, I'm on fire. He points at me and acts as if he's caught my kiss before he turns his attention back to the front of him. I'm so happy and excited that I feel like I can fly. What has this man done to me in such a short time? I can't believe he basically just staked his claim in front of thousands of people and I love it.

"Ladies and Gentlemen, it's time for the main event! Fighting out of the red corner, weighing it at one hundred and eighty-four pounds, and standing at five feet eleven inches tall, out of Stockton, California we have Lance 'The Hammer' Henderson." Some of the crowd cheers and claps, but I don't. "Fighting out of the blue corner, weighing in at one hundred and eighty-five pounds standing at six feet two inches tall, from Tempe, Arizona Jackson 'Hands of' Stone!" The guys and I scream our heads off with the majority of the crowd.

"Alright," Zane rubs his hands together, "here we go!"

When the bell rings signaling round one, both guys immediately come out aggressive. There's no feeling each other out or dancing around the other. They simply come out throwing shots. Jax gets in some good combinations, landing some decent blows. Lance, his opponent, manages to do the same. Each blow that connects with Jax's face and body makes me cringe. It amazes me how they are able to take a hit and keep on going. Jax takes shots to the side of his head, face, eye and cheek. Part of me wants to cover my eyes so I don't see him getting hurt and the other half couldn't look away even if someone tried to force me.

They keep trading blows, one after the other. Jax's cheek is already starting to swell making it hard for me to swallow. "Please tell me this round is almost over."

"He's doing good, Row. Hang in there," Cole reassures me.

Jax and Lance each look like they're starting to get a little winded. Jax is pressed against Lance, the cage at Lance's back, trying to put weight on him. They almost look like they've taken a break and decided to hug it out instead. I almost giggle at the thought. I breathe a sigh of relief when the bell rings signaling the end of round one.

They each return to their corner. Gil is in Jax's ear coaching him while another guy wipes him clean, dries him off and gives him water. We are close enough that I can hear Jax and Gil talking. Jax says, "I'm hitting him with everything I've got, and he keeps coming. I don't think I've hurt him at all."

"Oh yes you have," Gil replies, "You just keep your head in the fight and keep going after him. You're doing great."

Jax looks at Gil with frustration, "What fight are you watching?"

Gil just pats Jax on the back, and holds out his mouthpiece for him once again.

When the bell signals for round two, it seems like they hardly had a break. I brace myself for the next round.

When round two begins, Jax and Lance meet in the center of the ring. They circle each other for a few beats until Jax comes out with a left right combination, followed by a kick to Lance's leg. The impact makes Lance take a couple steps back, at which point Jax gets closer to Lance, and dives at his knees for a take down. We all start screaming our heads off when Jax gets Lance to the ground.

"Fuck yeah, end it Jax. End it now!" Zane is screaming.

"It's over! It's all over! He doesn't have a chance, Jax. Bring it home!" Dylan yells.

Jax and Lance roll around on the ground, grappling for position. It looks like Jax is trying to get into a good position in order to make Lance submit. Lance keeps evading him, but Jax manages to move behind Lance anyway. Jax keeps taking blows to his head and arms as Lance does his best to defend himself. A cut on Jax's cheek causes blood to run down his face, creating splashes of crimson against the white canvas floor of the cage. A particularly hard jab to his head makes me gasp.

"He's okay," Zane tells me with a rub on my back.

Jax uses one arm to punch at Lance from underneath him and Lance blocks his punches trying to stay in a safeguard position where Jax can't reach him. This continues until suddenly Jax slips to his rear side and looks like he's choking Lance.

"He's choking him," I say with a twinge of uncertainty.

"It's called a rear naked choke hold. He's applying pressure, making Lance uncomfortable and unable to move so he submits."

No sooner does Zane explain that to me when Jax locks in the hold and the pressure becomes too much for Lance. The crowd starts going nuts and is screaming louder knowing a submission is likely coming. We all hold our breath and watch Jax wide eyed as he continues to squeeze and not give up, his muscles trembling. Lance holds out until he can't any longer and has no choice but to tap out.

"Oh my god! He won! He won!" I start screaming. I can't help it. It's exciting! I'm clapping and screaming and the boys are next to me doing the same.

"Yeah baby! You're the shit!" Levi screams making me laugh harder.

Jax shakes Lance's hand then turns to us and points with a huge smile on his face. I keep jumping up and down in excitement. The announcer goes to his arm, pulls it up and puts the microphone to his mouth, "Jackson Stone wins due to a rear naked choke hold submission in the second round! Ladies and gentleman, let's hear it for Jackson 'Hands of'' Stooooooooone."

We all scream and clap, then hug each other in celebration while Jax gets taken away for an interview. We hang out and watch as he eventually makes his way back up the aisle to return to the dressing room to be checked out, but I can't get to him as he's surrounded by people. I stay with the guys like he asked me to and we hang out until the crowd thins out a little.

"So, what did you think of your first fight, Rowan?" Zane asks.

"I loved it! I mean, it's kind of scary and I hate watching Jax get hit, but the winning part is awesome."

"I agree with that, definitely. Losing sucks ass," Cole mutters.

"I'm sorry, Cole. I didn't mean anything-"

"No," he holds up a hand stopping my words, "I know you didn't. No worries."

I give him a tentative smile still feeling bad that I spoke without thinking. "So, how soon will he fight again?"

"Anxious for the next one, already? You have to let the man heal first," Dylan teases.

Levi replies, "He probably won't have a big fight like this one for another six months or so, but we will have a fight night through the gym before that."

I nod my head, "Got it. Can we go back now?"

"Anxious to see your man?" Ryder asks as he walks up to our group.

"Hey, Ryder!" We all greet.

"Congrats, man!" Dylan says.

"Great fight, Ryder," Zane adds.

The other guys nod and clap him on the back or fist bump and all that guy stuff. I just watch them with a smile on my face until Zane remembers I'm anxious to see Jax. "Come on, Rowan. Let's go back and see him."

I excitedly follow Zane down the aisle and to a back area that's designated for people with VIP passes. Zane takes my arm, as we work our way through the crowd. He looks all around likely making sure we don't accidentally pass Jax on our way, but then stops when he gets to a door and knocks.

Gil throws open the door and smiles, "He's just finished with the doctor, come on in."

As soon as I pass the threshold, I see Jax standing from a couch to greet me. Without thinking I run into his arms and throw my hands around his neck, "Congratulations! That was so awesome." His grunt makes me back up and curse under my breath, "Oh god, Jax. I'm so sorry. Are you okay? How sore are you? What did the doctor say?"

He leans down and pecks me on the mouth likely to shut me up. The other guys surround us and I can hear them chuckling and Levi muttering something about "crazy girlfriends' but I ignore them. "I'm fine. Just your typical bruises and cuts – nothing serious. I'm a little sore, but nothing I haven't dealt with before, I'm fine."

All the guys start congratulating him and they all talk about various moves and other fight talk that I barely listen to. Running my eyes over Jax, I can't take my eyes off of him. He does look okay like he said. The swelling on his cheek around his cut has gone down, but there's already some slight bruising showing there. He's got some various red marks on his torso and another bruise showing on his side, but none of it seems to bother him as he shakes hands, gets hugs, and moves around. I breathe a sigh of relief. "Row?"

Focusing on Jax I realize he must have said my name more than once, "Yeah?"

"You okay?"

"Yeah, fine. Just checking you out, making sure you're really okay."

"I promise, I'm fine. I'm going to go jump in the shower really quick. I'll be right back."

"Okay."

Taking a seat on the couch, I listen to the guys chat around me. They discuss Cole's fight in detail and what they think he did well, and what they think went wrong. Cole seems to take it all in stride which I admit surprises me considering how his coach was acting before.

"Too bad for you, Cole. Sorry you totally ate it. I, however, am a champion. You all can bow down and kiss my feet now." Levi brags about his win again. Boys are weird. He doesn't even consider the fact that his words may bother Cole. Girls in comparison overthink everything and would never dream of saying something like that in front of the person that just lost a fight in case it hurt their feelings. Well at least the girls that aren't complete bitches.

Cole doesn't look bothered by it though, and if he is, Dylan quickly puts him in his place. "Whatever, Levi. You looked like a goddamn fool in the octagon jumping around like a kangaroo on crack."

I laugh out loud and Cole smiles, but Levi frowns for a moment before he shrugs his shoulders. "Dude. That's called skill."

Rolling my eyes, I look over at Ryder. He and Zane are chatting until his attention is diverted by a couple of blondes in bikinis. *Seriously, what is up with the bikinis?* They start to walk by the door and look in on their way, they stop when they see Ryder, and giggle. Ryder totally leaves Zane midsentence in order to flirt with the girls. I'm quite entertained by these boys and their antics.

It isn't long before Jax comes back in the room fresh out of the shower, his hair glistening with moisture, dressed in jeans and a white MMA t-shirt and smelling edible. I don't know what cologne he wears, but I need to find out and spray it all over my pillows. And my blankets. And my couch, maybe? Possibly just everywhere. It's captivating.

"Are you ready to go?" He walks to me and puts an arm around my shoulders.

Zane interrupts, "To Fred and Blarney's like usual?"

"Fred & Blarney's?" I ask

"It's an Irish pub and grill we usually hit up after every fight. They stay open really late," Levi informs me while he jumps from foot to foot. Does he ever stop? Meanwhile, Jax is sighing next to me in irritation. I don't think he intended to keep with tradition tonight. I hate that because of me he's second-guessing whatever his normal routine would be with the guys. The last thing I would ever want is to come in-between their friendships.

"That sounds great," I reply with a smile at Jax.

"You sure?" He whispers in my ear. "We can ditch them and go do our own thing."

"It's okay. Besides, I could eat."

He kisses me on my forehead, "Yeah me too, but when we are done eating we are out of there babe, cool?"

I nod, "Cool."

Dinner's really fun. Sitting back and listening to Jax interact with his friends makes me feel an emotion I don't know how to express because I'm not sure what it is. I just know I feel happy, safe and content. I love their camaraderie. They all discuss Jax's fight and relive all their favorite moves Jax orchestrated and talk about strategy and things they'd like to work on in their training. I don't mind the shoptalk, as I barely take my eyes off of Jax the whole time. I'm mesmerized by his every movement; his ever word. Truth is, as far as I'm concerned no one else is there. Jax keeps looking at me and each time he catches my eye he smiles.

I've kept my hand on his thigh through most of dinner, but I keep inching it up bit by bit. He's in the middle of a conversation with Dylan about another fighter right now and I decide to make it clear I'd like to leave. After all, I've finished my meal and he's basically finished with his too, and he did say we wouldn't stay long. "No, I heard that he was going to be fighting in Las Veg-" he clears his throat in surprise, but somehow manages not to jump as my hand slides up his leg until I reach his hardness and stroke him. His eyes find mine and now it's my turn to give him the smirk he's always giving me.

Jax takes a drink of water and Dylan having no clue what's transpiring between us, continues as if Jax never stopped. "Las Vegas? Yeah, I heard that too. I guess they're having some kind of fight night…" the rest of his words become insignificant as I lift an eyebrow at Jax, the look on my face clearly saying, "let's go."

"Alright guys, Rowan and I are heading out. I'll see you all when I see you." Jax puts money on the table, stands, then immediately places himself behind my chair pulling it out for me, but I think also to cover up the bulge in his pants. He keeps me in front of him as we say goodbye to everyone and when Ryder, who we managed to pull away from his bikini babes after they exchanged numbers, hugs me a bit too long in a blatant attempt to irritate Jax once again, it works. Jax pushes Ryder off of me. "Alright playboy, go find your own girl. How many times do I have to tell you? This one's mine."

We aren't far from his place and when we walk inside, I immediately turn to him. "So, be honest. Are you too sore for us to-"

"No," he interrupts me and I barely take a breath before his mouth is immediately on mine. Knowing I should be careful, but not able to contain myself, I jump into his arms which causes him to take a step back as he braces my weight, then immediately turns around and pushes me against the door. My legs wrap around him making my skirt hike high on my hips, but I could care less. He rips his mouth from mine and kisses down my jaw, neck and collarbone.

"Jax, I want you. Watching you fight, my name on your mouth guard, the kiss before you began. God, I've been turned on for hours."

He groans and grinds his hips into me as his lips return to mine, and I gasp in his mouth from the feeling of his hardness. The only thing that separates us from joining is the thin cloth of my panties. His hand reaches out and he flips the lock on the front door, then he makes his way down the hallway to his bedroom. When we're through the door, he places me on the ground, and I immediately lift his shirt over his head taking it off, so I can place my lips to his chest. I place kisses all over him, even the bruise on his side before, standing on my toes to reach his tattoo better. I begin tracing it with my tongue, causing him to hiss with pleasure. I smile through my kissing and licking, but it falls when he pulls away and steps back.

"I just need to tell you that you look totally hot in my sponsor shirt." He smiles as he eyes me up and down.

"That reminds me. I'm mad at you."

"Babe. You could have fooled me what with all the kissing and grinding. If that's how you are when you're angry, then I'm okay with it."

"I'm serious. How could you not tell me that you were headlining the event tonight? And not only that, you're like some big time fighting God." He laughs and I glare making him try to stop, but he sucks at it. "You have your own t-shirts!" I pull mine away from my body like he needs evidence of my declaration.

"It's not a big deal. And I'm definitely not a 'big time fighting God'."

"Not a big deal? How can you say that? Do you need me to show you my t-shirt again?"

He shrugs, "Because it isn't. I didn't want any of that shit to influence the way you feel about me." He looks at me and suddenly the look I'm seeing in his eyes registers. He's worried.

Frowning, I step into him again and look into his eyes, holding his stare, making sure that he sees me clearly before I speak. "All that stuff doesn't matter to me. I'm giving you a hard time because it was quite the shock, but it doesn't have anything to do with whether or not I have feelings for you. It's too late for that. I think it's obvious I've had feelings for you before tonight. At least, I hope so." My brow furrows now because I don't know how or why he could think differently. "To make it clear, I have feelings for you because I like *you*. Not what you do for a living. You're sweet, thoughtful, caring, funny, sexy as hell, intelligent, protective, and *so* much more. You set me on fire with just one thought, one touch." He brushes his thumb across my cheek, "There's fireworks, Jax. Besides, I think I know the exact moment I was a goner for you."

"You do?"

"Well, I was already well on my way when you were so amazing at the hospital, I just didn't know it yet. But I think the first time you kissed me on the forehead, I was yours."

He grins showing me his cute dimples, "You like it when I do that?"

"No. I love it. It's such a simple act that shows everything about you. I've fallen for you," I declare simply.

In answer he kisses me again claiming my lips with his own. He pulls away for a second, and whips my shirt over my head, then the tank top under it. He wastes no time getting rid of my bra too and as he places me on his bed, his lips close around one of my nipples. He sucks and teases, then leaves a trail of love bites as he makes his way to the next one giving it the same attention.

"Jax, now. I want you now."

He stands to take off his clothes and while he does, I remove the rest of my own, then lay bare before him. When his body comes over the top of mine, the hair on my arms stands up anxious for the moment his skin touches mine. When it does, I sigh in pleasure. Taking me at my word, Jax doesn't waste anymore time. He positions himself and enters me with a deep thrust. "Fuck," Jax murmurs under his breath overcome with the feeling of our joining.

His hips push into mine over and over and my hips rise to meet him each time. I drag my nails down his back and throw my head back in ecstasy. "So good. It feels so good," I sigh. After a few more strokes, he surprises me by flipping me onto my stomach. Immediately, I know what he wants, so I get on all fours, shaking my ass enticingly back and forth.

He teasingly gives it a smack, "Tease," he admonishes. Then he runs the head of his erection over my opening before easing back into me nice and slow. Once I adjust to the new feeling of fullness, he grabs my hip with one hand, and wraps his other hand around me to rub my clit. He pumps into me, matching the movements with his fingers. It only takes a minute at most before I'm coming so hard I see stars and scream his name.

"You might want to hang on for this," Jax informs me and I laugh and place my hands, palms down, on the headboard. With one hand still on my hip, he reaches the other into my hair and grabs a handful. He pounds into me so hard, his hips smack into my ass making a loud slapping sound. Immediately, another orgasm starts to unfurl in my belly shocking me. His balls slapping against my clit with his movements stimulate me, as well as his thrusts inside.

"Oh fuck, Jax. I'm coming! I'm coming again." I announce as I clench around him tightly. With a loud groan Jax yells, "Rowan!" and empties himself inside of me. After removing himself he sits on the side of the bed and pulls me into his arms. I melt when he kisses my forehead and whispers, "I've fallen for you too."

My heart soars.

CHAPTER TWENTY

Jax

These few days since my fight have been good ones. The soreness in my muscles is much better and my bruises are already changing colors from purple and blue, to yellow and green, as they fade. This last weekend with Rowan was one of the best weekends I've had in a really long time. I've been replaying it in my mind over and over. Surprisingly, winning the fight has hardly crossed my mind. Rather, I can't stop thinking about her. It makes me happy, if not a bit taken back, that Rowan has easily become the most important thing to me – and has easily taken the place of other things.

When I woke up the morning after winning, Rowan had already left. She called a cab to get home choosing not to wake me. I know she needed to get back to Lily but her absence created a heavy feeling of loss and I found that I hated it with a passion. So, I quickly employed a solution. As soon as I showered and ate something, I was out the door and at her place standing on her doorstep. She was surprised to see me, but let me in right away. I'd like to think she was missing me as much as I was already missing her. I'm finding that I hate it when I'm not with her. I crave her companionship like an addict does his drug of choice.

When I arrived, she'd just hung up the phone with Ty. He'd called to tell her the specifics of his release and to make arrangements for her to pick him up. She was ecstatic and shyly asked me if I would go with her and Lily to get him. I was flattered that she'd think to ask me, and would want me to go, so I immediately agreed.

Now, a couple days later, we are sitting in my truck, waiting for Tyson to walk out the door of the jail. Rowan's knee is bouncing and she's hardly able to sit still, squirming in her seat and staring out the window.

Placing a hand on her bouncing knee, I squeeze around the knee cap making her jerk it away and laugh. Then I ask her a rhetorical question. "Are you nervous?"

She looks at my hand, then at me, and smiles with a touch of embarrassment. "Yeah, I guess I am. I haven't seen him in a while, and our conversations have all been quick and much the same these last few months. He asks how I am, and if I have enough money. There's really no time to get into anything else."

"I'm sure it will feel like you pick up right where you left off though. Don't worry," I tell her and hope it helps.

"You're right. I just know he's going to ask questions that I'm nervous about answering." She sighs and looks out the window for a beat before returning her gaze to me, smiling, "I am really excited for him to finally meet Lily though."

Looking in my rearview mirror at the car seat, I see little socked feet kick at the air as if the little one inside is just as excited to meet her uncle as her mom is to introduce her. "He's your brother and he loves you, he's only going to ask because he cares. Besides, I'm sure there isn't anything that you can't tell him."

She gives me a saucy look as her eyes travel over my body and she licks her lips, "Want to bet, sexy?"

I bark out a laugh, her sassy mouth taking me by surprise. "Okay, then. I will rephrase. I'm sure that you can tell him *most* anything anyway."

She smiles, "You're right. He has always been my best friend and I know that no matter what, he doesn't judge me. I just want him to be happy and stress fee. Not angry the second he gets home."

"He'll be fine, babe. Don't borrow trouble. And, if he's not fine, I've gotta tell you, that's not your problem. You aren't responsible for the actions and feelings of your brother."

"I know, but I don't want to be the catalyst, either."

"I get that, but you can't let the possibility of his reactions influence the way you treat him, or talk to him. You should always be one hundred percent you. If you aren't, and you censor yourself all the time, your relationship with him will become strained and disingenuous. He doesn't want that, and neither do you. If you can't be yourself with him, then that's a big problem. He's one person you should always be able to be yourself with. Trust in him and in your love for each other."

She leans over and kisses me on the lips. It's sweet and soft, "How did you get so smart?"

I want to prove how smart I am by deepening the kiss, but when a figure catches my eye over her shoulder, I decide now is not the time. Nodding my head towards Ty, Rowan catches the gesture and spins in her seat. As soon as she sees him walking out of the building, she gasps in excitement, gets out of the truck, and starts running to him. He drops his bag on the sidewalk and runs to her too. They meet half way and he twirls her around in his arms. Her head is thrown back in laughter and I can hear the tinkling sound of it from here. When he sets her down, he's grinning ear to ear, and kisses her on the head. He quickly backtracks to his bag, then catches up to her again and throws an arm over her shoulder. The affection they have for one another is obvious.

As they walk towards the truck, I get out and come around the front in order to greet him. Seeing them side-by-side makes their likeness, as well as their differences, apparent. They have the same dark hair, hazel eyes and smiles. But, Tyson's nose is a little crooked, maybe from being broken, and he doesn't have the same freckles across his nose Rowan does. There are other subtle differences, but those are the most obvious.

Stepping forward I hold out a hand, "Good to see you again, Ty."

"You too, Jax. Thanks for coming with Rowan to pick me up. It's nice to see you two together."

"Rowan's been anxious to see you."

"Let me guess… she was bouncing her knee like crazy, huh?"

I laugh, "You got it."

"Um, hello. I'm standing right here!"

Ty and I laugh, and he tells me how she's always had that nervous habit, but his laugh breaks off when he turns to Rowan in his laughter and sees she's taken Lily out of her car seat. He sets eyes on her for the first time, and the sight is nothing less than moving. Once again his bag is dropped and forgotten as the sweet girl in front of him takes all his focus. Lily reaches out and pulls on Rowan's hair and gurgles. Ty's face is lit up with love and adoration.

"She's gorgeous, Row, just gorgeous. I mean, I knew she would be, but seeing her in person is… well it's better than I imagined. Can I hold her?"

Rowan has tears in her eyes and swallows hard before nodding. Her eyes haven't left Ty as he takes in the sight of her daughter. Putting Lily in his arms, we both watch as Ty places a kiss on her head. Smiling at her when she reaches out and grabs his nose, he laughs and says, "Hi, beautiful. I'm your Uncle Ty or Uncle Tyson since your mom always calls me Tyson you probably will too. I am so, so, happy to meet you. I'm sorry I haven't been around for a few months, but I promise I'm going to make it up to you."

As if Lily knows what he's saying to her, she gives him a big gummy smile. While Tyson is smiling and completely enamored with her, he has tears in his eyes. "Row, she's amazing."

"I know she is."

"And she looks like you."

I laugh, "She looks like both of you."

They both look at me and laugh. "Yeah, I guess so," Ty says. "Wow."

"Come on," Rowan says. "Let's get you home. I don't know what you might want to eat, but I stocked up on your favorites at the store."

"Oh, did you buy nutty bars?"

She smiles, "Yes, I got you two value pack boxes."

"Awesome! I love me some nutty bars."

"I know," Rowan laughs and looks at me, "Tyson's a chocolate and peanut butter addict."

He shrugs, "No two things are better together. Well except maybe you and me, Row. Damn, I missed you."

"Me too. Come on, let's get home."

We all climb into the truck, Ty in the back next to Lily. Ty asks Rowan how work at the diner is going, and she asks him the details of how and why he was able to get out of jail a little earlier than sentenced. He asks if she's got everything she needs for Lily as well as if she's making ends meet okay. She seems a little embarrassed he's asking this in front of me, but she quickly lets go and answers him, "Everything is fine. Our next-door neighbor, Audrey, helped me out a lot when I was struggling at first. She's been great and I'm a lot better now."

Knowing Audrey helped Rowan, through things that I bought, makes me feel happy. I feel as if I helped contribute to her getting better, even if she doesn't know it. I'm never going to tell her either. It doesn't matter. I'm just happy I could be there in some way.

Once we get home, Ty carries Lily's car seat inside and Rowan goes immediately to the kitchen. While Ty takes Lily out of the seat, I follow her. "Hey," I say softly getting her attention, "do you want me to leave so you and Ty can have some time alone?"

She frowns, "No. I'd like you to stay. I mean, unless you want to go. I don't know if you need to get back to the gym."

"Nope," I quickly answer. "I just didn't want to be rude."

"I want you here."

I nod, "Good."

"Tyson, I have stuff for lunch meat sandwiches for now, but I got steaks and potatoes to make for dinner. Sound okay?"

Ty's comes into the kitchen with Lily on his hip. He looks like a pro holding her and Lily looks perfectly content. "That's fine with me."

"Can I help?" I ask Rowan, but she shakes her head at me. Ty shrugs his shoulders and the two of us make our way into the living room and turn the TV on to the sports channel to get updated on the latest games and sporting news. We're discussing the latest coach firing when Rowan calls us to the table. She takes Lily from Ty and buckles her into her highchair, then places Lily next to her at the table so she can feed her and eat at the same time. We make small talk in between eating, but mostly watch Lily and laugh as she spits out the carrots Lily's feeding her. Then, Ty asks a question that makes Rowan freeze.

"Alright, I'm done waiting. I want to know. What the hell happened to Jason?"

"Tyson... I really don't think that now..."

"No!" Rowan and I startle when Ty slams his fist on the table. Even Lily looks at him wide-eyed. "I want to know now, Rowan. No more putting me off. Tell me what the hell happened."

"Dude, calm down. Don't yell at her," I demand.

Ty looks chagrined, "Sorry," he mumbles.

"I just don't want to upset you when you just got home."

Ty just stares at her and she finally sighs. I'm sure she's wishing she had sent me on my way now. Crossing my arms over my chest, I sit back in my chair and wait for her to explain too. I'm not about to act like I don't want to know the answer to this myself. Her eyes meet mine and I hold her stare steadily hoping that I convey that not only do I want to know the answer, but that she can talk in front of me as well.

I can tell the exact moment that she chooses to finally let go and talk about what happened. Her body deflates and it's almost as if shame covers her face and it instantly makes my back straighten and my fists clench. Anyone that can make her feel this way deserves to have their ass kicked in my opinion. Ty and I quickly exchange a glance and the fact that we are thinking the same exact thing is apparent. Staying silent, we wait for Rowan to begin.

"My water broke in the middle of the night. I had been staying at Jason's place that night so I woke him up. At first he didn't believe my water had broken," Ty makes a noise that sounds like disgust. I don't say anything or move an inch, my eyes fastened on Rowan's face. She continues to feed Lily and doesn't make eye contact with either of us. "When I finally got him out of the house-"

"What do you mean when you 'finally got him out'? What took so long?" Ty asks.

She tucks her hair behind her ear in a nervous gesture before answering, "He got in the shower first and took his time getting dressed." She glances at Tyson after she answers, but he doesn't respond, his jaw ticking the only indication of his feelings.

"We pulled up to the hospital and he let me out at the emergency room entrance which I thought was strange. I told him where the maternity entrance was and that we should go there. In fact, I'd told him like a month before my water broke that I had my bag packed, my pre-registration papers submitted and everything ready to go. All we'd have to do is check in at registration when the time came, and we'd be set. But he wouldn't listen."

"What do you mean?" I ask.

"Well, he just told me to get out at the emergency room entrance because he was going to park the car in the covered parking spot. I was irritated but just figured he wanted to park out of the sun while we spent a couple days in the hospital."

"So, he told you he was going to park the car, and then what?" Ty asks.

"Why?" she asks.

"No, Rowan. Don't even try that shit on me. I'm not playing the why game with you. It's an insult. Don't you dare suggest I have a selfish motive for asking you these questions."

She sighs in defeat, looks at Ty, and what I see in her eyes makes my gut clench. It's sadness combined with an acceptance that breaks my heart. A part of her isn't surprised that he did this to her, and that fact makes me want to both shake some sense into her, and get her alone to cherish her until she believes how amazing of a woman she is. "Fine. What did he do, Tyson? He didn't come back. He didn't fucking come back."

"What do you mean he didn't come back?" Ty asks disbelieving.

"I mean, he told me he was going to park the car and three hours later I was still sitting in the emergency room by myself realizing that he abandoned me. Me and Lily both."

Ty stands abruptly knocking over his chair, "Three fucking hours, Rowan? You sat waiting for him for three hours?"

Rowan's face still holds the look that's threatening to break my heart and I look angrily at Ty. "Sit down and lower your voice. You're scaring Lily, and Rowan doesn't need your anger."

"Doesn't need my anger? Then who's going to be angry for her? You? Rowan? Jason needs to be taught a lesson. Who does he think he is leaving my sister in labor like that? Abandoning his daughter! He has responsibilities! I'm going to find him and make him live up to them."

"You will do no such thing, Tyson James Martin." Rowan is standing now too and the look of fury on her face shouldn't turn me the hell on, but it does. She looks fucking glorious. Her hands on her hips, head and shoulders back, body language full of confidence and eyes full of fire. She's amazing. "This isn't your problem. This isn't something I need or want you to straighten out or deal with. If Jason doesn't want Lily, then it's his loss. I will not force him to have responsibility and ownership in something he clearly doesn't want. She is better off without him. *I* am better off without him. And he is missing out. As much as I may have wanted a normal family, it isn't in the cards for us. So screw him. I'm done."

Her words are like a strike against my face. For all her brave words, a part of her feels that she deserves this. I know it's because of the shit her mom fed her, but there's also a part of her that still aches for him anyway. I don't think that it's Jason exactly that she's wishing for, but the idea of what he represented – the promise of normal that she so wants. The fairytale of the mother and father that created the child, raising it together and living happily ever after. How do I get her to understand that a family comes in many shapes and forms? That normal is a matter of perspective? In that moment, I envy Jason. I envy his history with Rowan. I envy the fact that he's Lily's father. Hell, I just envy the fact that he created a baby with this amazing woman and that I didn't get here first. I hate that they will always have a connection because of Lily, no matter where he is. But, all I can do is fight the pull that he has on her and stake my own claim.

Ty sits back down and runs his hands through his hair, "Did he give any indication that something like this might happen?" Rowan looks down and doesn't answer. "I'm not making excuses for him, do not misunderstand, I'm just wondering if this came completely out of nowhere, or if you weren't surprised because there's more to the story?"

Rowan stays quiet so long that I can't help but reach over and take her hand. She looks up at me and I smile encouragingly. "You know that he was never happy about the pregnancy." Ty nods his head. "I think he may have been cheating on me," she blurts.

"What?" I ask in surprise at the same time Tyson says the same thing.

"There were just some weird things that happened that made me suspicious. Whispering on the phone. Hang up calls. Spaces of time when he would be unavailable to meet or even talk. I found a receipt for a necklace I never received. Just weird things like that. No proof, but just an instinctual feeling. I honestly kept ignoring it figuring I had enough to worry about with getting through the pregnancy."

"I'm sorry, Row. I don't mean to lose my temper and act like an ass. I just hate thinking about you going through that and being left alone like that."

"You know what, Tyson? I wasn't alone. I met Jax." She looks at me and smiles making my heart beat faster at the look she's giving me. "As much as I absolutely hate what Jason did. I can't help but feel grateful for it too, which is weird and honestly a feeling I'm still trying to work through, but it brought me Jax. How can I be truly mad when I've so clearly won in the long run?"

I don't give a shit that her brother is there. I get up out of my seat, and pull her up from hers. Taking her in my arms, I kiss her soundly on the lips. In that moment, I realize I'm already half way to winning the fight. "I'm glad that you can see the wonderful thing that came out of something that hurt you so much. I hate that this happened to you too, but hell if I'm not thankful as well since it brought me to you." I kiss her again and start to lose myself until I hear Ty laugh.

"So, it's like that is it?" he asks.

I turn to him with Rowan still in my arms, "Yep. It's like that. I figured the whole me being along for the ride today made it obvious."

Ty nods and smiles, "I was hoping, but wanted to see more evidence before I assumed. I approve."

"Well that's good but truth is Ty, if you didn't, I wouldn't care. I'm not going anywhere." I state.

Rowan smiles so huge that I lean forward and plant a kiss on her cheek as if that was the period at the end of my statement. Ty just laughs, "Yeah, I definitely approve then."

CHAPTER TWENTY-ONE

Rowan

The rest of last night was filled with catching up with Tyson. He asked Jax questions about the gym, Jax's recent fight and the upcoming fight nights. Not surprisingly Tyson is anxious to get back into training. When I asked him why he never told me about it, he told me he was nervous about how I would feel about fighting as a competitive sport. He got a kick from finding out that I not only attended Jax's fight, but that I loved it. Moreover, he was surprised that I think fighting would be therapeutic for him. I promised him that when it was his turn in the cage, I would be there as well cheering him on as one of this biggest fans.

It was a nice evening and it feels so good to have him home. I really missed him. Having him home drives away the emptiness I felt with him gone. It's not the same emptiness that Jax fills with his presence; it's the kind that can only be filled by my twin.

Ty wanted to take some time to get settled and to go look for a new job. His previous job as a mechanic is gone; he knew it would be. They told him if he was sent to jail they couldn't hold it. He's hoping to find another shop that's hiring. He loves fixing cars, and one day wants to buy a '67 Mustang and fix it up. Jax asked if he could take Lily and I to the park to give Tyson some space and I readily agreed. Dressed in cut off shorts, a tank and flip-flops, I was sure to dress Lily in a cool sundress and to smother our skin with sunblock. It's a necessity in Arizona. There are so many more sunny days than cloudy ones and even the cloudy ones can't be trusted.

"Before we go to the park, I need to stop by the gym really quick. I need to make sure new stock of our supplements that came in is correct. They screwed up the last order. I could ask one of the guys, but it would be faster if I did it myself."

"It's no problem. I feel bad because I feel like I've kept you from the gym a lot lately."

"If it was a big deal, I'd be there. One of the guys is almost always there and so it's not a big deal for them to keep an eye on things. Other than that, the front desk staff is well trained and the place pretty much runs itself. Most of what needs done is accounts payable, order management, membership stuff, and machine repair when needed. Most of that can be done on my laptop, so no more worrying."

I nod my head and take him at his word. When we get to the gym, I prop Lily on my hip and head inside, following Jax. "You can come in my office with me if you want." I'm just about to do that when I spot Cole and change my mind. "Actually, do you have a pad of paper and pen I can borrow? I see Cole and I want to remind him to send me his bio for his social media page. He's the only one that hasn't responded to the email I sent the other day. Maybe I can get some of the other information I need from him now."

"Yeah sure." He hands me a paper and a pen from his desk and surprises me when he takes Lily from me. "Hi sweet girl, wanna play in your bouncer while I go through an order? Do you?" His baby talk is adorable.

"Are you sure you want to keep her in here? I can bring her and her bouncer with me."

"She's fine." He kisses me on my cheek and walks to her seat to buckle her in. He keeps smiling and talking to her the whole time and my heart lurches. *I love him. I am in love with this man.* The thought hits me like a freight train, but it makes complete sense. He has completely taken over my heart and clearly that of my daughters given the way she's taken to him. She greets him with squeals when he comes over and reaches for him to hold her. Standing there with the realization that I'm in love makes me immobile.

Jax turns around and a puzzled look crosses his face when he sees me still standing there. "Are you okay?"

I blink several times, "What? Oh. Yes." I hold up the paper and pen, "Thank you…for these. So I can write. And talk to Cole. Yeah." I walk away feeling my cheeks flush at how stupid I sound. Love has made me stupid. Wonderful.

Walking up to Cole I try to shake my realization from my mind so I can focus on what I need to get from him, "Hey, Cole."

He's punching the hanging bag in front of him and has sweat pouring down his face. He lowers his hands and turns to me with a smile, "Hi, Rowan. How are you? Came in with Jax, huh?"

"Yeah, he just had to check on a shipment I guess. I saw you over here and I'm sorry to interrupt your work out, but I want to ask you about your social media information. I never received the basic information I asked for like your hometown, birthday, favorite bands, movies you like and all that. I also don't have your bio. I'm wondering if you still want my help? And if so, I thought maybe I can get some of your information now." I poise my pen over the paper showing him I'm ready for any information he wants to share.

"Oh, yeah, um about that…."

"He doesn't need your help," a sharp voice behind me barks making me spin around. Jerry Stone, Jax's dad, is standing there with his arms crossed over his chest giving me a nasty look.

"I'm sorry?"

"Yeah you should be. Haven't you ever heard of professionalism? Begging Cole to hire you when he already has a coach and manager is pathetic. Is that the method you always use to get your clients?"

My mouth drops open in disbelief. It takes a moment for the fog to clear my mind in order for me to comprehend what he just said to me. "I didn't beg Cole to let me help him. I offered to help since I'm familiar with social media and he doesn't have any accounts yet."

"Don't you worry about what he has, or doesn't have. It isn't your place. I know what you're doing!"

"Um," I stare at him in complete loss. I have no clue what he's thinking. "I'm trying to help the guys build their social media presence. That's all. If that's what you're suggesting, then you would be correct."

"Don't even try it, little girl. You're hoping to get close to Cole so you can find out information to take back to Jax. It isn't going to work."

I laugh. He's got to be joking. "What the hell kind of information would I get to bring back to Jax? That makes no sense. Cole's birthday? A bio that Jax is likely already familiar with? You're delusional."

"You know, it's only a matter of time before Jax gets the shit storm that he deserves. With any luck it will start with Cole kicking his ass and putting that self-righteous prick in his place. Followed by this gym tanking. You may want to consider backing out now while you can. You're a pretty girl, I'm sure you can find another man easily."

I see red. Nothing he's saying makes a lick of sense, and calling Jax names just pisses me off. "Who the hell do you think you are? This is Jax's gym and as far as I can tell he's doing you a courtesy by letting you in here. Don't you dare stand here and disrespect him to me. You're a piece of shit for a father. You know, I actually felt bad for Jax because he doesn't have you in his life. But now? Now, I'm just happy he's gotten a disease like you out of his life. Jax is an amazing man and you don't deserve to have him in your life. It's only a matter of time before Cole comes to his senses as well." I spare Cole a brief glance and he makes eye contact with me briefly. I see a flash of regret flicker across his face before he looks down again.

Unfortunately, shifting my focus makes me unaware of Jerry moving closer to me until he grips my arm tightly. "Let go of me."

"You can't talk to me like that, you bitch. You're just a piece of pussy to my son. That doesn't grant you the right to talk to me like that."

"Get you're fucking hands off my girl right the hell now." Jax's voice is low, distinct and cold. You can hear his vicious feelings in each word. He's holding himself back from punching his own father. Shooting my glance over Jerry's shoulder to his face confirms my thoughts. He's standing there with Lily in his arms, looking absolutely livid. His jaw is clenched and his eyes are shooting daggers at his father. Dropping the pen and paper at my feet, I walk to him and take Lily from his arms. He immediately puts an arm around my waist and pulls me to him. "Get your shit and get the hell out of my gym," Jax demands of Jerry.

Jerry takes a step towards Jax, "You can't kick me out of here. This place is as much mine as it is yours. It belonged to MY father, you son of a bitch, and you cannot make me leave."

"I sure as hell can. Pops left this to *me*, not both of us. I've had enough of your hate and manipulations, and you sure as hell are not going to talk to Rowan like that. That's absolutely the last straw. Get. Out. Now."

"You'll regret this. Who's going to help organize your fights and get sponsors for everyone now?" Jerry seethes.

"It's not your concern. We'll figure it out just fine."

"If I go, that means Cole goes with me."

Jax looks at Cole, and Cole returns his look with apology written all over his face. Not once does he open his mouth to defend Jax, but he doesn't defend Jerry either. "That's up to Cole. He's always welcome here any time. You, are not."

Cole nods, walks to Jerry and takes his arm, "Let's go."

With a final stare at Jax, Jerry walks away. "This isn't over," Jerry throws over his shoulder as he leaves. Cole mouths the word "sorry" over his shoulder before turning back around.

Turning to Jax with apology in my eyes, I hold Lily tightly to me. She seems to feel the tension in the air and remains quiet. "Jax, I'm sorry. I was only trying to get Cole's information. Jerry didn't like it."

"Don't you dare blame yourself. This has been a long time in coming. It's actually a relief to kick his ass out. All I feel when he's around is tense, angry and frustrated. I'm tense waiting for his next rude comment. Angry because he can't get past his ridiculous feelings and for once be grateful that he has a son his own father loved enough to help take care of. And frustrated because nothing I've ever done is good enough for him. I can't get through to him. And I've tried long enough. I thought still having him around was better than never seeing him at all. I was wrong. It's best he's not here any longer."

"I'm still so sorry. This can't be easy and my heart is aching for you."

"It's not easy, you're right. But, I refuse to let his hate affect me any longer. This is his issue. I've already spent far too much of my life trying to change things, and I'm not going to do it anymore. I don't know why my grandfather did what he did, and it doesn't matter. I'm not going to carry my father's problems with me into the future. It's time to move on. I'm not going backward emotionally or mentally for him."

"I'm proud of you and I really respect your ability to do the right thing for you."

"Well, if you don't look out for your own heart, no one else will, right? Except, I promise to always help guard yours," he smiles at me and brushes his thumb over my cheek. I love it when he does that. He touches my heart with so many sweet gestures.

"And I yours," I promise.

"Come on. I've checked that order and it's all good. Let's get the hell out of here."

Jax insists we still eat lunch at the park. He doesn't want his father to mess up our day. Lily's propped in Jax's lap and trying to reach for his food. He hands her a cheerio and she happily brings it to her mouth. She looks adorable in her little sun hat, but her best accessory is the man holding her. "This was a great idea," I smile happily at Jax.

"I thought so too. It's a nice day out today. Not too hot yet, but it's coming."

"Yeah it is. We always skip the Spring and dive right into Summer here."

"Do you miss California?"

"No, not really. We've been here long enough that it's become home. When we first moved I was sad to leave a couple friends I had, but leaving was far more important. I've never been very good at making new friends. Tyson always fills that role for me, so I guess I've never really felt an absence of that in my life."

"That makes sense. He's your best friend so you never really needed anyone else."

I shrug, "I guess. I've never really thought about it. Besides, not everyone can have friends as great as yours."

"And yours now too. I'm pretty sure they like you more than me now."

Laughing, I take a drink of my lemonade. "I can't help it. I'm charming."

He laughs but it quickly fades. "By the way, I'm sorry that I had Lily in my arms when I came out and yelled at my dad. When I walked past the door of my office and saw my dad standing there, I knew that couldn't be good. The look on your face proved it. I just grabbed her and came over. I thought for a minute about asking Cindy at the front desk to hold her, but hell if I know if she has any experience with kids."

I almost choke on my lemonade. "So you're apologizing to me for not giving Lily to someone you weren't comfortable leaving her with? You never have to do that. Jax, do you have any idea how much it means to me that something like that would even cross your mind?"

He shrugs and looks away embarrassed and I reach out and grab his hand silently thanking him. "I care about her too."

Smiling softly I know that he more than cares for her, "I know." Knowing a change in subject is in order, I remember to ask him something I've been meaning to all week. "Oh, by the way, I would like your help with something."

"Name it."

"Tyson's birthday is coming up and I was wondering if you can help me pick out some MMA stuff for him? I don't know if he may need new gloves or work out clothes? I don't know. That's why I'm asking you."

He laughs, "I think I can be of assistance, no problem." His face falls, "Wait. If Ty's birthday is soon that means that yours is too. Why didn't you tell me?"

"It's not a big deal."

"Yes, it is. When is it?"

"Saturday."

"Saturday? As in the day after tomorrow?"

"Yeah," I smile sheepishly hoping he isn't mad at me.

Shaking his head, "Good thing for you we have a few things in my shop at the gym I can suggest and I can also show you a few things at the sports store in the mall. They actually carry some MMA items – cool t-shirts, hoodies, that kind of thing."

"Okay, that will be great. Do you have time now?"

"Absolutely, let's go."

A little while later, Lily is happily in her stroller and we're browsing through the racks of clothes. Jax is showing me the stuff he recommends and it's also giving me ideas for things I could maybe get for him at some point too. I end up with a couple t-shirts and shorts for Tyson that Jax says are great for training and a cool MMA brand shirt.

Walking out of the store, I stand on my tip toes and kiss him on the cheek, "Thank you for your help."

"You can thank me more properly later."

I laugh, "Sounds like a plan to me."

"I'm going to duck into the coffee shop and get a coffee. Would you like one?"

"Yeah, that would be great. Thank you."

"Alright, I'll be right back. Don't go far."

"I won't. I'm going to go check out that clothing store," I tell him point to it.

"Okay."

Walking over I window shop before I start to make my way into the store but a woman walks out of the store with a baby in her arms. I stop so suddenly, almost running into them with my stroller. I'm seriously not very good at maneuvering the damn thing; it's like me in a car with a stick shift - impossible. "Oh, I'm sorry."

"That's okay. Oh, your baby is so cute! How old is she?" She leans over a little to talk to Lily, "You're so cute. Yes you are."

"She's five months. How old is your little girl?" She's quite cute too. She's looking down at Lily and smiling. I love how babies are completely fascinated with other babies.

"She's eighteen months. Aren't they so much fun? Such little blessings." She smiles at me and I see she's quite pretty. Blonde hair, blue eyes that almost look grey and a sweet voice.

Right then, Lily starts fussing and I lean down to dig into my diaper bag, just as I see someone walk up to the girl out of the corner of my eye, "Oh there you are," she says. "Look at the baby, isn't she so cute? Katie is making friends."

"Hey babe. Here's your coffee." I spin and smile at Jax, taking the coffee from his hand.

"Thank you," I reply just as I hear, "Yeah, she's cute," from the man who walked up to the blonde.

Spinning around I stare in disbelief. Jason is standing next to the blonde, arm wrapped around her waist, staring at our child. Three things happen at once in what feels like slow motion. His eyes meet mine, Lily stops fussing, and my coffee hits the ground with a loud smack spraying everywhere.

"Rowan?"

Two men say my name simultaneously for two completely different reasons.

CHAPTER TWENTY-TWO

Jax

"Rowan?" I ask again. Her face is pale and her mouth is open. It finally dawns on me that she's staring at the guy in front of Lily's stroller. Instinctively, I move closer to Rowan and look down at Lily. Lily's fine, oblivious to everything around her except for the man across the way carrying dozens of balloons.

"Babe?" I ask again looking at her worriedly. Finally, she looks at me, and I see anger and panic in her eyes. "What's wrong?"

"Jill, why don't you go on over to the coffee place and get us our usual. I'll meet you there," the guy that's upset Rowan says.

Jill looks from Rowan to this guy and back again, nodding her head. "Okay." She takes her baby's hand and makes a waving motion, "Katie, say bye daddy, bye daddy," she says in a singsong voice. Then she smiles and walks away, the sound of her babbling to her baby getting quieter and quieter in her retreat.

Rowan makes a choking sound and I feel alarmed. She's looking at the man once again, and he's looking at her. "Daddy?" she whispers. "Is that your baby?" The man just stares at her, then his gaze moves to Lily. He reaches out as if to touch Lily and Rowan immediately reacts. "Don't you dare touch her!" She pulls the stroller back, out of his reach.

"What is going on?" I demand. I glare at this unknown person who is clearly upsetting my girl. What is he? Some child loving perv? . What did I miss? "Who the hell are you?" Rowan's look of astonishment and fear are worrying me.

"Answer me," Rowan hisses. "Is that your baby?"

The man stares at her before answering, "Yes."

"Oh my god. Oh my god. And the woman?" He just stares at her and doesn't answer. Rowan waits a beat before hissing, "It sure took you an awfully long time to park your fucking car, asshole. But now, it all makes sense."

What. The. Fuck.

Taking two steps forward, my fists automatically clench in realization. "You're the prick who left Rowan at the hospital in labor. You left her sitting and waiting for you. She sat there three hours waiting for your sorry ass to return. You left her, and you left your baby, and you have the guts to stand here and try to reach out to touch her? To even look at them? Get the fuck out of here."

He holds up his hands in a gesture of surrender, but instead of retreating, takes a step forward. "Wait. I can explain."

"It's taking all I have to not plunge my fist through your face. You can't offer an explanation good enough. If I were you, I'd back the hell up right now," I threaten.

He doesn't. He stares at me for a beat, before returning his attention to Rowan. I take it as pure defiance and take a step forward intending on following through with my threat. That is until Rowan places a hand on my chest silently stopping me. And that's when I catch the look on her face – she's pissed – but she's in control. I relax a little, her touch calming my innate need to protect and defend - for the moment. "Rowan, I-"

"You what, Jason? Got lost? Suffered from amnesia? Went crazy? Was in a coma until yesterday? Or how about, you have another baby with another woman that you never told me about? Suddenly, it's all clear. There's nothing you could possibly have to say that I want to hear right now. It's been five fucking months. Five months." She shakes her head in disbelief, "Just go. Pretend you never even saw us, because as far as I'm concerned, this never happened."

She grabs the stroller, and starts walking away, but not before she reaches for my hand. She doesn't look back, but I do. He's still standing there watching her walk away as if he has the right. There are so many things I would like to say to him, but she's more important right now. She's shaking badly, so I grab the stroller and steer us to the side, stopping for a moment. Without a word, I loop her arm through mine, kiss her forehead, then push the stroller towards the exit. We don't say a word until we are inside my truck. "Quite the day we've had. I'm thinking we should go back to my place and stay there for the next three days or so at least," I suggest.

Looking at me with a small smile she turns her body towards me. "That sounds like a good plan to me. I'm sorry, Jax. I just... I wasn't expecting that. To say the least."

"I don't understand why you're apologizing."

"I'm apologizing because I let him get to me so much that I left in the middle of our shopping trip. And because I didn't let you punch his face."

Laughing softly, I reach out and take her hand. "It's okay, Rowan. You're shocked, angry, and I would expect you're sad too. Do you want to talk about it?"

She sighs, "I'm just... so angry. Jax, when he disappeared, I sat in that waiting area and I tried calling him over, and over, and over. I left messages. Initially, I actually thought something might have happened to him." She laughs sardonically. "Then, at my emotional lowest, I actually went to his place and beat on the door. I cried on his doorstep, with our daughter in my arms, and begged him to open his door. I begged until his neighbors told me they'd call the police if I didn't leave."

Staying quiet, I stroke the back of her hand with my thumb, while I let her work through her emotions. Sneaking a peek at Lily, I'm happy to see she's sleeping. Her little hands rest on her chest and a pacifier moves in her mouth as she sucks it on and off in her sleep. My heart squeezes thinking about the man that abandoned her. I can't comprehend walking away from her, or her mother.

"I know I was deep into my post-partum depression when I acted that way, but I think I would have done it regardless. I felt so lost and confused. And you know what? Yes, I'm angry he abandoned us, but truly, I'm angrier for Lily. She doesn't deserve this."

"No, she doesn't. But neither do you."

She continues as if I never spoke, "Did you see the way he was looking at her? As if he was moved by how cute she is, like he wanted to touch her and hold her. And that baby… oh god, Jax. That baby is his. And that woman… I feel sick." She starts breathing hard and I help her push her head between her legs, taking deep breaths with her until she relaxes again.

"Better?" I ask.

She nods. "I never want to see him again."

"With any luck you won't. Give yourself time to process this and don't beat yourself up for feeling angry, sick and shocked."

"Yeah, you're right. I am that. Shocked. Running into him is not something that's crossed my mind. Maybe at first I thought about it, but not in a long time. Not now that I'm happy and Lily and I are good, you know?"

Not able to hold it in any longer, I lean towards her and give her a small kiss on the mouth, letting my lips linger for a moment as I hold her chin with my fingers. Tucking her hair behind her ear, I smile in reassurance. "You and Lily are great, not just good. You are the most amazing mom. Be proud of everything you've done. Don't let him mess with any of that. Don't second guess any of your decisions."

"No, I don't. Really, I don't. Like I said, I'm just angry. I will never, ever, understand how he could just abandon his child, whether he has another one or not."

"I hope you don't ever understand that, babe."

Suddenly she laughs prompting me to look at her curiously, "He didn't want Lily because he already had a baby. That's why he told me to get rid of my pregnancy."

"He did what?!" I slam my hand on the steering wheel in anger. That asshole.

She smiles sadly, "Really are you surprised?"

"I'm so sorry you had to endure all of this, but I'm so happy you aren't falling for his bullshit anymore."

"Me too." She smiles and then initiates a kiss on my lips. "Thank you for being here for me."

"Always. I'm guarding your heart, remember?"

"I remember. And I yours."

We share a smile and without another word I head back to my place.

That Saturday evening, I'm sitting in the diner waiting for Rowan to get off work. I'm taking her back to her place when she's done to spend the evening with her. It's her birthday, and I have a surprise. I hate that she's working on her birthday, but she insisted, so I let it go. I'm anxious to get her out of here.

When Zane casually walks in and sits at my table I smile at his nonchalance even though the meeting is planned. We just don't want Rowan to know. "Hey," I greet him.

"Yo. How's it going?"

"It's going. Is everything ready?"

"Yep. She gets off in the next half hour, right?"

"Yeah."

"Do you think she knows?"

"No. She thinks we're going back to her place to have dinner together with Ty."

"Cool."

"Thanks for all your help."

"No thanks needed. She's yours, that makes her ours too."

"Yeah, I know. I'm glad. Shh, here she comes."

Not a moment later, Rowan is standing at our table, "Hey, Zane. How are you?"

"I'm good, beautiful, thanks."

"Can I get you something to drink or eat?"

"I'll just have a water, please. I texted Jax and he told me he was here so I came by to talk to him."

"Oh, is this about all that stuff with Jerry?" She assumes.

"Huh?" I kick him under the table, "Oh yeah. That's why. We're just working out how we're going to move forward."

"Any ideas?" She looks back and forth between both of us.

"No," I reply and Zane shakes his head.

Her brow furrows, "What's involved in linking up sponsors and organizing the fights? Is it hard?"

"No, not hard," I reply. "It's basically like sales as far as the sponsors go. You have to give them a reason to want to collaborate and lining up the fights is just being persistent and having contacts in the industry. Fortunately, all of us have those contacts. My dad's went a little deeper because he's been in the industry longer, but technically we could call them as well and work with them."

Rowan sits next to me and I scoot over a little making room for her, "Well, can I help?"

I stare at her for a minute, and then look at Zane who's smiling ear to ear. "You would do that?" I ask.

"Well sure. If it's something that can be learned, I'm happy to help out."

"I think it's a great idea. " Zane adds. "Rowan you would be a great person to represent us."

"I like this idea, babe. Let me think on it some more, and we'll talk about it later."

Her face falls, "Oh, okay. I mean, of course. You need to think about it. I just thought I would offer because I'm happy to help. You know… if you want me to."

"No, you misunderstand. I think it will be a great fit, I don't doubt that at all. I just want to put together a formal offer with what exactly the position will entail as well as monetary compensation information. I just need to work out the details."

"I don't want to get paid for helping you, Jax. It doesn't feel right."

"You wouldn't just be helping me. Let's talk about it later, okay?"

"Yeah, okay. We'll talk." She gets up to check on another table.

"Really, Jax. She really would be great."

Smiling I nod my head, "Yeah, I think so too."

"Are you worried about having her integrated even more into your life?"

"Not at all."

"You really like her," he says.

"I more than like her, Zane."

"Whoa," he rubs his hand along his jaw. "Have you told her that yet?"

"No. I don't want to scare her. It isn't time yet."

"Wow. I'm happy for you man."

"Do I sound like a chick if I say that I just hope she feels the same way?"

"Yeah, a little, but I don't think you have to worry about that. Is she doing okay after everything your dad said to her? I still can't believe he actually said that shit to her."

"He definitely went too far. I couldn't let him get away with that."

"Definitely not. You know, we've all been hoping for a while you would finally do something about him. All he does is cause trouble and run his mouth. I know he's your dad, but enough is enough."

"Well, I told him not to come back. Cole is welcome any time. I still don't get what the hell he's doing, but it's his choice. He can come in whenever he wants, but not with him."

"I told the other guys too, so they're aware of the situation as well. If he comes in, he'll be asked to leave."

"Good."

"What else is going on?"

"What do you mean?"

"Dude, I've known you since we were kids. You're stressed. What else is bugging you?"

I sigh. I'm not really comfortable talking about Rowan's business with anyone, but it would be nice to talk to someone. "Rowan and I ran into her ex at the mall."

"Her ex? As in the asshole that left her and Lily?"

"Yes."

"Oh fuck. Are the cops going to show up any time to arrest you for assault and battery?"

"No," I smile at Zane's assumption. "I didn't punch him - didn't even touch him. Not that I wasn't tempted, but Rowan's emotions were more important and I just wanted to get her the hell away from him."

"I don't know how you refrained yourself."

"It wasn't easy, but it would have scared Lily and that was the last thing Rowan needed. It would have felt really good though."

"No doubt. Do you need anything? Does she? Are you worried he's going to come around now?"

"I really don't know what he's going to do. Before he could say or do much we walked away. She asked me not to tell Ty, because she's afraid he'll show up at Jason's place and beat the hell out of him putting him right back in jail. Can't say I blame her for that worry."

"Definitely not. He's completely hot headed. He's already been at the gym again since he's been out of jail and dude has some serious anger issues."

"I know. Hopefully he can channel them in the right direction and win some fights for gym promotion."

"Let's hope. Alright, I'm going to head out. I'll see you shortly."

"Alright, see you soon."

Not long after he leaves, Rowan is off work. She's tired, but thankfully it isn't too bad since she worked a short shift. "I hope you're planning on feeding this birthday girl because she's hungry."

Smiling, I back her up against the side of my truck. "Just what kind of hunger are we talking about here?"

She laughs and pushes her hips against me and sighs softly, "Both, definitely both."

"That can be arranged." I lean down and put my mouth on hers. Gripping my hand in her hair, I tilt her head and open my mouth to deepen the kiss and moan when she responds in kind. Each and every time I kiss this woman I feel fireworks. I hope it never stops. Pulling away I adjust myself with a smile. "Come on let's go."

We hop in the truck, and I start heading to her place. "I've already got dinner arranged for you. It's a surprise."

"Yeah? Sounds fabulous. Dinner, kisses from my baby, and you. Perfect birthday if you ask me."

Smiling, I pull into her driveway and am about to get out of the truck when she stops me. "Wait." She unbuckles her seatbelt and takes me by surprise when she straddles me in my seat. Before I can say a word, she puts her mouth on mine and kisses me hard. When she grinds her center into me, it's all I can do not to reach under the skirt she's wearing, yank her panties to the side and stroke her until she comes.

Remembering where we are, I pull away breathless. "Wow," I murmur.

"Just a preview for later," she winks saucily making me laugh. She climbs off of me and hops out the door. I open my door and she laughs when she comes around and finds me adjusting myself.

"Don't laugh. I doubt Ty would appreciate me walking inside with a hard on no matter how much he may approve of us."

"Come on, lover boy." We walk to the door and I make sure to stand behind her when she opens it. Stepping into the house she flips the light on, then screams when several people jump out at her and scream, "SURPRISE!"

CHAPTER TWENTY-THREE

Rowan

Jumping out of my skin I throw my hands over my mouth and look around the room in complete and utter surprise. Tyson, Zane, Dylan, Cole, Levi, Ryder and Audrey are all here. There are a few people I don't know, and I find myself anxious to meet them. "Happy Birthday!" Tyson calls out while bouncing Lily on his hip, which is followed by everyone else calling out their wishes too.

"Thank you so much!" Spinning around I put my hands on Jax's shoulders and smile, "You did this?"

"I had some help."

"But this was all your idea wasn't it?" He just shrugs his shoulders. "Thank you so much! I don't even know what to say. I've never had a surprise party before. My mom never…" I stop knowing an explanation isn't needed.

"Well, then it was way past due. Come on, let's go get some food. I had the Italian place cater in, and Zane helped with a last minute alcohol run, while Tyson decorated and assisted with the food delivery. It was a group effort."

When we turn to head to the table, Tyson catches my eye and I mouth a "thank you" to him. He smiles and takes Lily's hand and waves it at me in hello making me laugh. Taking plates off the table, we begin filling them, then everyone else follows suit. As I'm walking towards a seat, Ryder stops me, "Happy birthday, Rowan. This is my friend, Abby."

"Hi Abby, it's nice to meet you." Abby looks like Ryder's kind of girl - blonde hair falling in waves down her back, bright red lips, and huge boobs. She even has tattoos inside her wrists and one on her upper arm. "Thank you for coming."

She smiles at me briefly, then wraps her arms around Ryder, burying her face in his neck. I take that as my cue to walk away. I don't get far before Levi, and the girl next to him, stop me. "Rowan, I'd you to meet my sister, Sami. Sami, this is Jax's girl, Rowan."

"Hi, Sami. It's great to meet you." She's super cute. She has the same blonde hair and green eyes as Levi and the blonde streaks and tan skin she's sporting gives her the same surfer look Levi has. It's obvious they're related.

"You too, Rowan. Levi has great things to say about you."

"Sami's home from college for a long weekend. She's attending California State University."

"Ah, I confess I'm envious of your tan. Do you spend a lot of time on the beach?"

She smiles, "As much as I can. When Levi comes and visits me for the weekend, you all should make it a group road trip. It would be fun to hang out."

"That does sound fun. I'll have to talk to Jax about that." They're attention is diverted by Dylan calling their names, so they head to the table where he's standing.

"Happy birthday, Rowan." Looking into the kind eyes of Audrey, I smile and set down my plate on an end table so I can give her a hug.

"Thanks for coming, Audrey."

"I wouldn't miss it, sweetie. I was excited when Jax asked me to come."

Finding Jax across the room talking to Zane, I smile at him. "He's so great, isn't he? I can't believe how lucky I am to have him. He's been a huge blessing to Lily and me from the very beginning."

"Oh good," Audrey claps her hands. "I'm so glad he finally told you." Audrey smiles and bounces on her feet in excitement and I feel confused. "I didn't like that he asked me not to tell you, but he made me promise and said he would tell you eventually. When he would drop off all the packages for you, he'd sit and visit with Lily. I knew even then how much he adored your little girl. I could see it in his eyes. So, I trusted that he would tell you when the time was right."

Doing my best to follow along I realize the worst thing I can do is let her know I have no clue what she's talking about. Not if I want to find out more. "Yeah, I was so surprised. I still don't know how to thank him," I watch her closely hoping she buys my response.

"I was always blown away by the amount of stuff he would buy. You know, I asked him once how he knew what things you'd need for Lily. Considering he doesn't have any kids of his own, because I asked you see, I was always surprised he purchased just the right things. Diapers sure, everyone knows that, but burp cloths, pacifiers, bottles, extra nipples, blankets, teething rings, you name it, he got it. He told me he actually bought some parenting magazines and asked the people that worked at the baby store. Can you believe that?"

"No, no I can't."

"Anyway, I hated lying to you, but I hope you understand. He was just trying to look out for you the only way he knew how. I thought it was admirable of him."

"I'm not angry, Audrey. Not at all. Will you please excuse me?"

"Of course, sweetie."

Immediately walking in Jax's direction I do my best to hold my tears at bay. He looks up as I approach and his smile drops when he sees my face. Before he can say a word, I look at Zane. "I need to steal him away for a few minutes, please."

"Of course." Zane looks at me curiously, but then grabs the beer Cole is handing him and turns away.

Taking Jax by the hand, I lead him to my room and close the door behind us, locking it. It's dark in the room, the only light coming from a small night-light I have plugged to assist if Lily awakens during the night. "What's wrong, babe?"

Twisting him around so his back hits the door, I look up into his face. It's covered in shadows but I can still make out his eyes and they are staring worriedly at me. "Audrey had something interesting to say."

His brow furrows, "Yeah?"

"Yeah." I wait a beat to see if he says anything, but he just stares at me waiting to hear what I know. "Were you ever going to tell me?"

Looking at me blankly, I'm sure he's going to tell me he doesn't know what I'm talking about, but he surprises me. Dropping any façade he was hoping to keep, he lets out a breath, and runs a hand through his hair. "Maybe. Probably. I don't know. It doesn't really matter."

"Doesn't matter? How can you say that? What you did…" I look away and blink my eyes repeatedly holding back tears.

"Please don't be mad at me," he begs.

Snapping my eyes back to his I look at him in disbelief. "Mad at you? How could I possibly be mad at you? God, I am *so* in love with you already and this just makes me fall even harder, and I didn't think that was possible. What you did for Lily and me? It's everything, Jax. It means *everything* to me."

Without another word I launch myself at him. I can't wait any longer; I need my lips on his, our bodies to touch, and his hands on me. As I kiss him, I hope that each movement of my lips, and every touch of my tongue, is a testament to showing him with actions what I said with words. I put everything I have, everything I feel into that kiss. He's still for a moment and then it's like we're kindling set ablaze. He turns and presses me against the door, my legs wrap around him and I twist my hands into his hair. He pulls away from me with a question in his eyes. His breaths are just as heavy and rapid as mine, conveying his desire. "I want you," I tell him and reach my hands down to undo his belt.

"Are you sure? There's people-"

"We'll be quick," I promise.

He doesn't say another word. After I undo his belt and release him, he rips my panties to the side and enters me with a deep upward thrust. Throwing my head back with a moan, it bangs against the door. If anyone heard, I could care less. All my thoughts and focus are completely on the man moving between my thighs. Kissing him again I nibble on his bottom lip then pull away. Running my hands down my breasts temptingly, I wish they were bare for his mouth, but this is supposed to be fast. Moving my fingers between my own thighs, I begin rubbing my clit while looking into his eyes.

His reaction is instant, "Oh, fuck. You're so sexy."

Smiling at him, I continue circling my fingers feeling sexy as hell. He clutches my hips as he keeps up his pace and the movement of his hips. "Yes. God. Jax. So. Good."

Just as I fall off the ledge, losing myself to nothing but sensation, he stiffens and releases almost immediately with a whispered, "I love you so much."

Looking into his eyes, I know he sees the question in mine when his lips turn up at the corners. "I've loved you for a while, I've just been waiting for you to figure out how you feel. I was afraid of telling you too soon and scaring you off after everything you've been through."

Laughing I squeeze him and place kisses all over his face. "I'm not going anywhere," I promise.

He walks me to the bathroom, keeping us joined. Placing me gently on the sink, he pulls out of me and uses a cloth to clean us up. When he's finished and we're dressed once again, I look deep into his eyes, "I can't believe everything you've done for me. I feel like I'm always thanking you. I'm not sure what I bring into this relationship, but I promise to do my best to give you everything that you've given me."

"You already do. Don't you see that? Before you, I pretty much had no life. It revolved around fighting, the gym, and making a conscious effort to put my dad's shit and drama behind me. You... you're a game changer. The gym and fighting come second; you and Lily are everything to me. Putting you first has never even been a question, but almost a necessity. I felt a connection to you from the minute I saw you and it's only grown since then. You help me feel worthy, needed, wanted, and loved for the first time, in a long time. At least not since my grandfather passed away, and even then showing emotion wasn't easy for him."

"I love you so much. As crazy as it is, I'm glad for the circumstances that led me to meeting you at the hospital."

"I know what you mean, in a weird way, I'm thankful for them too even though I hate it at the same time. And, I love you too. Now let's get back to your party. We're already going to get enough shit from the guys."

"Okay," I smile feeling light and happy.

"Oh, wait." I spin around and look at him. He pulls a small flat box out of his pocket. "Since we're alone, I'd like to give you this."

Looking at him shyly, I take the box out of his hand and open it. Inside is a beautiful silver necklace that is the form of a mother embracing a child. "Oh. It's so beautiful."

"I want you to have a constant reminder of what a wonderful mother you are. I know with everything you experienced with your mom it's easy to fear you could be like her, but you are nothing like her. You love your daughter with a passion that grows every day. I'm honored to be a part of it. Whenever you doubt yourself, wrap your hand around this and remember. Remember that you are loved. Remember that you are worthy. And remember that as lucky as you are to have Lily, she's just as lucky to have you."

Tears are falling down my face. He couldn't have said anything more perfect. "I love it. So much. Thank you."

"I love you."

"I don't think I'll ever get tired of hearing you say that."

"Good. Get used to it babe."

He helps me put the necklace on, then we walk out of the room hand in hand. All the guys turn and look at us with ornery grins and smirks on their faces. Rather than embarrassment, a sense of pride runs through me. I wrap my hand around my necklace, loving the feel of it, the solid reminder of love around my neck. Then I confidently take Jax's hand and we tightly grip each other. Meanwhile, Jax gives them all death glares and flips them off, daring them to say a word, which makes me laugh out loud.

Grabbing my plate from where I left it, I take it to the kitchen to warm up my food, suddenly feeling famished. As flashes of our activity against the door come to mind, I realize why I'm so hungry. After I finish eating, while making small talk with Levi, I grab my drink and start walking to where Jax is sitting so I can plant myself on his lap. I stop when a knock sounds on the door. "I'll get it," I call out.

When I see who's standing on the other side, I freeze, shocked at the sight. So many thoughts enter my mind at once. What is he doing here? Why now? What does he want with me, with Lily? My mouth doesn't move as fast as my mind and all that comes out is a squeak.

"Hi," he gives me a timid smile that has no effect on me what so ever. "I'm sorry for just showing up like this. I remembered that today is your birthday and I brought you these," he holds up a bouquet of lilies, of all the flowers in the world, he brings lilies, "and was hoping we could talk."

I think it's the lilies that snap me out of it. I walk outside and close the door a little behind me trying to prevent the bomb that will blow if Jax and Tyson see this. "I don't have anything to say to you. just leave before Tyson or Jax sees you. They won't take kindly to your being here."

Before he can say a word, it's already too late. The door opens and Jax is next to me.

"What the fuck are you doing here?"

Jason looks at Jax and quickly dismisses him looking back at me, "Rowan, please. I just want to talk to you." He takes a step forward prompting me to immediately take one back. I'm startled when I feel hands at my waist steadying me. Looking over my shoulder, I see that Levi, Cole, Zane, Ryder and Dylan are all standing behind me as well, arms crossed, anger on their faces. Feeling choked up at the sight, it also makes me stand taller when I turn back to Jason. "Just leave. I don't want to talk to you. There isn't anything you can possibly say to justify your actions."

His face screws up in anger, "You can't just turn me away. She's my daughter too. I have rights!"

"It takes more than sperm to make a father, asshole," Jax says and I nod in agreement.

Jason opens his mouth to respond, but angry words halt his response. "What. The. Fuck. Is. He. Doing. Here?" Tyson makes his way through the guys and stands with his hands clenched into fists, glaring at Jason.

Immediately, I stand in front of him, but Jax doesn't like that. "No, babe. Get back."

"Get out of the way," Tyson demands. "I'm going to show this asshole exactly what I think about what he did to you and Lily."

"Lily? That's her name?" Jason asks.

Tyson takes a step forward, but Dylan and Cole are at his sides each grabbing an arm to hold him back. "He's not worth it, bro." Dylan says.

"Not here, not now," Cole adds.

"Just leave, Jason. All you're doing is pissing people off," I sigh worried about my brother getting himself thrown back in jail.

"I'm not leaving until you talk to me," Jason threatens.

"Go home to your other baby."

"Other baby? What the fuck does that mean, Row?"

Looking to Jason I ask, "Do you want to explain or shall I?" He remains quiet. "Jax and I ran into Jason, his girlfriend and their baby at the mall."

With a roar, Tyson lunges at Jason, but the guys hold him back. It was stupid of me to do that, I knew Tyson would react that way. I'm just angry. Levi and Dylan drag Tyson away kicking and screaming. I look at the remaining men in my life, "Guys, just give us a minute."

Jax spits, "Fuck that."

Reaching for Jax's hand, I turn to Zane, Ryder and Cole. "Jax is here. Just give us a minute." They all go back in the house, Zane the last one in. Turning back to Jason, I yell, "How dare you come to my home and start making demands of me. You want to talk me about your rights? Are you fucking kidding me? After everything you've done? You don't deserve to even look at her let alone try to suggest you should have access to her life."

"She's mine too. You can't keep her from me."

"She belongs to this man beside me, more than she's ever belonged to you. He's been her father in every way, taking care of us when he barely even knew me. Loving both of us and showing an interest more than you ever have before and after I had her. Don't you dare tell me that she's yours."

Jax catches my gaze and I see love, devotion and protection in his eyes. His hand tightens in mine and he asks Jason, "Why do you care? Why now?"

"I made a mistake because I was afraid."

Staring at him wide-eyed I begin to laugh. "Are you serious? *You* were scared? You? I'm the one who carried her for nine months. I'm the one who went to doctor appointments and birthing classes and visited the hospital by myself. Shit! I had to give birth. I'm the one that was left at the hospital. I'm the one that came home and had no clue what I was doing. I'm the one that had post-partum depression so severe, I thought about hurting myself. I'm the one that was left alone to figure all this shit out. Not you. And you have the nerve to stand here and tell me that *you* were scared? Fuck you, Jason."

"How many times am I going to have to apologize to you? I'll just keep showing up and bothering you until you talk to me and let me see her."

"Are you threatening my girl? Because I think you better rethink your words."

"Your girl? That's rich. How long have you even known her? How long have you been together? A month? Please, not only is that *my* baby, but her mom was *my* girl for over a year."

Jax takes a step forward, but I squeeze his hand. "You want to take me to court? Fine. Do it. I'll get you for the back child support you owe. Of course, that's after you pay for a paternity test."

"Why would I need a test? She's mine."

"The birth certificate doesn't say so."

"What? What are you talking about?"

"The birth certificate doesn't list you as the father."

"Why would you do that?"

"Are you seriously asking me that question? Maybe because I was angry and abandoned."

He sighs and a flash of irritation crosses his face and for a blink I see the real Jason, the one that I didn't see clearly, for far too long. "Look, I made a mistake. A mistake that I regret, okay?"

"Why?"

"Why what?"

"Why do you regret it?"

"Because I do, what do you want me to say? Haven't you ever done something that you regret?"

"First of all, if I have to tell you what to say, then that's a problem. Secondly, as to your second question, if it wasn't for Lily, I wish that the moment I'd seen you, I had walked the hell away. I'm done with this conversation. Jax, let's go inside."

"I'll be back, Rowan. I'm not giving up."

Ignoring him, I walk inside with Jax's arm around me.

CHAPTER TWENTY-FOUR

Jax

The next day, I'm still feeling angry that Jason interrupted Rowan's party. The rest of the night continued after he left, all the guys doing their best to make Rowan laugh and enjoy herself, but a heavy weight was in the room that wasn't there before. For a while, Ty even paced the room like a tiger trying to work out his anger. After everyone left he and Rowan had words. He was angry she wouldn't let him say his piece, or go after Jason.

Thankfully, Lily was kept away from all the drama. Audrey kept her close while we dealt with Jason, but when Rowan came inside; she made a beeline for her baby. Rowan held her close until she fell asleep in her arms. The three of us sat nestled together on the couch while we talked with everyone around us. I found myself frequently looking down at the two of them, reveling in the feeling of contentment that washed over me at the sight.

Smiling, while I wash my hair in the shower, I think about how Rowan woke me up this morning. A thank you for the party and gift she said. Damn but that woman is sexy. I tried to drag her in the shower with me, but Lily started crying in hunger so she went to care for her while I get ready. I need to head to the gym and take care of a few things.

After I'm dressed I walk out and head to the kitchen. Ty's door is open and he's not in there so either he's gone or with Rowan. When I hear her talking I assume she's talking to him or Lily, but when I hear her say, "Jason, I don't know about that," I realize she's not speaking to either of them. When she speaks again with no response,

I look around the corner into the kitchen and see she's on the phone. Ducking back out of sight, I unashamedly stand there and listen to her side of the conversation.

"I don't really know that meeting for lunch is going to help. I've already told you where I stand." She sighs and I hear a chair scrape across the floor, then creak as she sits down. "Yes, we did have some good times," she says and I clench my teeth. When she laughs, my fists follow. "No, I did not. That was your entire fault. I was an innocent bystander." Oh well isn't this sweet, a walk down memory lane? "No, stop distracting me from the point. I heard what you had to say, but I'm not in a place where I can get over what you did." Okay well that's better. "Yes, that is a good point and I will try to do that. I need time. I don't know about that. I'll call you back when I decide. Yes, we certainly did make a beautiful baby." My stomach clenches this time. "Don't say that to me, Jason, didn't I just see you with a girl at the mall? Plus, if that were true, you wouldn't have made the decisions you did. Alright. Bye."

Standing there for a moment longer, I walk around the corner and see her sitting at the table with her head in her hands. I can't help but feel anger. The thought of them together, the fact that they made a baby, all of it crushes me. I know she can't change any of this, but it's always going to be here between us.

"Well from this end at least that sounded like an interesting conversation," I say loudly. Rowan jumps in her seat and stands, knocking the chair to the floor. She spins around and stares at me open-mouthed.

"You were listening?"

"Yes," I answer without guilt.

"Jax, I can explain."

I hold up a hand to stop her. "I don't think I want to hear it. I don't understand why you continue to give him the time of day."

"I'm trying to put my own feelings aside and consider those of my daughter."

"She's a baby. She doesn't have thoughts on the matter yet."

"Which is exactly why I have to make sure I'm doing the right thing for her and not letting my personal feelings get in the way."

"What did he say to you at the end of the conversation that made you tell him not to say it?"

She stills and the tightening of her mouth and the way she bites her lip tells me she doesn't want to answer, but I wait it out, holding her stare. "He told me he still has feelings for me," she whispers and I freeze.

"Do you still have feelings for him too?"

"No," she says without hesitation. Truth is, I really don't think has feelings left for him. I don't even necessarily believe that he has feelings for her – not real ones anyway. It isn't even that she's trying to figure out what to do, I get it, I really do. But what I realize in that moment, is that I'm completely destroyed over their history together. No matter where she and I go from here, he will always be the father of her baby, not me.

"I need to leave," I announce before spinning around and walking to her room to grab my wallet and keys.

"What? What do you mean? You can't just leave."

When I turn around she's standing behind me. "I can't deal with this right now. I have stuff I need to do at the gym and I have feelings about this whole situation that I can't even…" I run my hand through my hair cutting off not able to finish the sentence. I push my way past her and walk to the door.

"Please. Don't leave me. Let's talk about this."

Looking at her with my hand on the doorknob I give her a sad smile, "I'm not leaving you, or us, but I'm not ready to talk about this either." Then I walk out the door.

Sitting in my office I stare at the same fucking invoice over and over not seeing a damn thing. Stupid thoughts have taken over my mind - thoughts of them together. I know Ty suggested to me what the reality of Rowan's relationship with Jason was like, but stupid images of them together haunt my mind. Her kissing him. Him rubbing her pregnant belly. Her legs wrapped around him. Her giving him the sassy, sexy smile she gives me. I pound the heel of my hand against my head hoping to bang out the images.

"Hey, bro, what the hell's wrong with you?"

I look up at Ryder. "Hey, nothing. Just a headache," I lie. "You here to work out already?"

"Yeah, getting an early start. Saw you in here and thought I'd ask how Rowan's doing?"

"She's doing okay. I'm worried about how far Jason is going to keep pushing this. She hasn't threatened to take him to court or anything yet, but it may not be long before we need to play that card."

"Understandable. I have to admit I'm surprised to see you here. What are you working on?"

"I need to get the fight night information to the printer to get signs made. I'm ordering the trophies and getting vendors here. Rowan had a great idea about getting local businesses to sponsor us, so I'm putting some of her ideas into action as well."

"You going to hire her, or what?"

"Yeah, hopefully. I'm not sure how stubborn she's going to be on me paying her to work here, but that's another thing I'm working on. I need to draw up a proposal."

"She'll be great. And I bet you'd like to put a desk for her in here right next to yours."

"Why the hell not? I think that's a great idea. Thanks, Ryder."

We laugh and he walks out leaving me to my work. A few hours later, I decide to head back to Rowan's. I've pouted enough and she and I need to talk this out. Fact is, I'd like to ask her to move in with me. I want our relationship to keep morning forward, and all this other stuff getting in the way is pissing me off. She may have reservations about it because she won't want to leave Tyson alone, but I would love to have her and Lily with me. Holding them last night and reveling in how whole it made me feel, I realize I want them to be with me twenty-four seven. Moving in with me would certainly facilitate that wish.

Pulling into the drive, I instantly feel rage when I see Jason standing at the front door again. What the fuck is he doing here again? Rowan's standing in the doorway with Lily in her arms. He's touching her arm and Rowan at least looks furious. They both look my way when I pull in and I fly out of my truck, slam the door and stalk up to the front door.

"Jax-" Rowan starts but I don't even look at her. Jason has that smirk on his face again and I'm done. I cock my right fist back and let it fly straight into his jaw knocking him flat on his ass. Standing over him, breath heaving, I point at him, "Leave, right now."

He stands rubbing his jaw and I feel satisfaction run through me. He looks from Rowan to me, and back again. "I need to get going anyway." The way he looks at Rowan and Lily before he stalks away makes me want to tear him apart limb by fucking limb, slowly so he feels excruciating pain.

We stand silently as he leaves giving Rowan a wave. Turning to her after he's gone I'm surprised to see fury covering her features. "What the hell was that, Jax?"

"Seriously? That's what you have to say to me right now?"

"What do you mean?"

"What do I mean?" I shake my head in disbelief and then raise my voice repeating myself, "What do I mean? Are you kidding me? What the fuck was he doing here? Why was he touching Lily?"

"Jax, calm down."

"Don't tell me to calm down. I'm gone for a few hours and come back and you guys are suddenly this cute little family?"

"Cute family? No, that's not true. He came by again, and I

answered the door holding Lily. What the hell was I supposed to do?"

"How about slam the door in his face? I don't want you talking to him or even around him when I'm not here."

"I can take care of myself."

"That's not the point!"

"Then what is? What am I supposed to do? Fact is, he is Lily's father. Whether I like it or not. And I'm just tired of dealing with this and worrying about what he's going to do next. I just wanted to hear him out and get it over with."

"Oh, now this I have to hear. Please tell me what he had to say."

"It was the usual crap. He apologized, he wants to see Lily and be involved. Said he just freaked out when he found out he was having another child."

"I reminded him that he's clearly in a relationship with someone else and that was also the problem. He claims he wasn't with her then, but I don't believe him, nor do I give a shit. He actually told me that I have some blame in this too."

"Are you kidding me?"

"No. He said when I was pregnant all I cared about was the baby. I stopped caring about what he wanted and our relationship changed because I put the baby first."

"Oh my god. He's blaming you for looking toward the future and a life with a new baby."

"Yeah, and I don't agree with what he said, at all. Right before you got here I threatened to take him to court for back child support and to settle this legally because I'm tired of dealing with all of this. I decided to hear him out because of my need to give Lily a normal family, with her mom and dad in her life. That's all it was."

"You've got to be kidding me."

"Please don't be mad. I'm just trying to put aside my own personal feelings and do the right thing for Lily."

"And where does that leave us exactly?"

"I don't understand the question."

"Well, while you, Jason and Lily are busy being a quote, unquote, normal family, where does that leave me and us?"

"It leaves us as we are. I love us. I love you. I want us to be together."

"But you also want Jason?"

Her brow furrows, "Not in the way I think you're suggesting."

I'm so angry I can't even stop to think about her feelings and where she's coming from right now. "And what if I told you that I don't want that asshole to have anything to do with Lily, or us?"

"I don't know that I have a choice in the matter. Like it or not he is Lily's father."

"I want to be her damn father!" I bellow surprised at my own outburst, but with the words I realize the truth behind them. "I love her. And I love you. And I don't want him or anyone else intruding on that."

"I understand, I do." She walks to me and reaches out a hand but I back up from her and hate the flash of pain I cause to cross her face. "I'm just trying to be smart here. I'm trying to do what I think is best all the way around."

"And if I don't agree with your choice?"

"I don't know. I'd like for us to talk about this and come to a decision together. Like I said though, I don't know how much of a choice I really have if Jason forces me to take him to court because he doesn't give up. I will say that he didn't take too kindly to that when I brought it up."

Staring at her and Lily, I want nothing more than to gather them into my arms and run away. Far away where no one else can threaten what we have. Where I can adopt Lily and make her mine. Where I can marry Rowan and make her mine too. I don't like feeling threatened, not one bit. As if Lily can sense my feelings she reaches her arms out for me and it breaks something inside of me to not take her from Rowan and hold her close, but I can't deal with this right now. "I need to go."

"Again? You just got back. We need to talk about this."

"I can't deal with this right now."

"Jax, please."

Spinning around I look her in the eye, "One thing I think you need to think about is your definition of a normal family. Your thoughts on the matter are screwed up. You may take Jason to court and he may end up getting visitation and all that shit, but what about the future? What happens when Jason freaks out and bails again? How will that affect Lily then? I know that isn't something you can control or anticipate but if Lily having her biological mother and father in her life is how you view a normal family, then I think that's a problem. You need to reevaluate your definition of an 'ordinary' family."

"What do you mean?"

I sigh and rub my temples, "That's the thing. If I have to explain it to you, then that's a problem."

With that I stalk to my truck and leave. I can't stay. I need to think and work out what I'm feeling. Deciding to head back to the gym, I try to shift my mind to the equipment I'm going to beat the shit out of to work out this aggression. It works for a second, until I look in my rearview mirror and see Rowan and Lily still standing where I left them.

CHAPTER TWENTY-FIVE

Rowan

Hours have passed since Jax left, and I'm lying in bed trying to get some sleep. Tyson came home for a little while and tried to cheer me up, but as soon as it became apparent his efforts were futile, he asked if I would be okay and then left. I have no idea where he went at this time of night, but he's a big boy and I'm too exhausted to worry about it.

My eyes are swollen, my head aches, and my nose is running from all the tears I've shed. I've started to call Jax several times, but have miraculously managed to refrain from doing so. He said he wasn't ready to talk and I'm trying like hell to respect that, even though it's so damn hard.

When Jason called this morning, he pushed me again to let him see Lily and to talk things out. When he showed up on the doorstep I knew that if I kept slamming the door in his face, this was just going to keep replaying over and over. I guess I thought trying to settle things was the best strategy for everyone. I'm the queen of asking why. All my life people have only done things because they want something in return, and I know that Jason is no exception. I've only ever had two people in my life that have been an exception to that, two people that truly love me, and their acts are based on love, not want. Tyson and Jax. I realize that it's been a long time since I've felt the need to ask Jax or Tyson why. It's progress because usually I automatically assume the worst, but I've come a long way and I know Jax is whom I have to thank for that.

Punching the pillow at my head, I reposition trying to find a more comfortable spot, but it's not working. I'm startled when my phone rings. Looking at the screen I'm disappointed when Jason's name is on the screen. With a sigh, I answer. "Hello?"

"Hi, it's Jason."

"Now isn't really a good time."

"Why? Because your boyfriend is there?"

"What do you want, Jason?"

"I want to know if you thought about me being able to see Lily. I really want this to work out."

"I really haven't given it any thought since I saw you to be honest. It's kind of been a crazy day."

"When are you going to figure it out?"

"I don't know. I told you that I need some time. You're asking me to just put aside everything and make a fair decision for you, for me, for Lily, for other people in my life and I don't know if I can do that. I really don't know if I can set aside my emotions and figure this out on my own. Maybe we should take this to court, Jason. Let a court decide what your child support should be, what you owe me for these last few months and what your visitation should be. I don't know what's fair, I don't know what's right here and frankly, I wouldn't mind someone else making the decision for me at this point."

"Are you fucking kidding me? Look, I've been patient, but the fact is, I can't afford to go to court. If you try then I will disappear. I can't afford to pay you back child support or support going forward. I have another kid and a wife to support."

"A wife? You're married?"

"Yep. Surprise! The reason I left you and the brat is because I'm married and didn't want my wife to find out."

"But your apartment, the time we spent together…"

"Yeah, not my only place. Not that it's any of your fucking business. Between my apartment, and supporting Jill and Katie, I can't add your kid to the mix too. Just let me help take care of the kid outside of court and we'll call it good, okay? I'll give you money any time I have some extra. I'm sure we can come to some kind of arrangement. No need to go to court."

I'm not able to answer him for a solid minute. I am so stupid. I should have known. Not surprisingly, I could care less about his wife and kid. I'm not surprised, but my love for Jax and Lily overshadow anything this asshole could do to me. I'm so over him and this whole situation. "So, that's what this has been about the whole time? You just didn't want me to take you to court, did you?"

"Look when you saw me at the mall I knew I was caught and you'd probably get pissed off enough to take action. I figured we could just work this out between the two of us. Jill doesn't need to find out anything."

"Unbelievable. You are a real piece of work." I don't even know what else to say.

"Yeah, sucks finding out that you were the other woman all along doesn't it?"

I hang up the phone. Nothing good can come from continuing this conversation and I don't want shit from him anyway. Jax's words from earlier were already resonating with me, but now they are beating against my mind like a drum. All this time I've told myself I'm doing this for Lily. I told myself working things out with Jason was the right thing to do for her, but that's not true. I've been doing this for me. Because I think I have something to prove. Suddenly, a flash of my sixteenth birthday comes to mind. My mom and I are sitting in a booth at a diner when she becomes angry because she sees me looking at the family across from us. I know now that she saw longing on my face, which angered her. I remember her telling me I would never have what that family across from us had, and ever since I've been determined to prove her wrong. But the thing is, I already have.

Family comes in many shapes and forms. It's a single mom that happily gives up the things she wants or needs in order to provide that extra special something for her child. It's the single father that's trying to be a mother and father to his kids. It's the parents that were never able to have children of their own and adopt a child. Family doesn't show prejudice based on race, age or sex. Family isn't only defined by blood; it's defined by love. Something that Lily and I have in leaps and bounds.

Family's what we make it, what we want it to be. I'm done living with my mother's jealousy of what she didn't have, because the truth is, she didn't want it. If she did, she would have realized that we were already a family. She wouldn't have let anyone else's definition stand in her way.

Needing to call Jax to tell him that I understand, that I'm sorry, that I love him, I grab my phone and type in my password. Just as I get ready to dial, I hear Lily start crying through the baby monitor. Waiting it out for a minute, I see if she just fusses her way back to sleep, but her cry changes. It isn't her sleepy, hungry or her I need changed cry. It's her something is wrong cry. Hurrying to her room, I look into her crib. "What's wrong, sweet girl?"

She looks hot. Her cheeks are flushed and wet from her tears. Picking her up, she feels warm to the touch. Switching on a lamp, I lay her down so I can check her diaper. She's still crying and putting her pacifier in her mouth doesn't help. She sucks it for a minute and then starts crying again. As I work her pajamas off, I notice she's holding one of her legs stiffly and fusses more when I bend her knee to slip her pant leg off. Curious, I look at her leg and gasp in shock and surprise when I see a huge red knot there. Touching it gently, it feels warm to the touch. Something is wrong. She's definitely feverish and in pain and nothing I've read has ever talked about anything like this.

"It's okay, Lily, mommy's going to make it better." Picking her up, I wrap her in a blanket and start shoving random things into her diaper bag. Then, I grab a couple bottles out of the fridge, set her on the bed so I can throw on some clothes and shoes, then I pick her up again, grab my phone, and head out the door. After I buckle her into her seat, I get behind the wheel so I can get her to the emergency room. Tears slide down my face as her cries pick up and I start to feel panic inside my chest and my heart hurts as if her pain is also my own.

Taking out my phone, I call Jax. I know he's angry with me, but I pray he answers his phone. It rings once… twice… three times and I almost cry out in relief when he answers. "Hey," he says softly and I can hear longing I also feel clear in his voice.

"Jax?" My voice breaks on his name and I'm sure he can hear Lily crying in the background.

"What's wrong?"

"Something is wrong with Lily. I'm scared. We're on our way to the hospital."

"I'm on my way. What's going on?"

"I'm not sure. She woke up crying and she has a fever and a large swollen spot on her leg. I don't know what it is. I've never seen anything like it before."

"Okay, babe, it's going to be okay. Be calm so you can get yourself there safely."

"I know you're mad at me but thank you for being here for me."

"I'm not mad at you, and you don't have to thank me. People in love and in relationships are there for one another."

"Thank you anyway."

"We'll talk later, but first, we need to find out what's wrong with our baby."

With those words from him, tears pour down my face and I swipe at them quickly at a stoplight. "Yes. Let's take care of our baby," I whisper.

CHAPTER TWENTY-SIX

Jax

When Rowan calls I'm at the gym beating the shit out of a punching bag pretending that it's Jason's face. All the guys are there too and we're training and just hanging out. Someone even ordered pizza, which seems to defeat the purpose, but oh well. It's nice to hang out – it's just what I need. I'm not mad at Rowan, not really, I'm just scared. All of this is new to me. I've never felt about anyone the way I feel about her and Lily. There's a certain vulnerability to opening yourself up to feelings like this, and it's uncomfortable and nerve-wracking. I'm not the only one responsible for the well-being of my heart anymore. Rowan and Lily both hold it completely in the palm of their hands. I've given it to them and hell, that's more than a little scary.

During moments when my father was too busy for me, insulted me, ridiculed me and treated me like an annoyance, I told myself I would never give anyone power to hurt me ever again. That resolve only hardened after my grandfather died because he always did his best to protect me. Without that buffer anymore, things became worse. So, imagine my surprise when one look from a pregnant woman changed everything.

I'm just feeling threatened by Jason and his role in Rowan and Lily's life. I'm selfish enough to want them for myself and his presence threatens that, and I hate it. But, what I realize is that not having them would be much worse.

When my phone rings and I see Rowan's face on the screen, my heart races. I'm so glad she's called and I regret that it wasn't me that called her first. "Hey," I say softly, wishing I was with her right then, holding her close and kissing her lips.

"Jax?" The sound of her voice immediately has me on alert. As she tells me what's going on, I do my best to remain calm and to keep her calm as well. When I jump up and run to my office to get my keys, the guys all run after me knowing immediately something is wrong.

Covering the phone with my hand, I say softly so she doesn't hear, "It's Lily." That's all I have to say and they immediately spring into action. Levi starts shutting all the lights off, Cole makes sure the equipment is shut down, Zane takes his keys out of his pocket and starts running around making sure all the doors are locked. I see Ryder take off towards the locker room and I know he's making sure everything is shut off in there. We are all out of the gym and locking the doors in record time. I don't even blink twice when Zane and Ryder climb in my truck with me and Cole, Dylan and Levi pile in Cole's truck.

Keeping Rowan on the phone the whole way to the hospital, I hear when she speaks to a nurse explaining why she's there and when she's called back to a room. "I'm not far, babe. You go so you can talk to them and as soon as I get there, I'll come find you."

"Okay," she says weakly before she hangs up.

When I pull into the parking lot, I see her car and park next to it. Cole parks next to me and then we all run into the emergency room. "Go," Zane says. "We'll be here."

I nod and go through the sliding doors that lead back to the rooms. Walking up to a nurse behind a desk, I'm glad when she gives me her attention. "Hi, can you please tell me where Rowan and Lily Martin are?"

"Yes, they're in triage number 4. Just walk down that hallway. The numbers are next to the doors."

"Thanks." I walk past the rooms until I find number four and go inside. Lily is lying on a table getting her temperature checked and vitals taken by a nurse. Rowan is next to her, tears on her cheeks and worry in her eyes. She turns to me and gives me a weak smile. I walk up to her and kiss her forehead, and she squeezes me around my waist. When Lily sees me she gives me a weak smile that has my chest constricting with a combination of worry and love. Even in the midst of her pain, she tries to smile. Her eyes are bloodshot from crying and heavy with exhaustion. I lean down and kiss her on the head too. Her little hand touches my face. "Hi, baby girl. You don't feel good, huh? The doctors are going to make you all better."

When I get a look at her leg I clench my teeth. It's red, swollen and has an angry looking welt on it that's obviously the source of her pain. "She does have a slight fever. Have you given her any Tylenol already?" Rowan shakes her head no. "Okay, we'll go ahead and give her some right away to help with her fever. I'll be right back with that, and the doctor will be in soon, okay?"

"Okay," Rowan and I both say.

Amazingly, Lily's eyes are heavy and she starts to fall asleep while we wait. Occasionally, a little frown will come to her face and her bottom lip will stick out, but exhaustion is clearly winning out over whatever pain she's feeling.

I hate to ask her this but I know I need to be the bigger person here and do the right thing. "Babe, did you call Jason?"

"What?" She looks at me blankly.

"Did you call Jason to let him know about this? I mean, he's wanting to be involved and I guess you should let him know."

"No. I'm not calling Jason."

"Okay…can I ask why? I'm confused. I thought you were considering involving him?"

She sighs and rubs her eyes, "He called me earlier wanting to know if I made a decision yet regarding his involvement. I told him I hadn't and that frankly I wasn't sure I can set my emotions aside and make a fair one. I mean, with my emotions, yours and what's right for Lily versus whatever he has in his head, I just don't want the responsibility. Does that make sense?"

"Yes."

"So, I told him that we should just go to court and let them decide. They can figure out what he owes me and what he should pay going forward in child support. I didn't tell him this, but I'd want sole custody and they can help figure out visitation. Anyway, he got angry. Told me that the only reason he even contacted me was because after I saw him at the mall he knew he was caught and didn't want me to take him to court. He was hoping we could work it out on our own. He told me he has his wife and daughter to take care of."

My mouth falls open, "Wife? You've got to be kidding me. That asshole," I seethe. I want to hunt him down and put his head on a spike like they did in the old days. He deserves worse but that would satisfy me for sure. "Are you okay? That had to be a shock."

"I guess?"

"Why do you seem confused?

"Because, it didn't really bother me that much. Not like it would have four months ago. I'm just over it. I'm over him. I've moved on." She smiles at me, "I'm in love. I'm happy. I don't care about him anymore or anything about his life. I ended up hanging up on him. I doubt I'll be hearing from him again and that's just fine with me."

"It is?"

"Definitely."

Her statement both excites me and makes me want to kiss her, and confuses me, but before I can ask her anything the doctor comes in. An hour later, Rowan has a sleeping Lily in her arms and we're ready to leave. Both of us are relived to find out that it appears Lily's had an allergic reaction to some kind of insect bite. We know too well it could have been something much worse. We aren't sure what got her, but the doctor thinks it was something from our time at the park a couple days ago and it just got infected and became inflamed. They gave her a shot to fight the infection and other than that they rubbed some Neosporin on it, told us cold compresses will help, to keep giving her Tylenol to keep her fever down, and gave us a prescription for antibiotics. The shot is a good jump-start to the antibiotics and we have to give her the liquid kind over the next few days. The doctor told us that we should spray bug spray on her for future park visits and told us the safe kind to buy for babies.

When we walk out into the waiting room, Rowan stops and I look at her to see why and then follow her gaze. All the guys are sitting in the waiting room. Levi has his head resting on Cole's shoulder. Ryder's flirting with a nurse behind the nursing station, Zane's pacing the floor and Dylan is looking at his phone. "They all came?"

"Of course," I shrug. "We were all at the gym when you called."

Zane notices us first, "Guys," he says and everyone else hops up and makes their way to us, Ryder too. They surround us, each peeking at Lily and giving her kisses on the cheek while asking Rowan what happened. We fill them in and they all look as relieved as we do. When we start walking out the door, Rowan tugs my hand and holds me back for a second. "I get it now."

I look at her in confusion, "What do you mean?"

"Family." She looks at me, Lily, and all the guys in front of her. "I get it."

Nodding, I feel too choked up to respond. Placing a small kiss on her lips, I put my hand on her back and steer her to the truck. All the guys insist on piling into Cole's truck so Rowan and I can go back to her place. After Rowan kisses each and every one of them on the cheek, which I begrudgingly allow - even when Ryder looks at me and winks just to piss me off - we each get in our cars and I follow her home.

When we get to her place, we put Lily in her crib and then go to Rowan's room shutting the door behind us. We turn to one another at the same time, "I'm sorry," she says at the same time I say, "I need to apologize." We both laugh.

"I'm sorry I left earlier. I should have stayed and talked everything out with you."

She shakes her head, "I understand. I wish you had stayed too, but maybe we both needed a breather. It was actually good for me. It gave me some time to realize a few things."

"Me too," I reply. "Look, the way I acted about Jason is wrong. Regardless of how things ended up going down with him tonight, I just felt threatened by him and it make me act out."

"What? Why?"

"Because. I hate the history that the two of you share. I hate the fact that he's the father of your baby. I hate the fact that you will always be connected to him because of that. I was afraid. I was afraid that if he pushed hard enough that he'd use your past to get to you, and you'd want your ordinary family with him and babe, I don't want to lose you."

"Oh, Jax. I'm so, so sorry." She walks to her bed and sits and I do the same. "I don't want to lose you either, and I'm so sad that I made you feel and think otherwise. I never realized that while my mom's words have always stuck with me, what I've really been fighting against all along is the envy and anger *she* felt. She was angry at my dad for leaving, angry at Tyson and me for being born, angry at the kind of life she had. She was jealous of everyone around her that she felt had it better than she did, and she used it as a crutch her whole life. It was an excuse for why things weren't good for her. She told me I wasn't worthy of love. She said that I would always be alone and I believed her, Jax. Some of this I've told you before, but I don't know if I've ever confessed that. I said sometimes I was afraid she was right, but really I *believed* her. I told myself that I didn't, but I did. I've been clinging to this idea of a 'normal family' because in my mind it's been how I prove my mom wrong. But you see, what I failed to realize is that I've had it all along. I have the fairytale - it's just with an unconventional family. Tyson, you, me, Lily, the guys, we are a family. You, me and Lily, we are a family. I am surrounded by love. You are surrounded by love, and my god, it's so beautiful. Our family is *so* beautiful. My mom was wrong. I am worthy, I'm not alone and all I feel for her now is sadness that she wasn't able to look past the jealousy she had for others and realize that she could have had the same thing. I don't know what's going to happen with Jason. And I really don't care - truly I don't. How involved he is, or isn't, is on him and the court if it comes to that. If he decides to be involved, you and I will create boundaries and decide what works for us, because that comes first. Our family comes first. I love you, Jax. So much. You have nothing to fear, no reason to feel threatened, you and Lily - you're my everything.

"You're mine too, and you don't have anything to apologize for."

"Yes, I do."

"No, you don't. A relationship is full of love, faith, trust, passion, dreams and understanding. You and me? We have that in spades. But sometimes there will be disagreements, misunderstandings and uncertainties and that's okay. It's those other things that will help us get through them. You're right. We're beautiful and it's perfect."

I pull her to me and kiss her. I put all my love, need and passion into that kiss. I kiss her like I never want it to end. Everything she said, everything she feels is everything I've hoped for. Everything I've ever wanted. Pulling away, I pull her to standing and then I stand in front of her and slowly strip off her clothes. She reaches out and undresses me as well. We stand and look at one another for a moment, before I pick her up and place her on the bed. I begin kissing her again, but then pull away and trace kisses down her jaw, chin, neck and chest making my way to her breasts. Lavishing her breasts with attention, bringing each nipple to a hard peak, I groan at the sight, "Fucking beautiful, babe." I give it the same treatment.

She makes sounds that make my pulse race faster.

Kissing, biting and licking down her stomach, I start to make my way lower but she surprises me. "No." She pushes me back and gets me to roll on my back. I stare amazed at her beauty as she rises over me, straddles my lap and positions herself at the top of my cock. Looking into my eyes, she slams herself down on me in one quick motion making me grunt in surprise. Cocking a brow at me as if she dares me to tell her to stop, she says "I want you now."

All I can do is nod at her and stare into her eyes, lost in the love, desire, need and passion they hold. Gripping her hips I help her find a rhythm as she rises and falls on me. Throwing her head back in her passion she's fucking beautiful. Hair flowing down her back, tits proudly thrust forward, riding me up and down with complete abandon, her face is filled with desire. When she shatters around me, her pussy tightens on my cock over and over and I can't handle it a moment longer. Flipping her over onto her back I sit back on my heels. Pushing into her again, I lift her under her hips to get deeper access and moan at the feeling of her clenching around me. "God, Rowan, you feel amazing. You're so tight."

"Fuck me, Jax. Please. Fuck me."

I reach down and rub her clit hoping to bring her to a second orgasm. Her eyes are hooded with her passion and the sounds she's making tell me she's just about there again. I press harder onto her clit and feel satisfaction when she tightens around me again in orgasm. Thrusting once, twice, then three times, I release into her. Leaning forward, I kiss her all over her face. "Move in with me."

"What?!"

Her eyes flash open wide and it makes me chuckle. "I want you and Lily with me all the time. I know you may have doubts because of Tyson-"

"Yes."

Smiling wide, knowing I'm showing her the dimples she loves, I kiss her soundly on the lips. "Yes?"

"Yes. I would love to move in with you. Tyson will be fine. This is about us and I want to live with you. I love you so much."

Sighing into her neck, I kiss it, "I love you too."

Later, we sneak into Lilys' room and peek into her crib. She's sleeping peacefully, and we both breathe a sigh of relief, glad she's comfortable. Holding Rowan in my arms and looking down at Lily, I'm thankful that all those months ago when Rowan slammed the door in my face, that I didn't just give up and walk away. Obstacles are sometimes placed in our way to see if what we want is really worth it. What I know, what I've learned, is that love is always worth the fight.

THE END

Coming up next - FIGHTING WRATH
When Tyson meets the one girl that calms the constant, uncontrollable rage simmering inside, he'll do anything to make her his.

ACKNOWLEDGEMENTS

Thank you so much for reading the first book in my new series. I've been super excited for you all to read it, and I hope you enjoyed it. I have several people to thank for supporting me through this new journey.

To my husband and daughters, thank you for putting up with the fact that I live in my own mind the majority of the time. I can become a nightmare when I'm on deadline and you all love me anyway – you just throw chocolate at me like you're feeding a tiger. Thanks for getting me.

Mom, I find myself thanking you every book I write so I need to say thank you for being my constant support each and every time. I can't convey how much it means to me, but I'll continue to try. You and I make a great team.

Gypsy Rae Choszer, Cora Brent, Angela Corbett, Jennifer Domenico – your advice, support and brain storming sessions are priceless. Thank you all for being my friends. The InDivas – thank you for always answering my questions, sharing my posts and supporting me, no questions asked. I'm lucky to have such a great support group in you.

Tara Brown, you are a word master! Thank you for always helping me with my blurbs. I freaking hate them! You always know just what I'm trying to say. You're amazing.

Robin Harper, thank you for making me this gorgeous cover. I can't wait to continue the series with you. Elaine, thank you for making my books look great on the inside. You do an amazing job and your turn around time kicks ass! Jess Peterson, thank you for all your promo help.

Miller's Killer's – thank you for your unwavering support and all the dinosaur jokes. I love you girls!

Bloggers, thank you for always promoting me and sharing my posts time and time again. It gives me a thrill every time!

To all my readers, thank you for picking up my books and taking a chance on me over and over. My goal has always been to offer an escape from reality to readers for a few hours – I hope you were able to get lost in my book and enjoyed the ride.

Author Jennifer Miller was born and raised in Chicago, Illinois but now calls Arizona home. Her love of reading began when she was a small child, and only continued to grow as she entered adulthood. Ever since winning a writing contest at the young age of nine, when she wrote a book about a girl with a pet unicorn, she's dreamed of writing a book of her own. The important lesson she learned about dreams is that they don't just fall into your lap – you have to chase them yourself. Most importantly, she is a wife and mother, and is very lucky to have a family that loves and supports her in all things. She also has an unhealthy addiction to handbags and chocolate covered strawberries, neither of which she cares to work on. For more information about Jennifer Miller, please visit www.jennifermillerwrites.com.

Facebook – https://www.facebook.com/JenMillerWrites?ref=hl
Twitter – https://twitter.com/JenMillerWrites
Pinterest – http://www.pinterest.com/jenmillerwrites/
Sign up for my newsletter – http://goo.gl/JNRarR
Instagram - http://instagram.com/jenmillerwrites
Tsu - https://www.tsu.co/AuthorJenniferMiller
Goodreads - https://www.goodreads.com/author/show/7019978.
Jennifer_Miller

www.ingramcontent.com/pod-product-compliance
Lightning Source LLC
Chambersburg PA
CBHW060907250626
47159CB00008B/2903